DISCARD
PEANUTS®
by Schulz

DISCARD   DISCARD

Special Thanks to the Schulz family, everyone at Creative Associates, and Charles M. Schulz for his singular achievement in shaping these beloved characters.

Cover
Art by **Charles M. Schulz**
Color & Design by **Nomi Kane**

Trade Designer: **Grace Park**
Assistant Editor: **Alex Galer**
Editor: **Shannon Watters**

For Charles M. Schulz Creative Associates
Creative Director: **Paige Braddock**
Managing Editor: **Alexis E. Fajardo**

ROSS RICHIE CEO & Founder • MATT GAGNON Editor-in-Chief • FILIP SABLIK President of Publishing & Marketing • STEPHEN CHRISTY President of Development • LANCE KREITER VP of Licensing & Merchandising • PHIL BARBARO VP of Finance • BRYCE CARLSON Managing Editor • MEL CAYLO Marketing Manager • SCOTT NEWMAN Production Design Manager • IRENE BRADISH Operations Manager • SIERRA HAHN Senior Editor • DAFNA PLEBAN Editor • SHANNON WATTERS Editor • ERIC HARBURN Editor • WHITNEY LEOPARD Associate Editor • JASMINE AMIRI Associate Editor • CHRIS ROSA Associate Editor • ALEX GALER Assistant Editor • CAMERON CHITTOCK Assistant Editor • MARY GUMPORT Assistant Editor • MATTHEW LEVINE Assistant Editor • KELSEY DIETERICH Production Designer • JILLIAN CRAB Production Designer • MICHELLE ANKLEY Production Design Assistant • GRACE PARK Production Design Assistant • AARON FERRARA Operations Coordinator • ELIZABETH LOUGHRIDGE Accounting Coordinator • JOSÉ MEZA Sales Assistant • JAMES ARRIOLA Mailroom Assistant • HOLLY AITCHISON Operations Assistant • STEPHANIE HOCUTT Marketing Assistant • SAM KUSEK Direct Market Representative • AMBER PARKER Administrative Assistant

kaboom!™

PEANUTS Volume Eight, October 2016. Published by KaBOOM!, a division of Boom Entertainment, Inc. Peanuts is ™ & © 2016 Peanuts Worldwide, LLC. Originally published in single magazine form as PEANUTS: Volume Two No. 25-28. ™ & © 2015 Peanuts Worldwide, LLC. All rights reserved. KaBOOM!™ and the KaBOOM! logo are trademarks of Boom Entertainment, Inc., registered in various countries and categories. All characters, events, and institutions depicted herein are fictional. Any similarity between any of the names, characters, persons, events, and/or institutions in this publication to actual names, characters, and persons, whether living or dead, events, and/or institutions is unintended and purely coincidental. KaBOOM! does not read or accept unsolicited submissions of ideas, stories, or artwork.

A catalog record of this book is available from OCLC and from the BOOM! Studios website, www.boom-studios.com, on the Librarians Page.

BOOM! Studios, 5670 Wilshire Boulevard, Suite 450, Los Angeles, CA 90036-5679. Printed in China. First Printing.

ISBN: 978-1-60886-899-5, eISBN: 978-1-61398-570-0

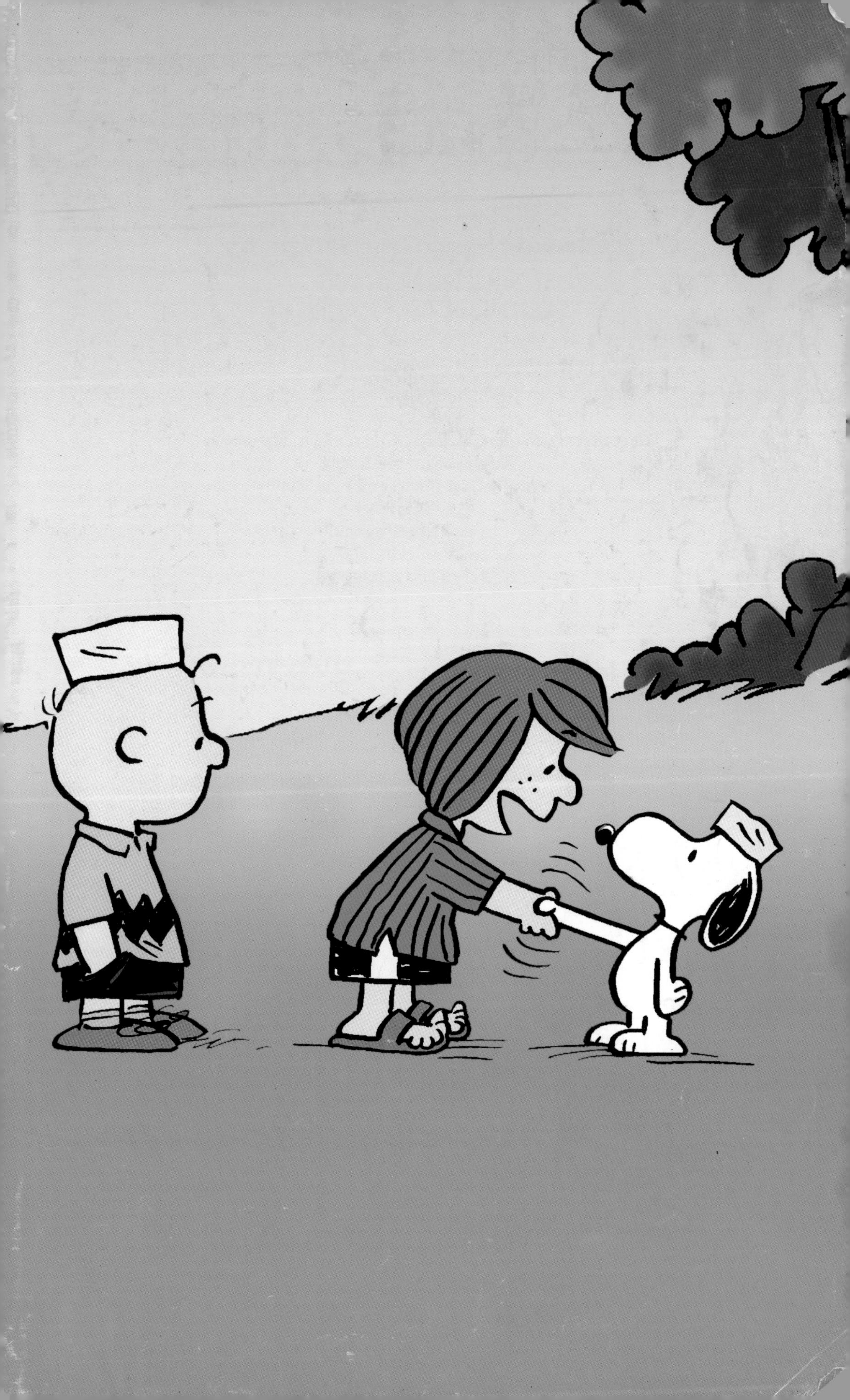

Table of Contents

Classic Peanuts Strips by
Charles M. Schulz
Colors by Justin Thompson & Katharine Efird

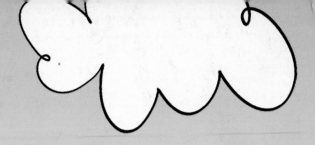

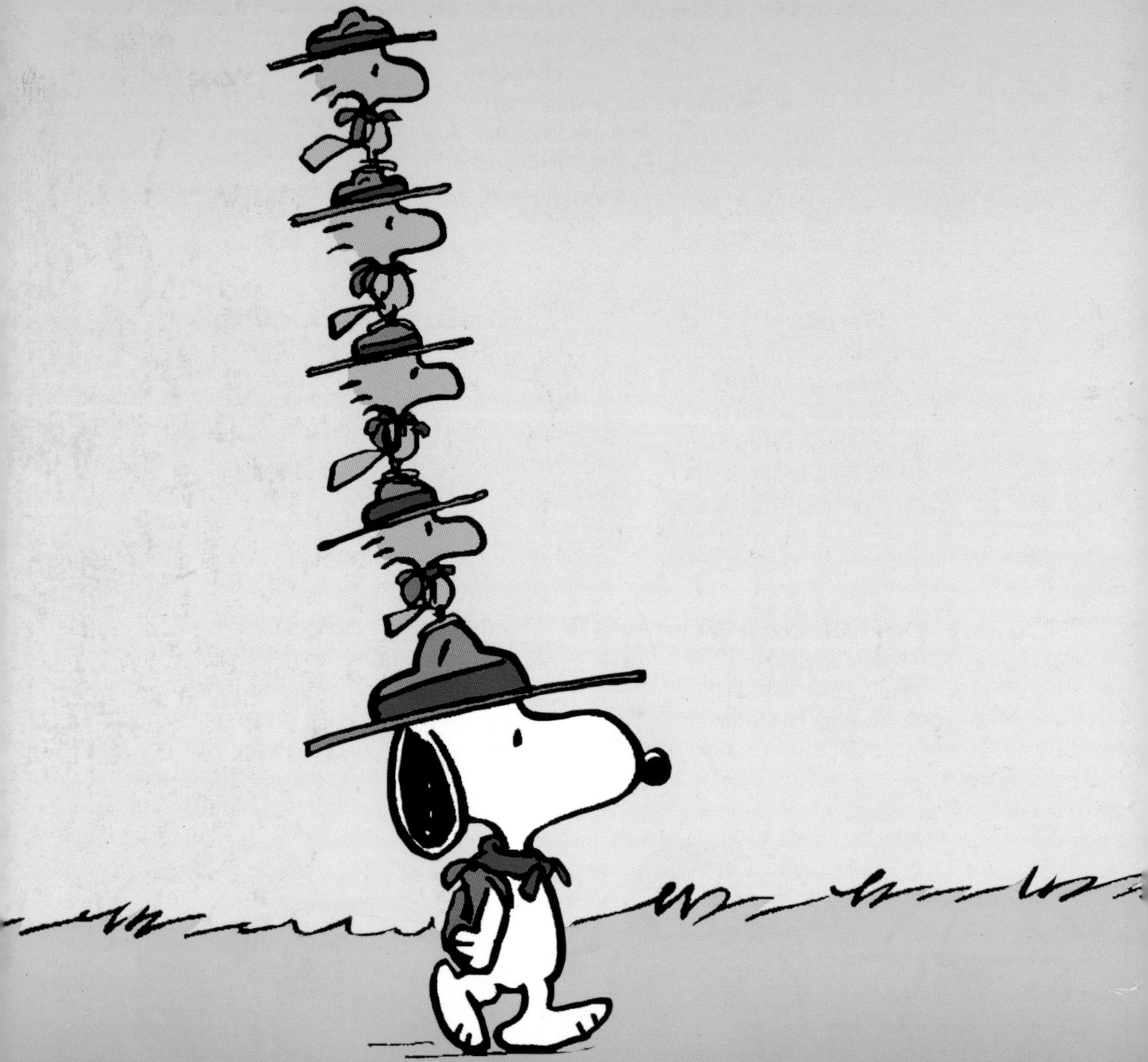

IT'S SUMMER CAMP, Charlie Brown

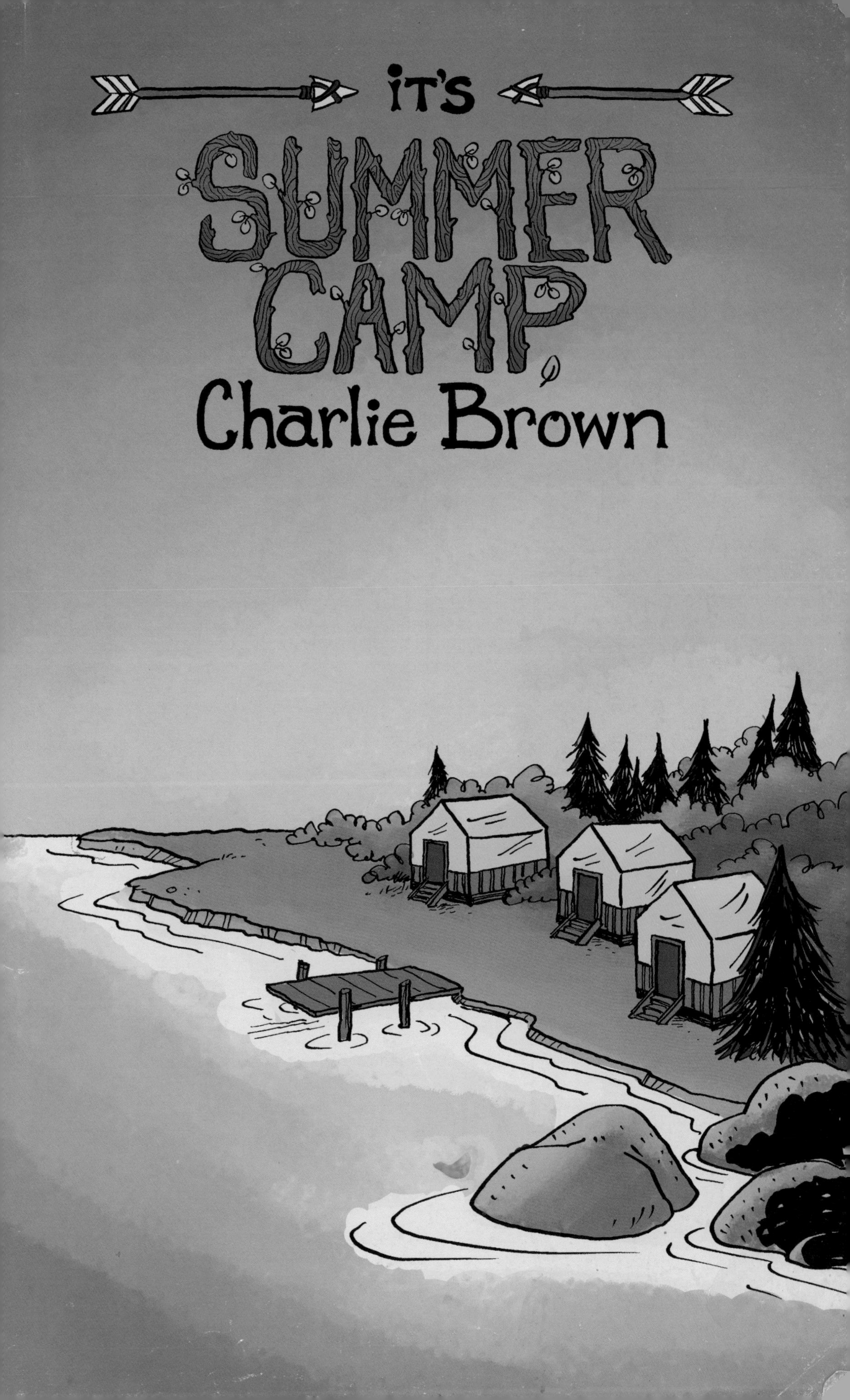

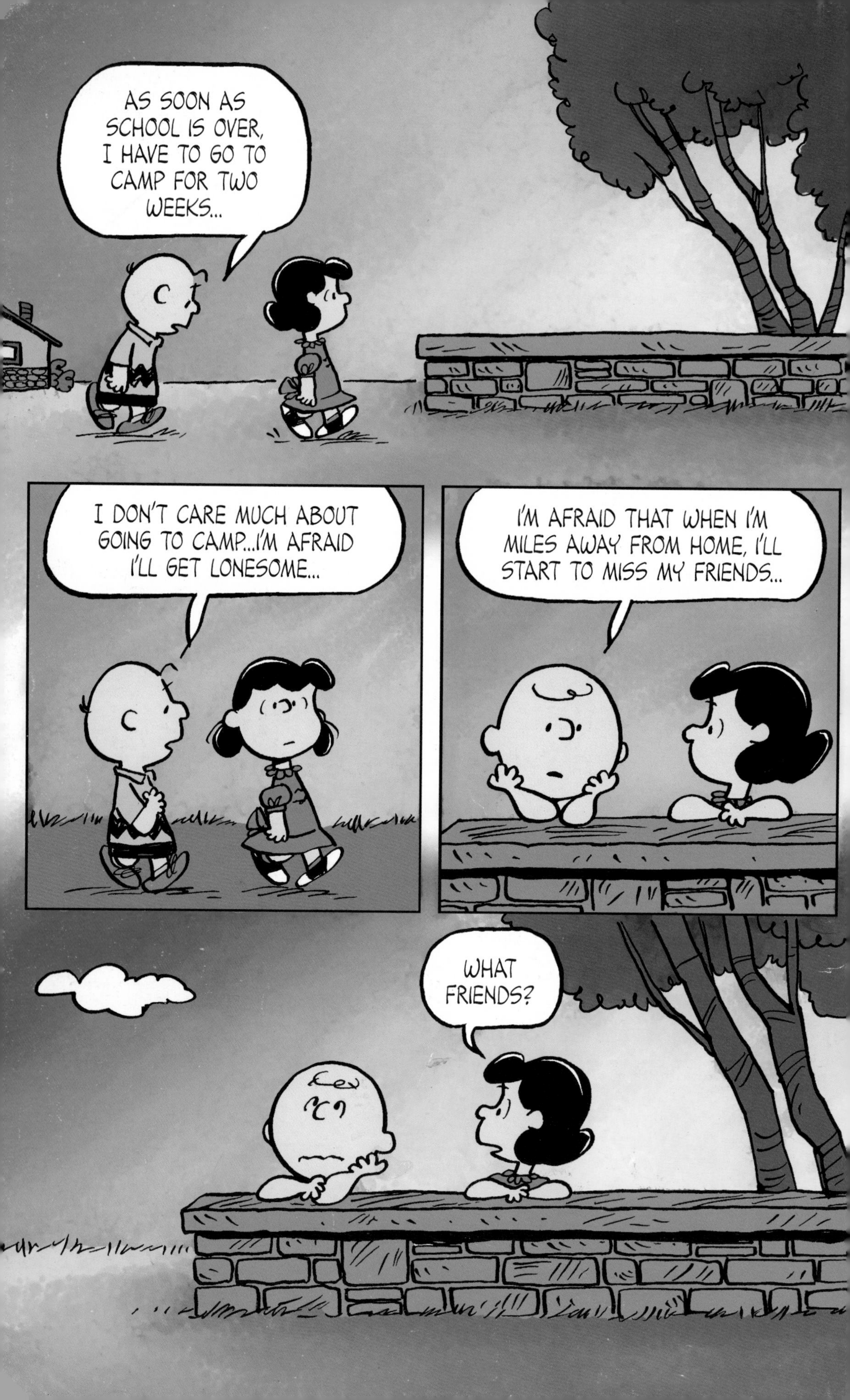
AS SOON AS SCHOOL IS OVER, I HAVE TO GO TO CAMP FOR TWO WEEKS...
I DON'T CARE MUCH ABOUT GOING TO CAMP...I'M AFRAID I'LL GET LONESOME...
I'M AFRAID THAT WHEN I'M MILES AWAY FROM HOME, I'LL START TO MISS MY FRIENDS...
WHAT FRIENDS?

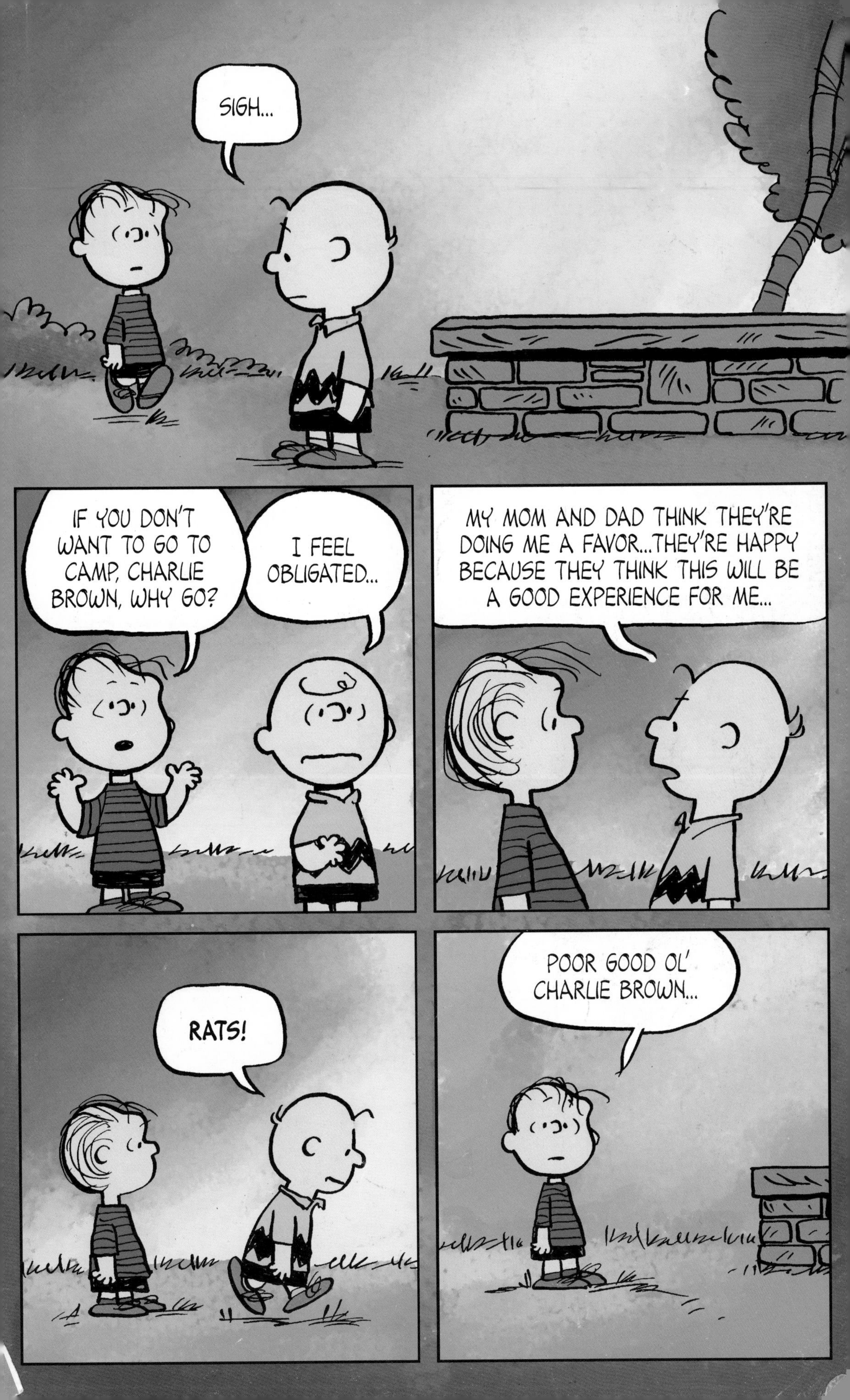
SIGH...
IF YOU DON'T WANT TO GO TO CAMP, CHARLIE BROWN, WHY GO?
I FEEL OBLIGATED...
MY MOM AND DAD THINK THEY'RE DOING ME A FAVOR...THEY'RE HAPPY BECAUSE THEY THINK THIS WILL BE A GOOD EXPERIENCE FOR ME...
RATS!
POOR GOOD OL' CHARLIE BROWN...

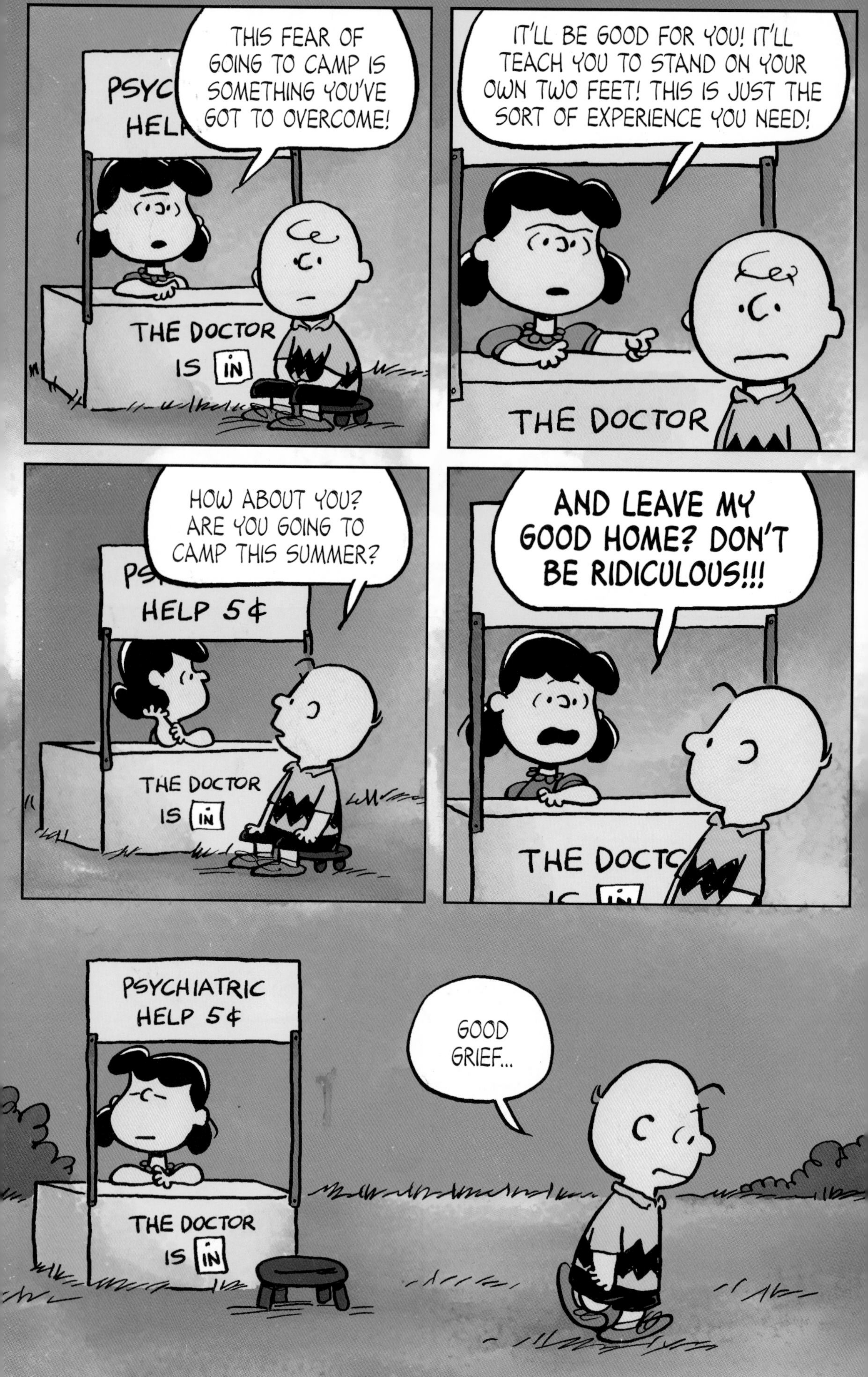
PSYC
HEL
THIS FEAR OF GOING TO CAMP IS SOMETHING YOU'VE GOT TO OVERCOME!
THE DOCTOR IS IN
IT'LL BE GOOD FOR YOU! IT'LL TEACH YOU TO STAND ON YOUR OWN TWO FEET! THIS IS JUST THE SORT OF EXPERIENCE YOU NEED!
THE DOCTOR
HOW ABOUT YOU? ARE YOU GOING TO CAMP THIS SUMMER?
HELP 5¢
THE DOCTOR IS IN
AND LEAVE MY GOOD HOME? DON'T BE RIDICULOUS!!!
THE DOCTC
PSYCHIATRIC HELP 5¢
THE DOCTOR IS IN
GOOD GRIEF...

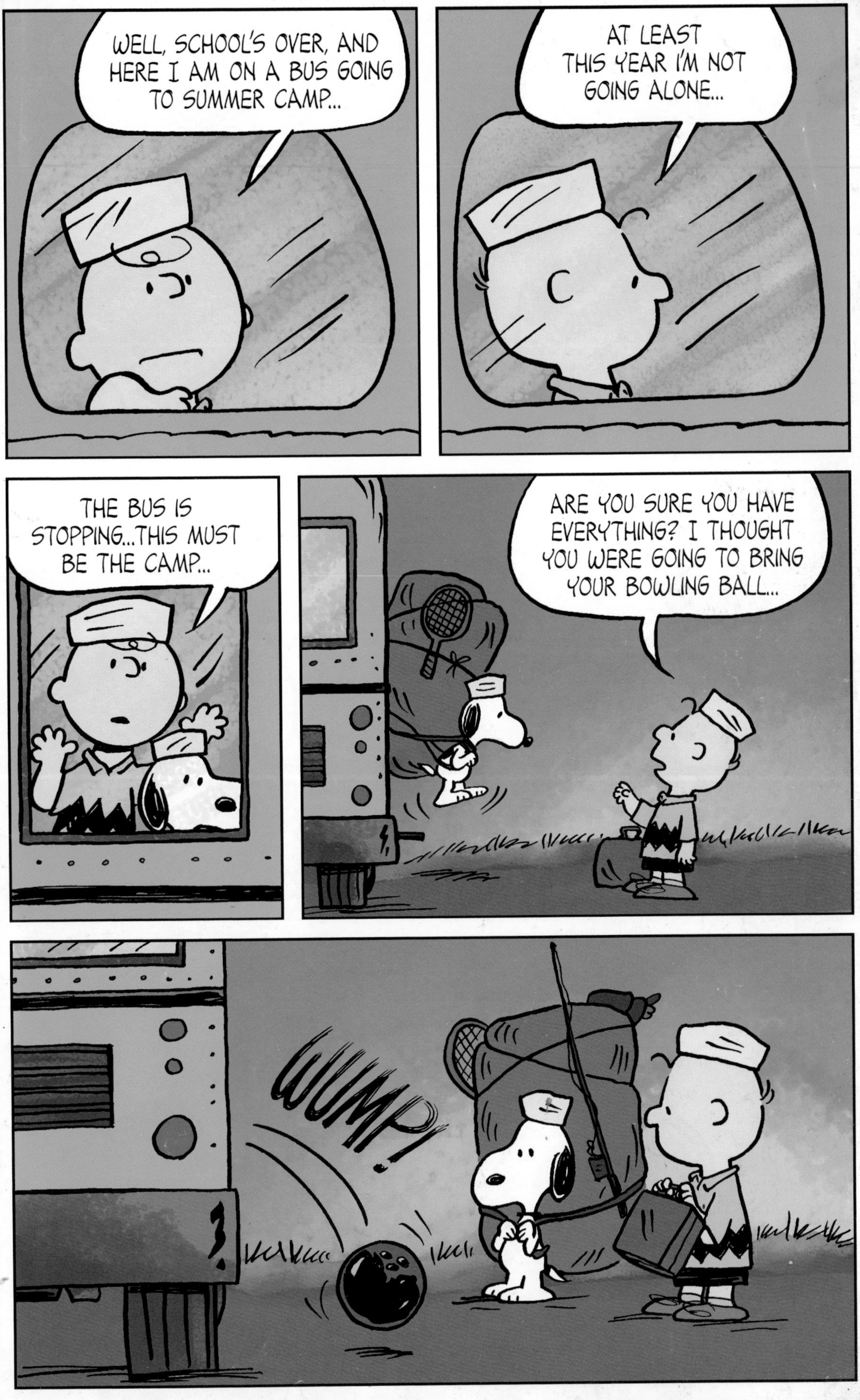
WELL, SCHOOL'S OVER, AND HERE I AM ON A BUS GOING TO SUMMER CAMP...
AT LEAST THIS YEAR I'M NOT GOING ALONE...
THE BUS IS STOPPING...THIS MUST BE THE CAMP...
ARE YOU SURE YOU HAVE EVERYTHING? I THOUGHT YOU WERE GOING TO BRING YOUR BOWLING BALL...
WUMP!

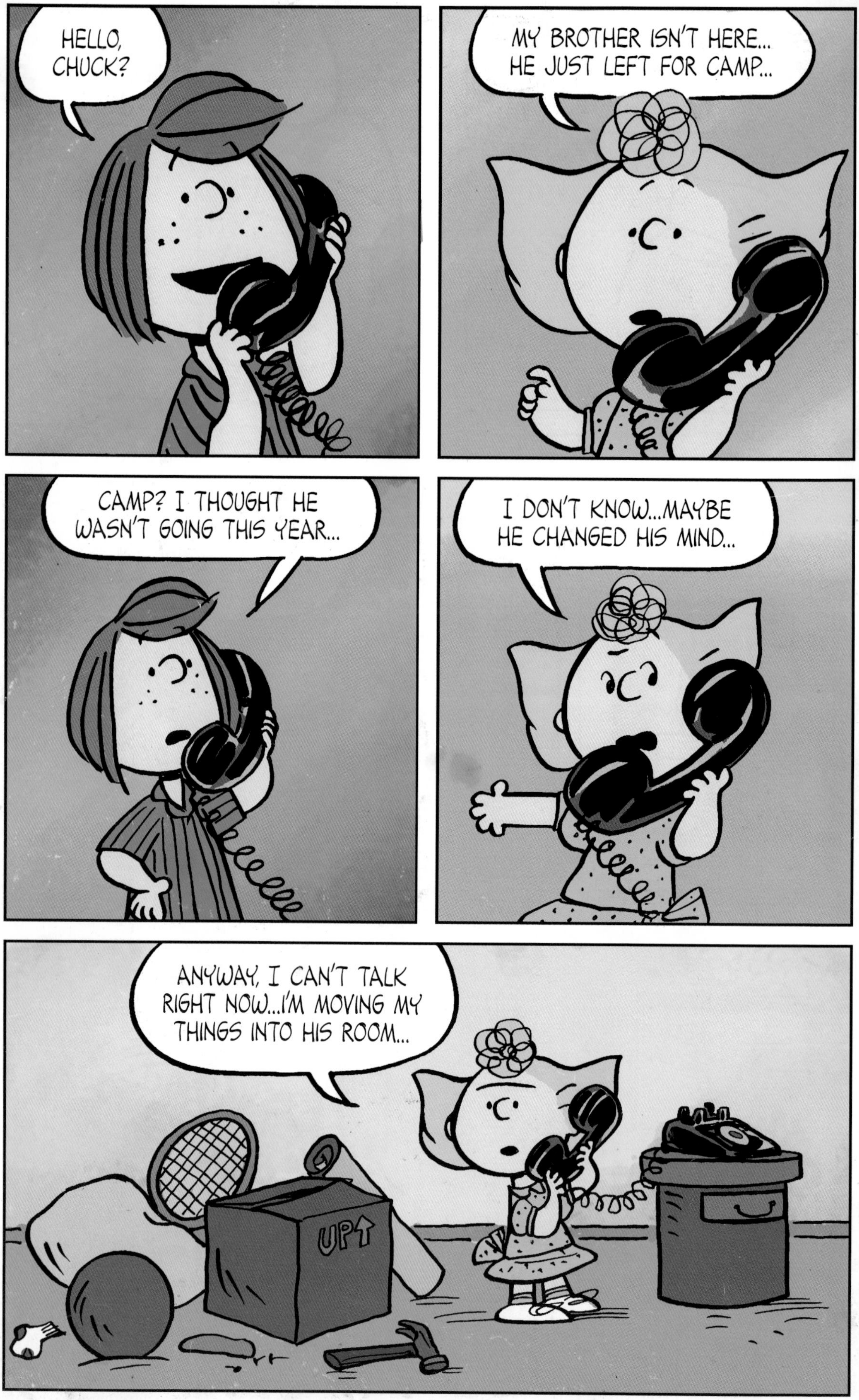

HELLO, CHUCK?
MY BROTHER ISN'T HERE... HE JUST LEFT FOR CAMP...
CAMP? I THOUGHT HE WASN'T GOING THIS YEAR...
I DON'T KNOW...MAYBE HE CHANGED HIS MIND...
ANYWAY, I CAN'T TALK RIGHT NOW...I'M MOVING MY THINGS INTO HIS ROOM...
UP

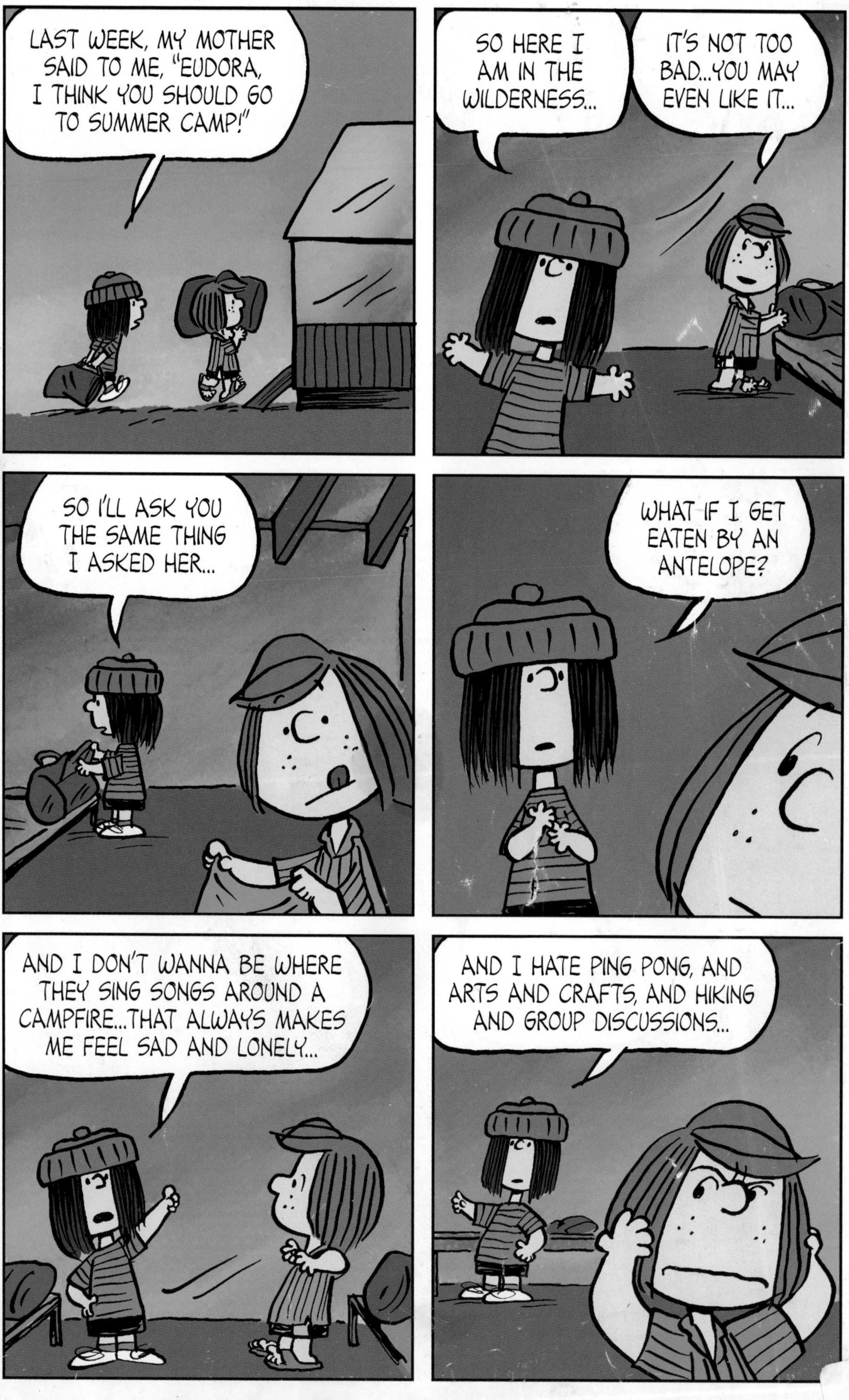
LAST WEEK, MY MOTHER SAID TO ME, "EUDORA, I THINK YOU SHOULD GO TO SUMMER CAMP!"
SO HERE I AM IN THE WILDERNESS...
IT'S NOT TOO BAD...YOU MAY EVEN LIKE IT...
SO I'LL ASK YOU THE SAME THING I ASKED HER...
WHAT IF I GET EATEN BY AN ANTELOPE?
AND I DON'T WANNA BE WHERE THEY SING SONGS AROUND A CAMPFIRE...THAT ALWAYS MAKES ME FEEL SAD AND LONELY...
AND I HATE PING PONG, AND ARTS AND CRAFTS, AND HIKING AND GROUP DISCUSSIONS...

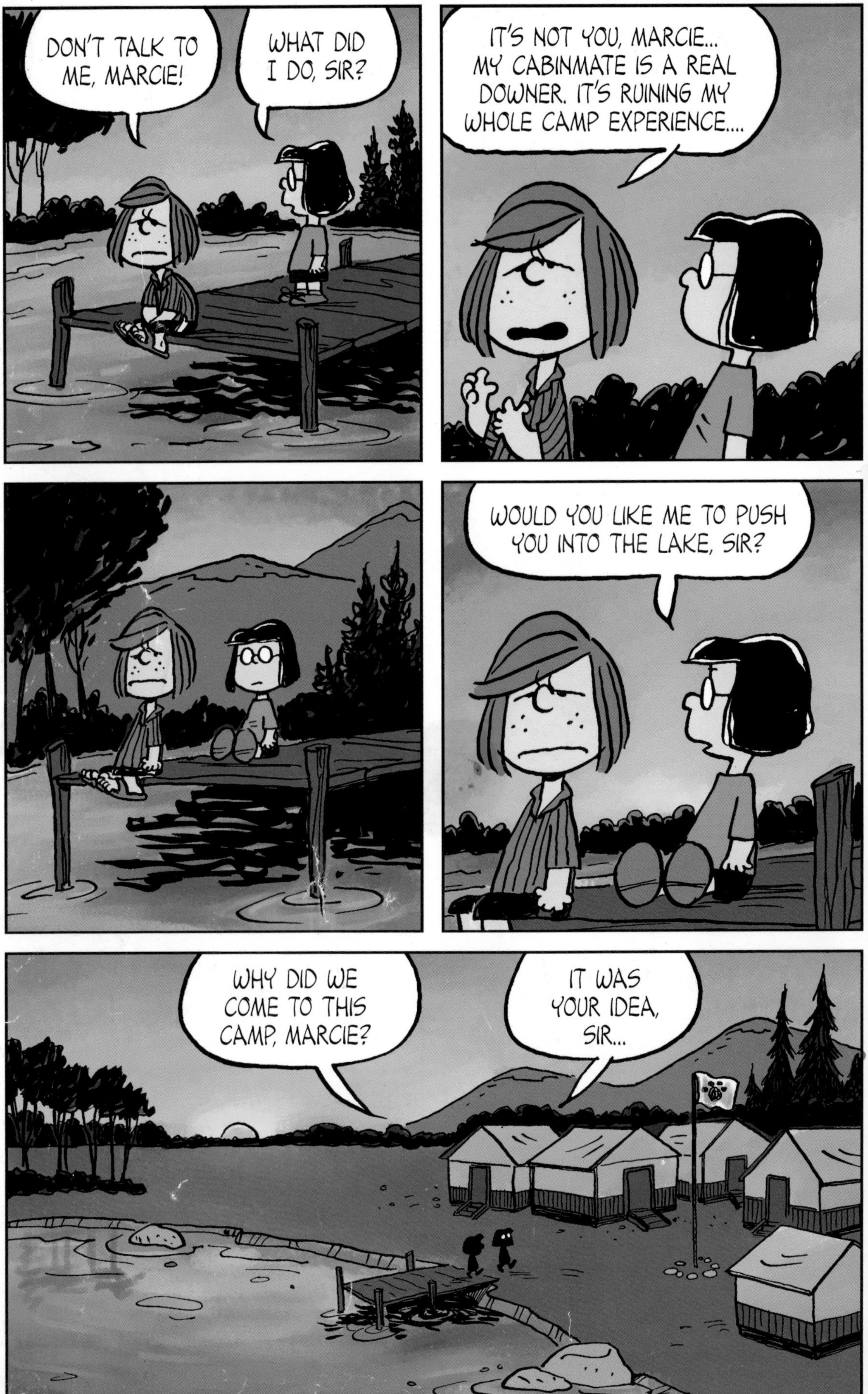
DON'T TALK TO ME, MARCIE!
WHAT DID I DO, SIR?
IT'S NOT YOU, MARCIE... MY CABINMATE IS A REAL DOWNER. IT'S RUINING MY WHOLE CAMP EXPERIENCE....
WOULD YOU LIKE ME TO PUSH YOU INTO THE LAKE, SIR?
WHY DID WE COME TO THIS CAMP, MARCIE?
IT WAS YOUR IDEA, SIR...

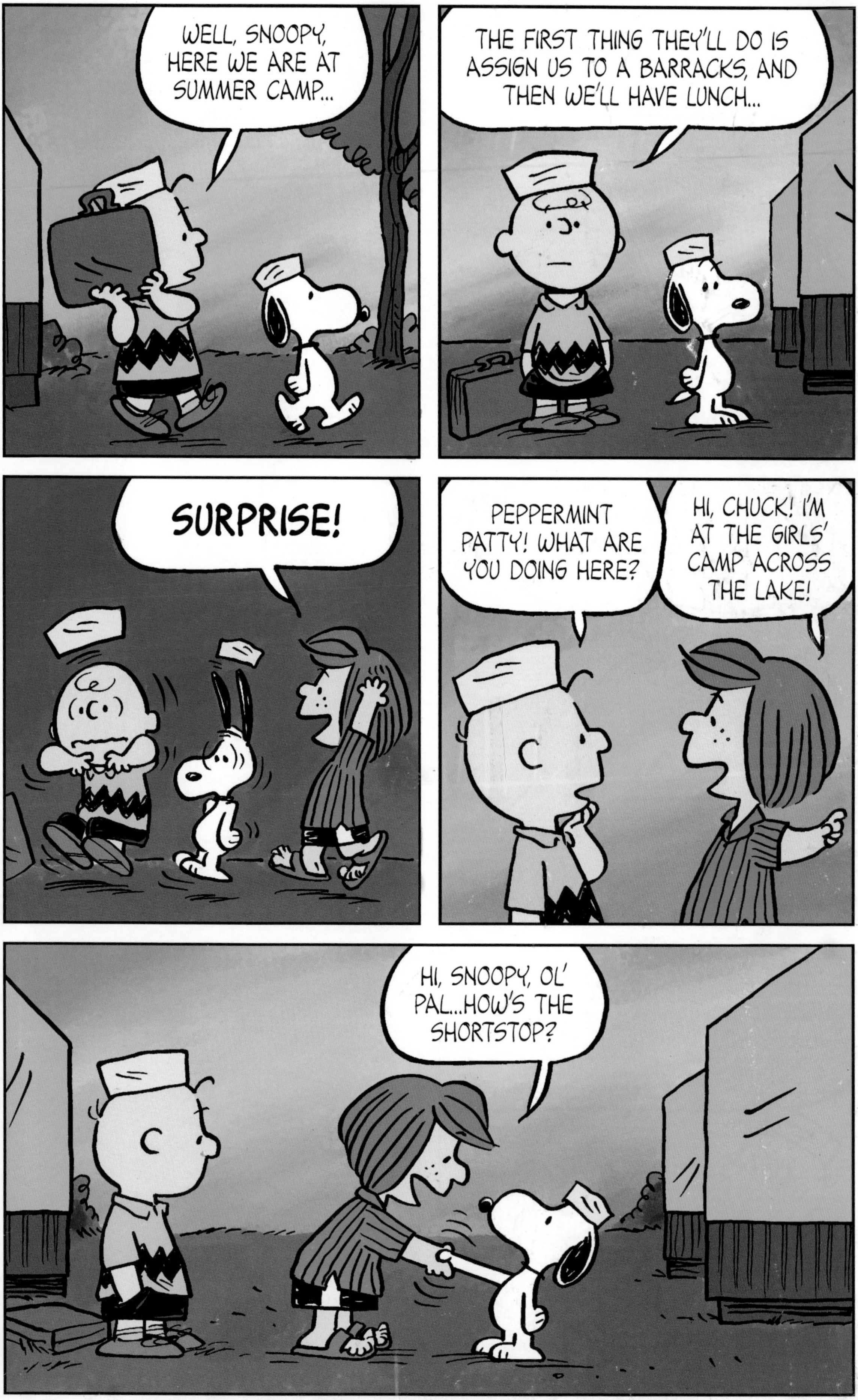
WELL, SNOOPY, HERE WE ARE AT SUMMER CAMP...
THE FIRST THING THEY'LL DO IS ASSIGN US TO A BARRACKS, AND THEN WE'LL HAVE LUNCH...
SURPRISE!
PEPPERMINT PATTY! WHAT ARE YOU DOING HERE?
HI, CHUCK! I'M AT THE GIRLS' CAMP ACROSS THE LAKE!
HI, SNOOPY, OL' PAL...HOW'S THE SHORTSTOP?

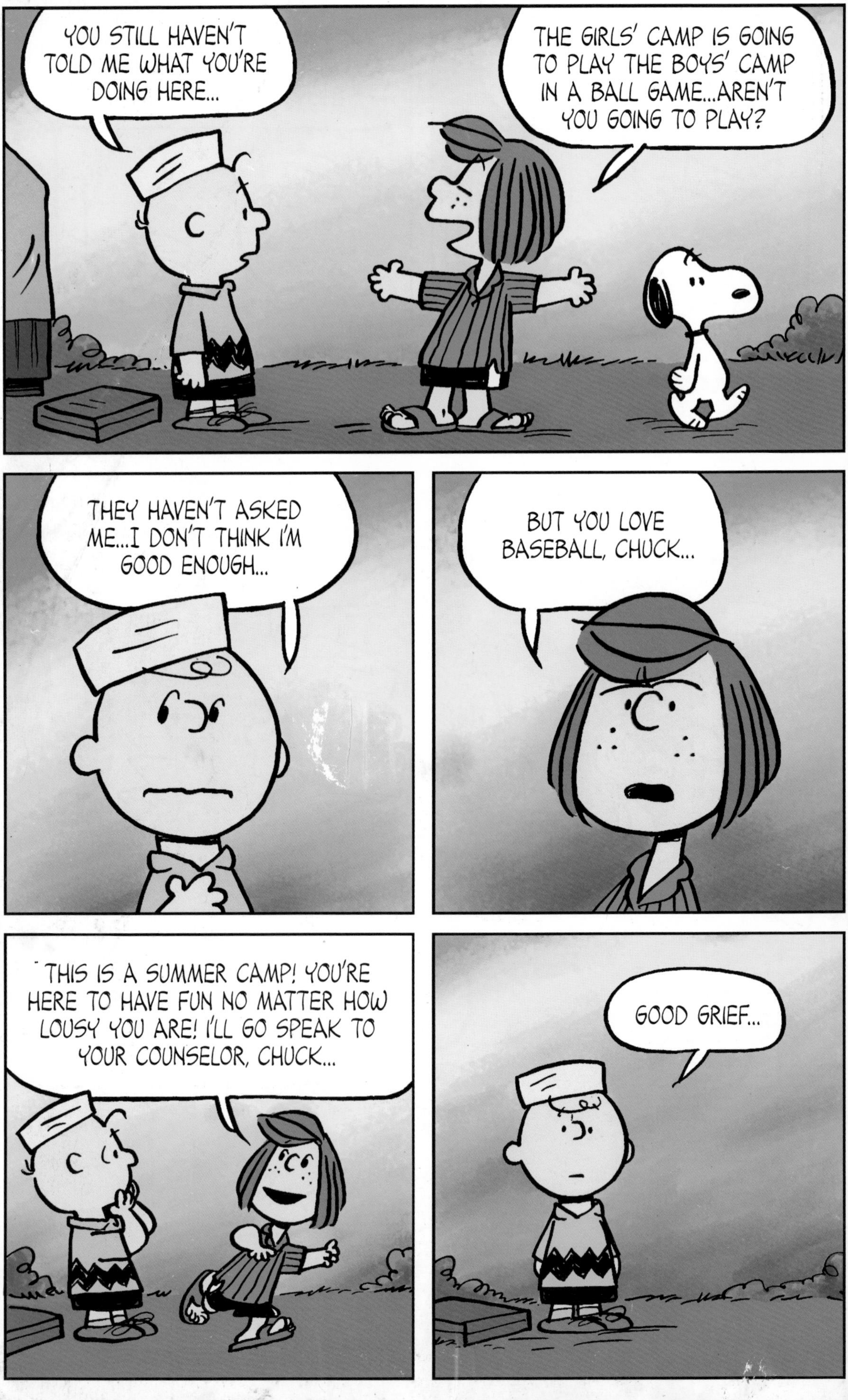
YOU STILL HAVEN'T TOLD ME WHAT YOU'RE DOING HERE...
THE GIRLS' CAMP IS GOING TO PLAY THE BOYS' CAMP IN A BALL GAME...AREN'T YOU GOING TO PLAY?
THEY HAVEN'T ASKED ME...I DON'T THINK I'M GOOD ENOUGH...
BUT YOU LOVE BASEBALL, CHUCK...
THIS IS A SUMMER CAMP! YOU'RE HERE TO HAVE FUN NO MATTER HOW LOUSY YOU ARE! I'LL GO SPEAK TO YOUR COUNSELOR, CHUCK...
GOOD GRIEF...

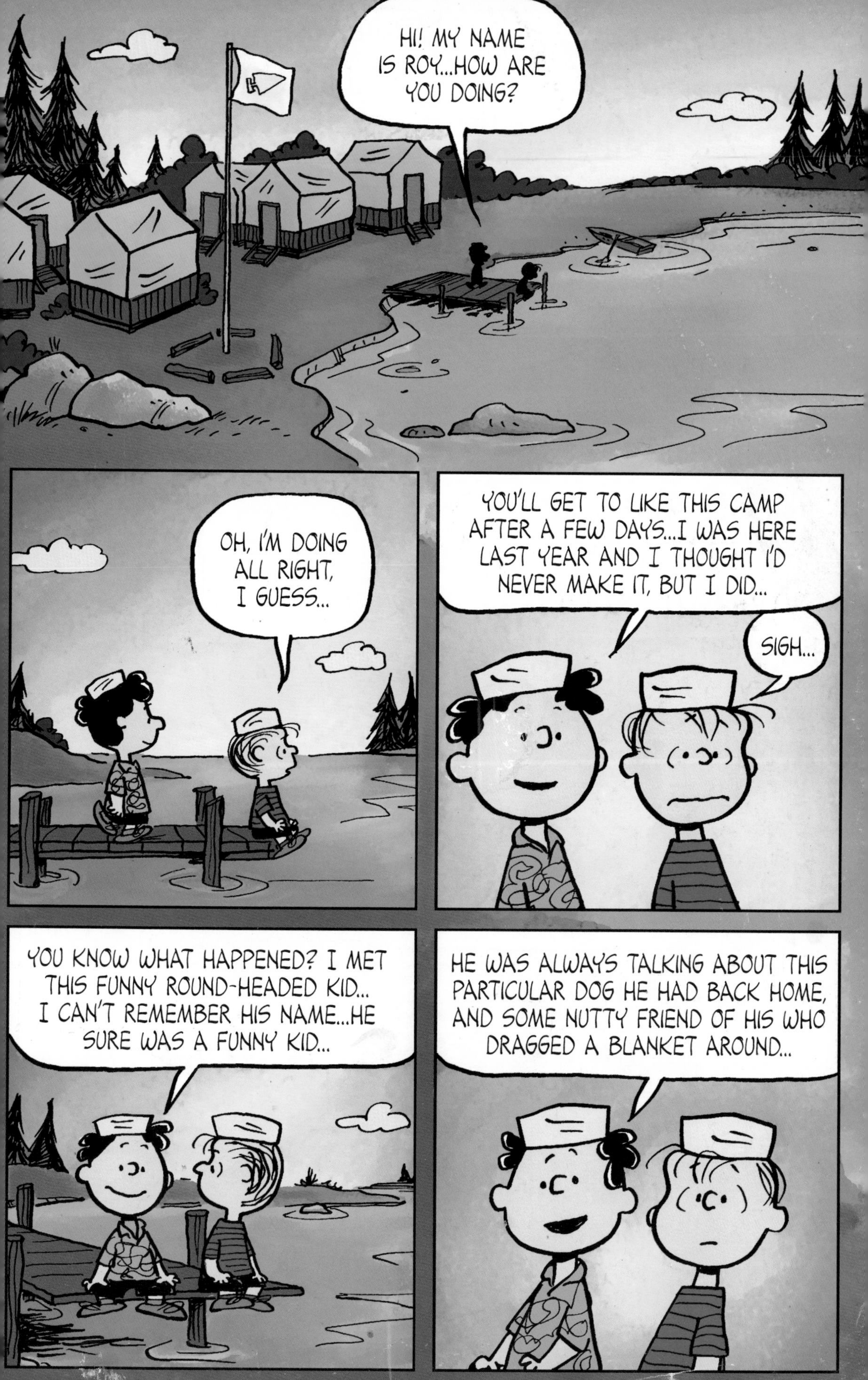
HI! MY NAME IS ROY...HOW ARE YOU DOING?
OH, I'M DOING ALL RIGHT, I GUESS...
YOU'LL GET TO LIKE THIS CAMP AFTER A FEW DAYS...I WAS HERE LAST YEAR AND I THOUGHT I'D NEVER MAKE IT, BUT I DID...
SIGH...
YOU KNOW WHAT HAPPENED? I MET THIS FUNNY ROUND-HEADED KID... I CAN'T REMEMBER HIS NAME...HE SURE WAS A FUNNY KID...
HE WAS ALWAYS TALKING ABOUT THIS PARTICULAR DOG HE HAD BACK HOME, AND SOME NUTTY FRIEND OF HIS WHO DRAGGED A BLANKET AROUND...

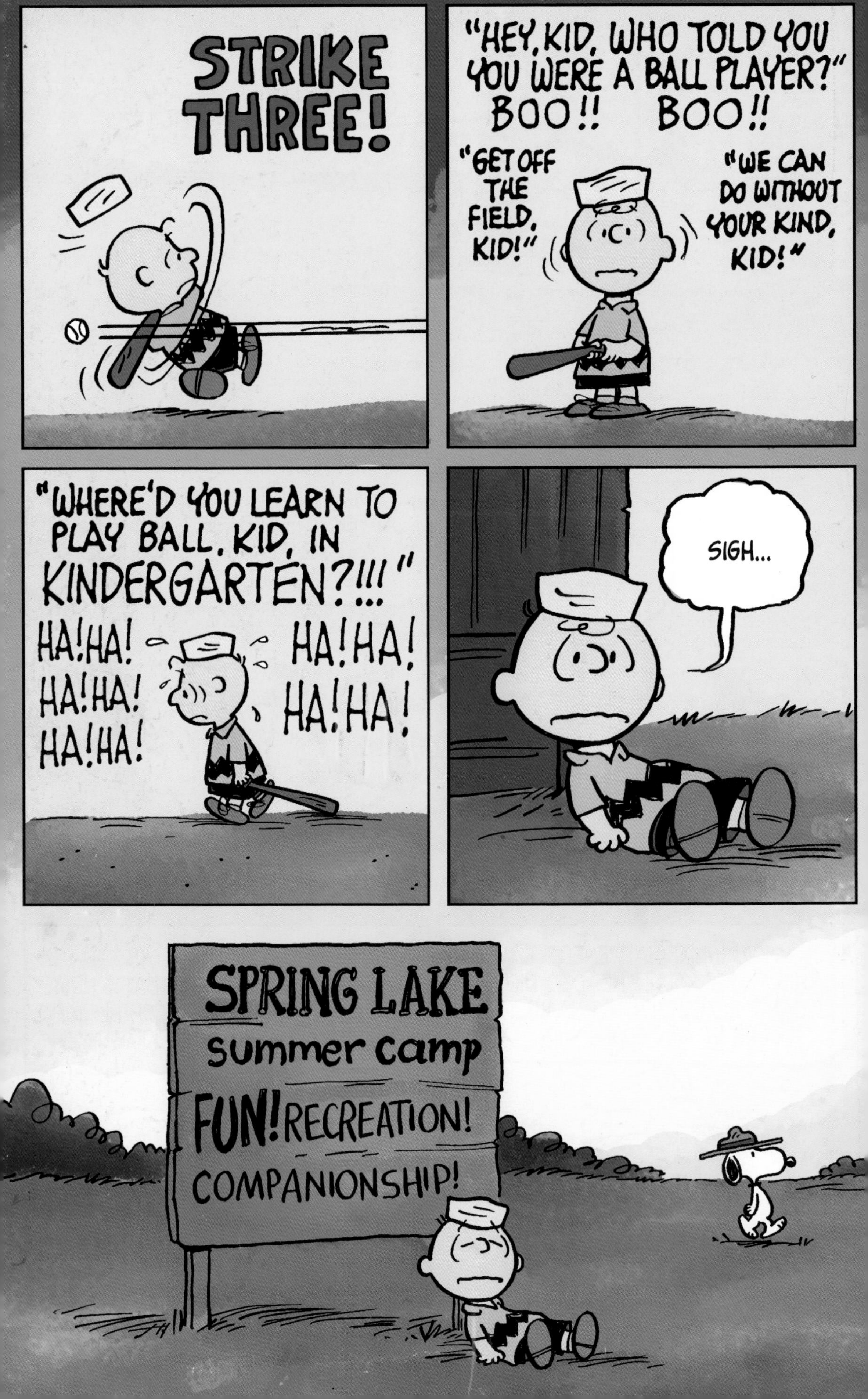
STRIKE THREE!
"HEY, KID, WHO TOLD YOU YOU WERE A BALL PLAYER?" BOO!! BOO!!
"GET OFF THE FIELD, KID!"
"WE CAN DO WITHOUT YOUR KIND, KID!"
"WHERE'D YOU LEARN TO PLAY BALL, KID, IN KINDERGARTEN?!!!"
HA! HA! HA! HA! HA! HA!
HA! HA! HA! HA!
SIGH...
SPRING LAKE
summer camp
FUN! RECREATION!
COMPANIONSHIP!

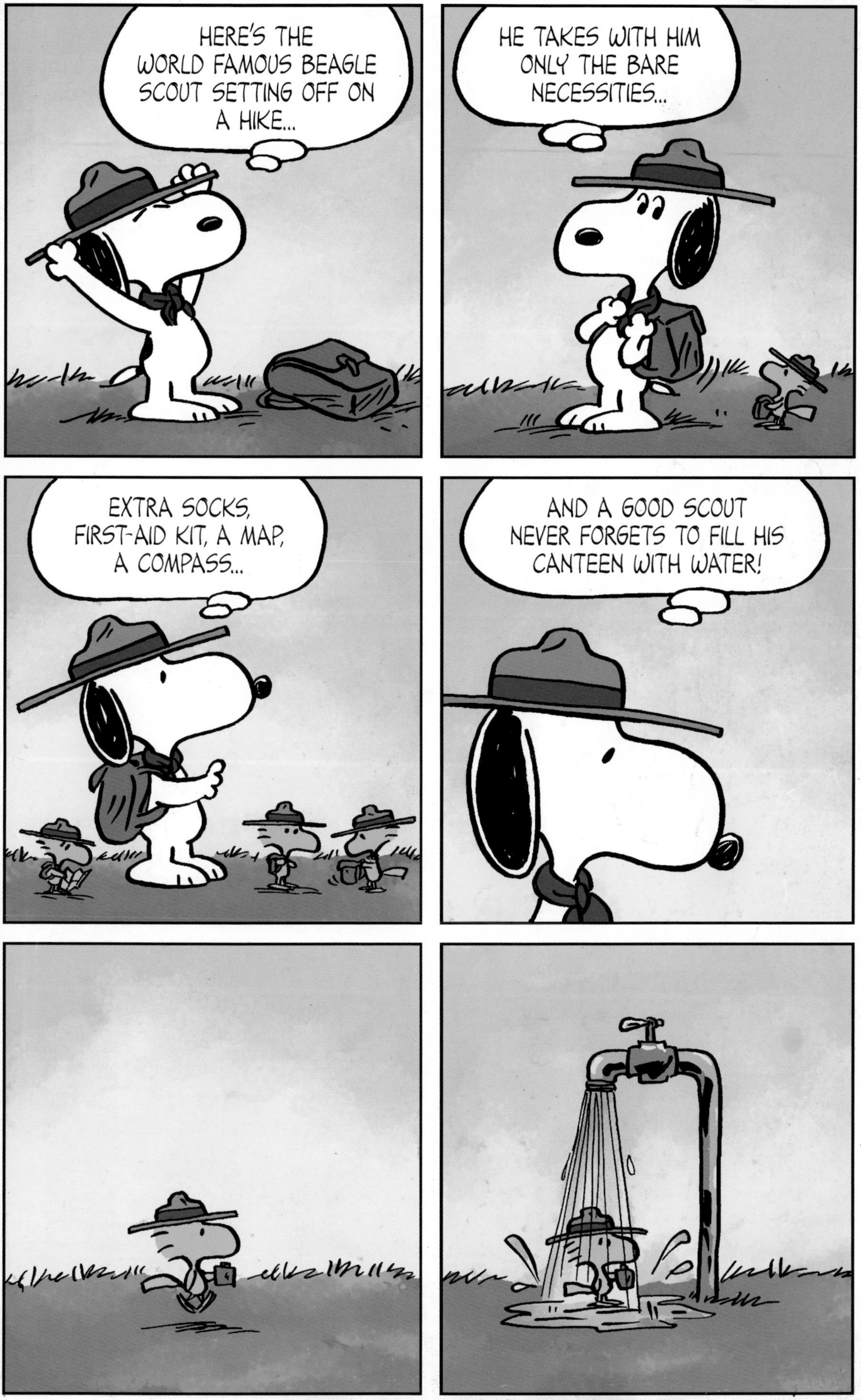
HERE'S THE WORLD FAMOUS BEAGLE SCOUT SETTING OFF ON A HIKE...
HE TAKES WITH HIM ONLY THE BARE NECESSITIES...
EXTRA SOCKS, FIRST-AID KIT, A MAP, A COMPASS...
AND A GOOD SCOUT NEVER FORGETS TO FILL HIS CANTEEN WITH WATER!

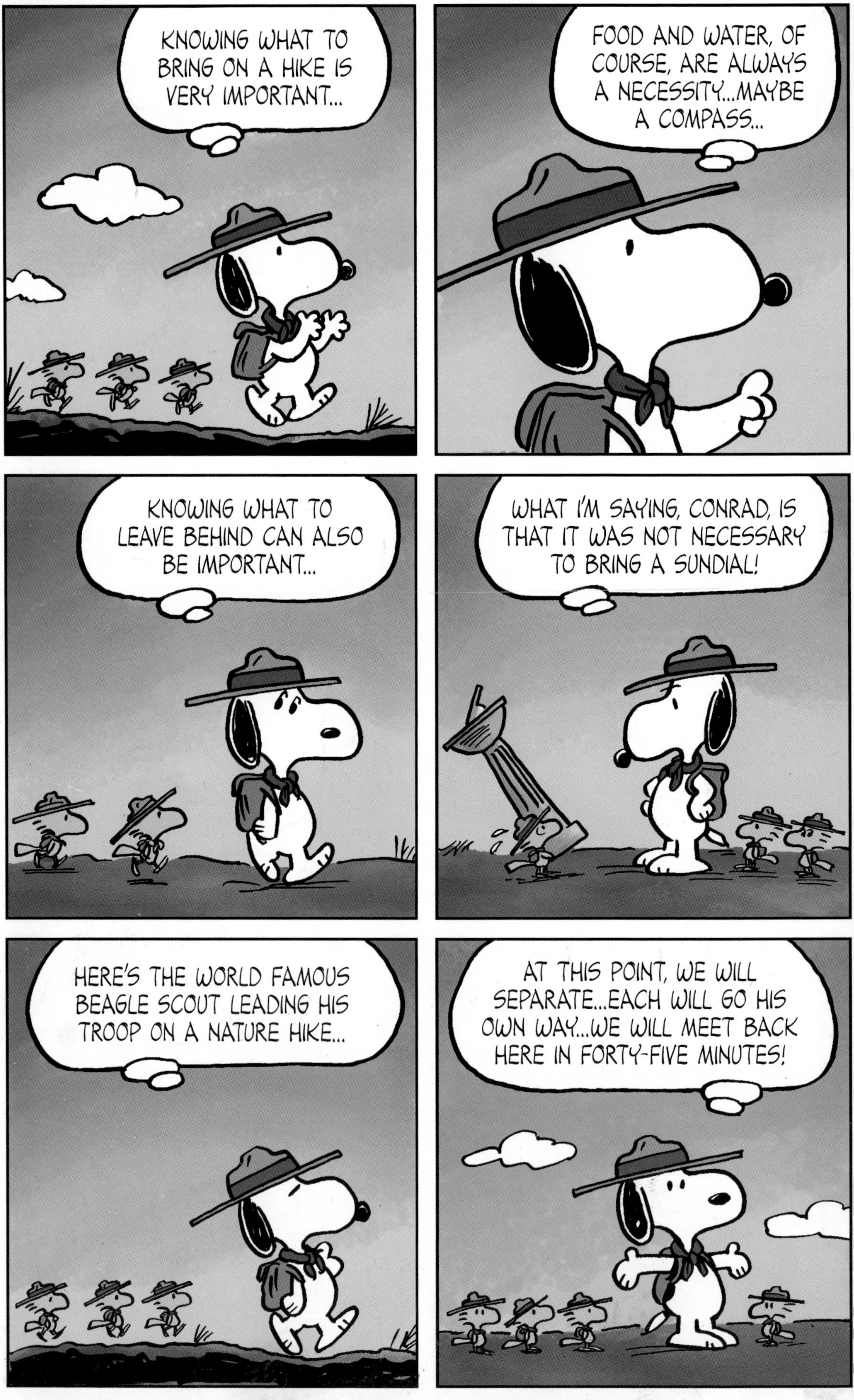
KNOWING WHAT TO BRING ON A HIKE IS VERY IMPORTANT...
FOOD AND WATER, OF COURSE, ARE ALWAYS A NECESSITY...MAYBE A COMPASS...
KNOWING WHAT TO LEAVE BEHIND CAN ALSO BE IMPORTANT...
WHAT I'M SAYING, CONRAD, IS THAT IT WAS NOT NECESSARY TO BRING A SUNDIAL!
HERE'S THE WORLD FAMOUS BEAGLE SCOUT LEADING HIS TROOP ON A NATURE HIKE...
AT THIS POINT, WE WILL SEPARATE...EACH WILL GO HIS OWN WAY...WE WILL MEET BACK HERE IN FORTY-FIVE MINUTES!

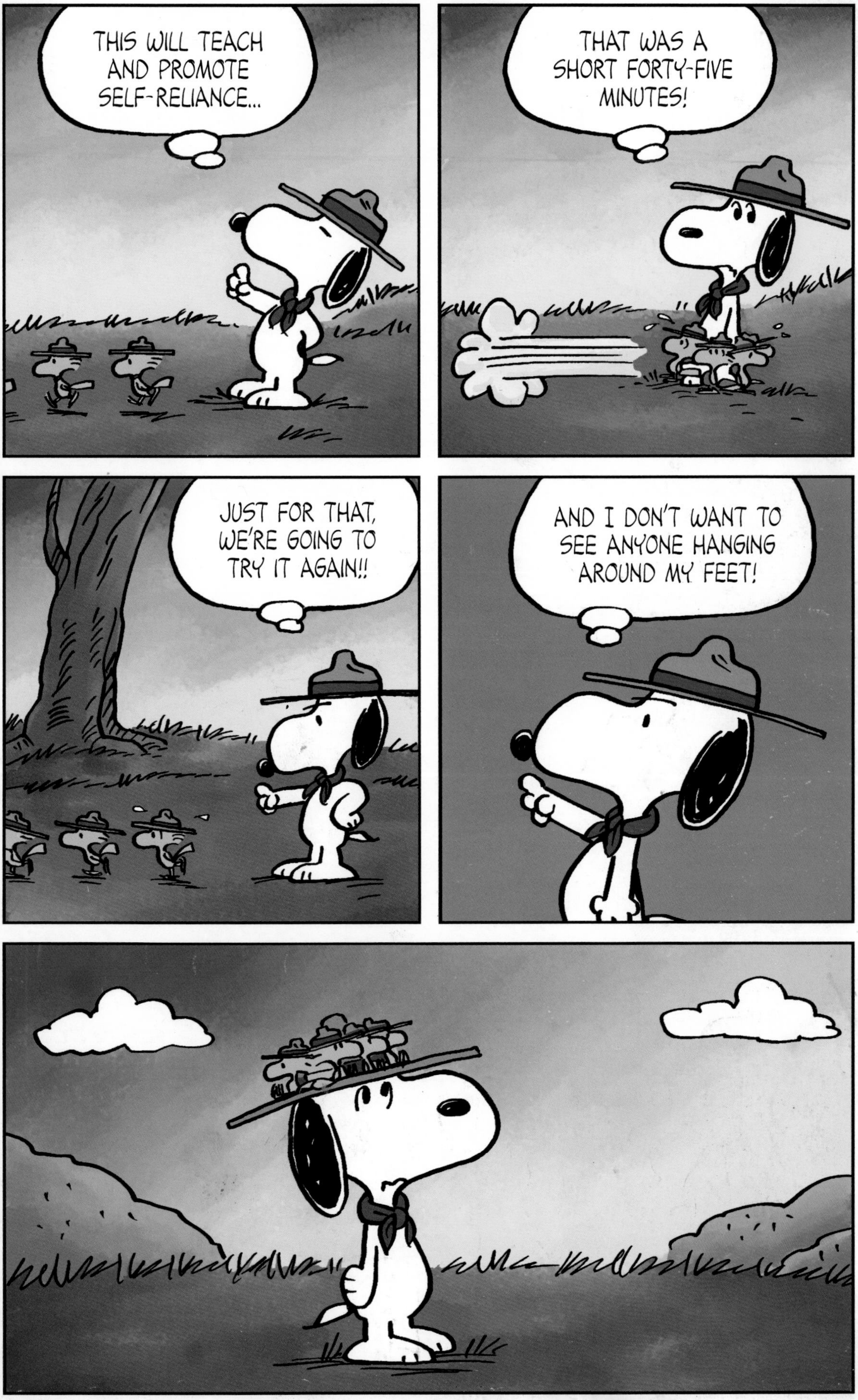

THIS WILL TEACH AND PROMOTE SELF-RELIANCE...
THAT WAS A SHORT FORTY-FIVE MINUTES!
JUST FOR THAT, WE'RE GOING TO TRY IT AGAIN!!
AND I DON'T WANT TO SEE ANYONE HANGING AROUND MY FEET!

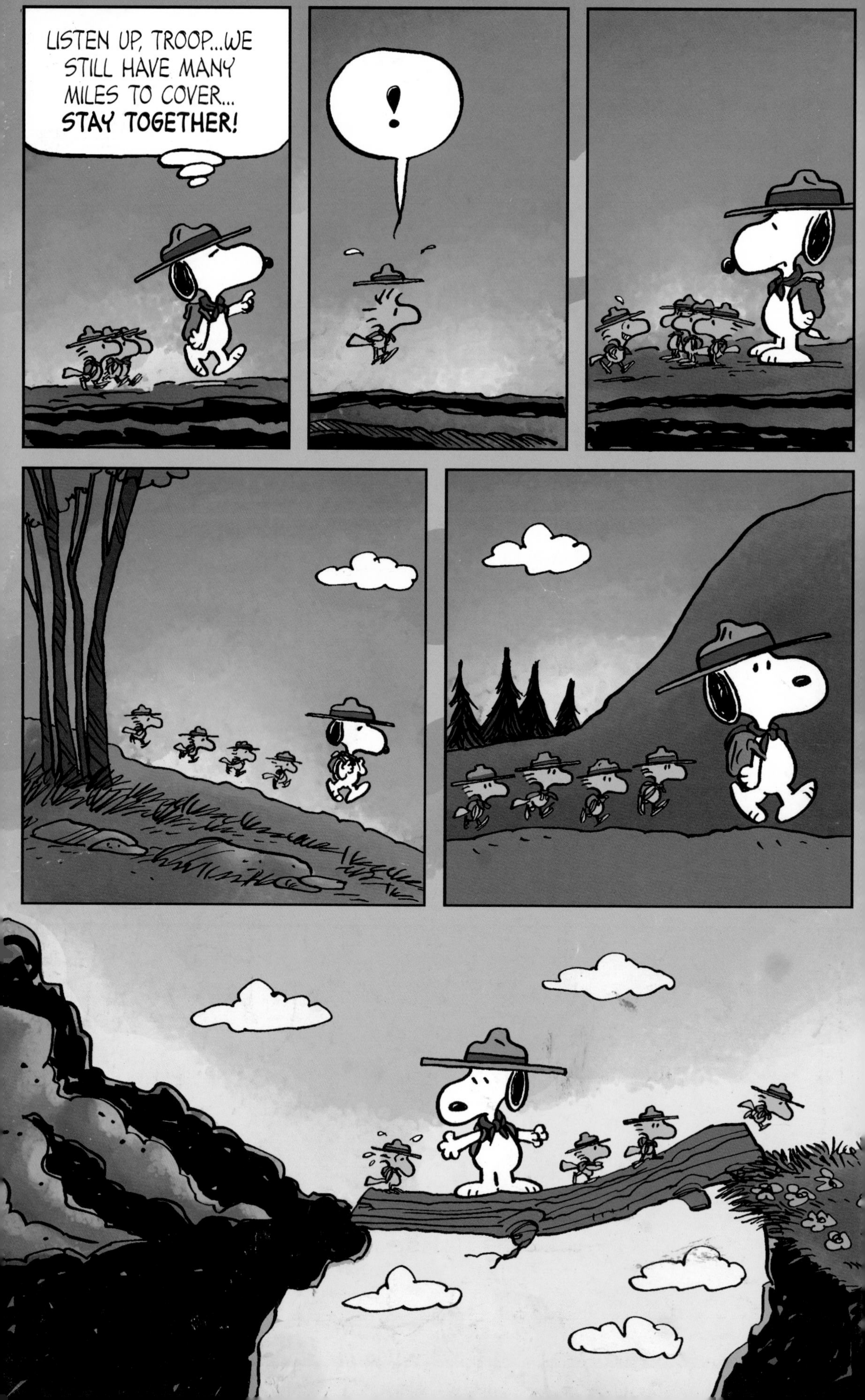
LISTEN UP, TROOP...WE STILL HAVE MANY MILES TO COVER... STAY TOGETHER!
!

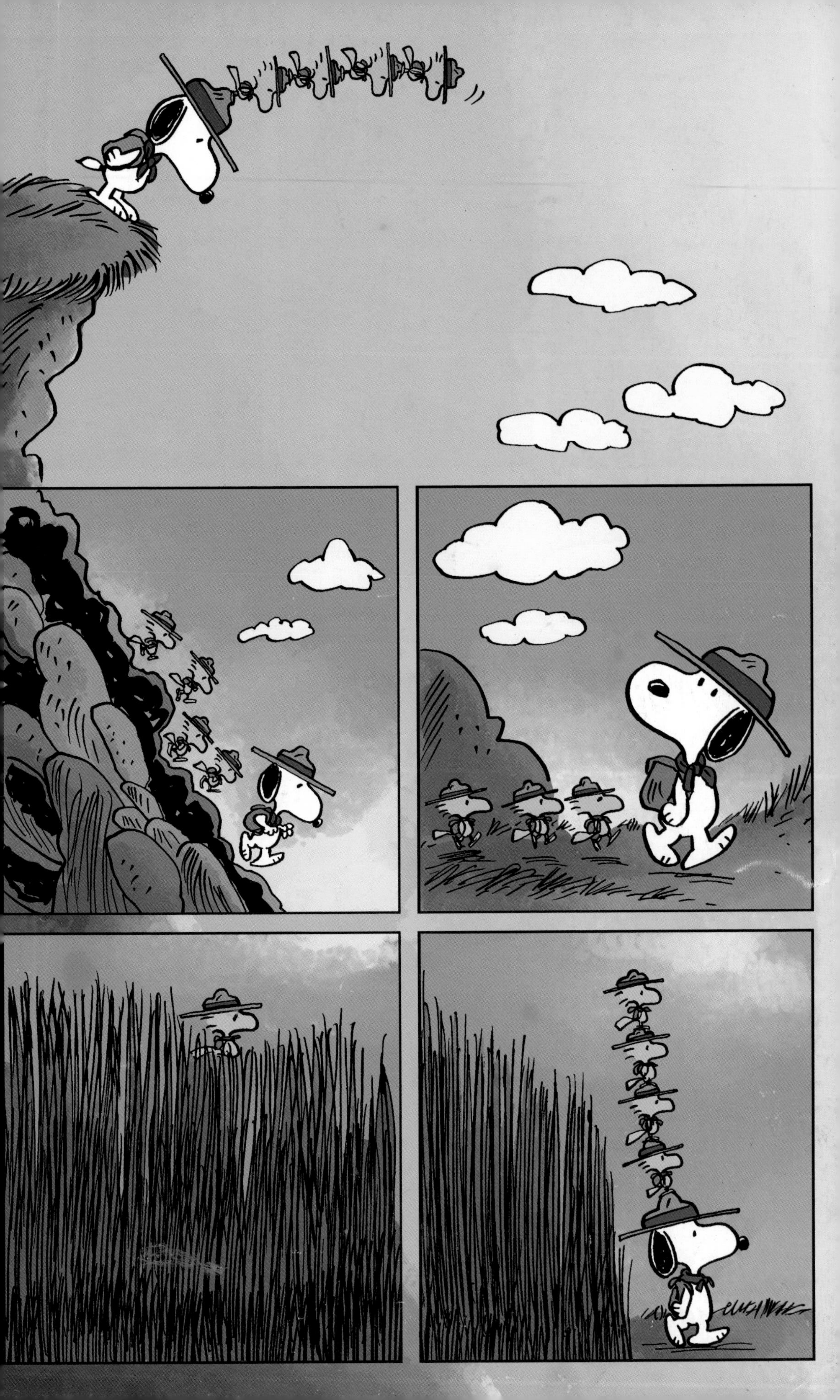

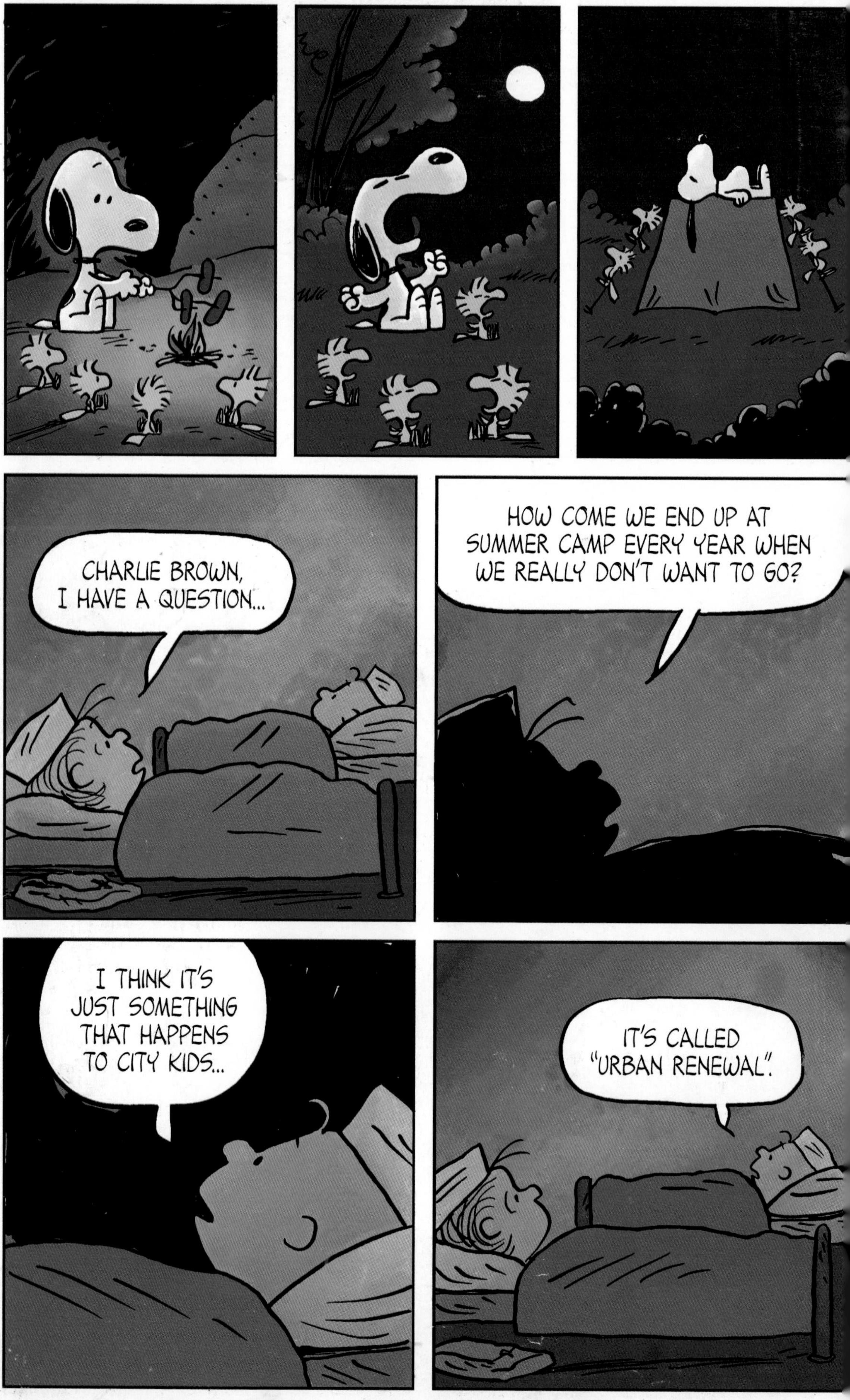
CHARLIE BROWN, I HAVE A QUESTION...
HOW COME WE END UP AT SUMMER CAMP EVERY YEAR WHEN WE REALLY DON'T WANT TO GO?
I THINK IT'S JUST SOMETHING THAT HAPPENS TO CITY KIDS...
IT'S CALLED "URBAN RENEWAL".

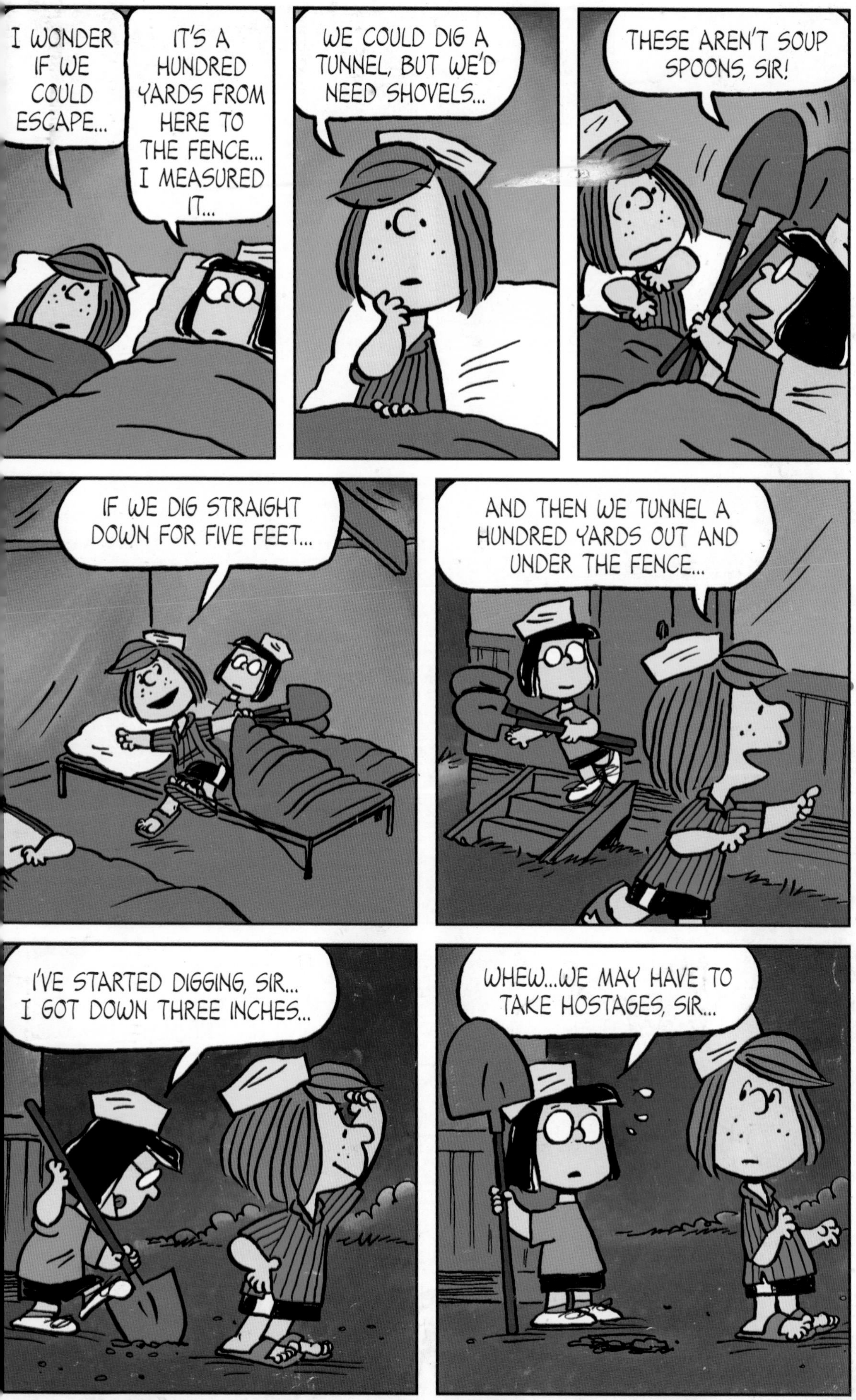
I WONDER IF WE COULD ESCAPE...
IT'S A HUNDRED YARDS FROM HERE TO THE FENCE... I MEASURED IT...
WE COULD DIG A TUNNEL, BUT WE'D NEED SHOVELS...
THESE AREN'T SOUP SPOONS, SIR!
IF WE DIG STRAIGHT DOWN FOR FIVE FEET...
AND THEN WE TUNNEL A HUNDRED YARDS OUT AND UNDER THE FENCE...
I'VE STARTED DIGGING, SIR... I GOT DOWN THREE INCHES...
WHEW...WE MAY HAVE TO TAKE HOSTAGES, SIR...

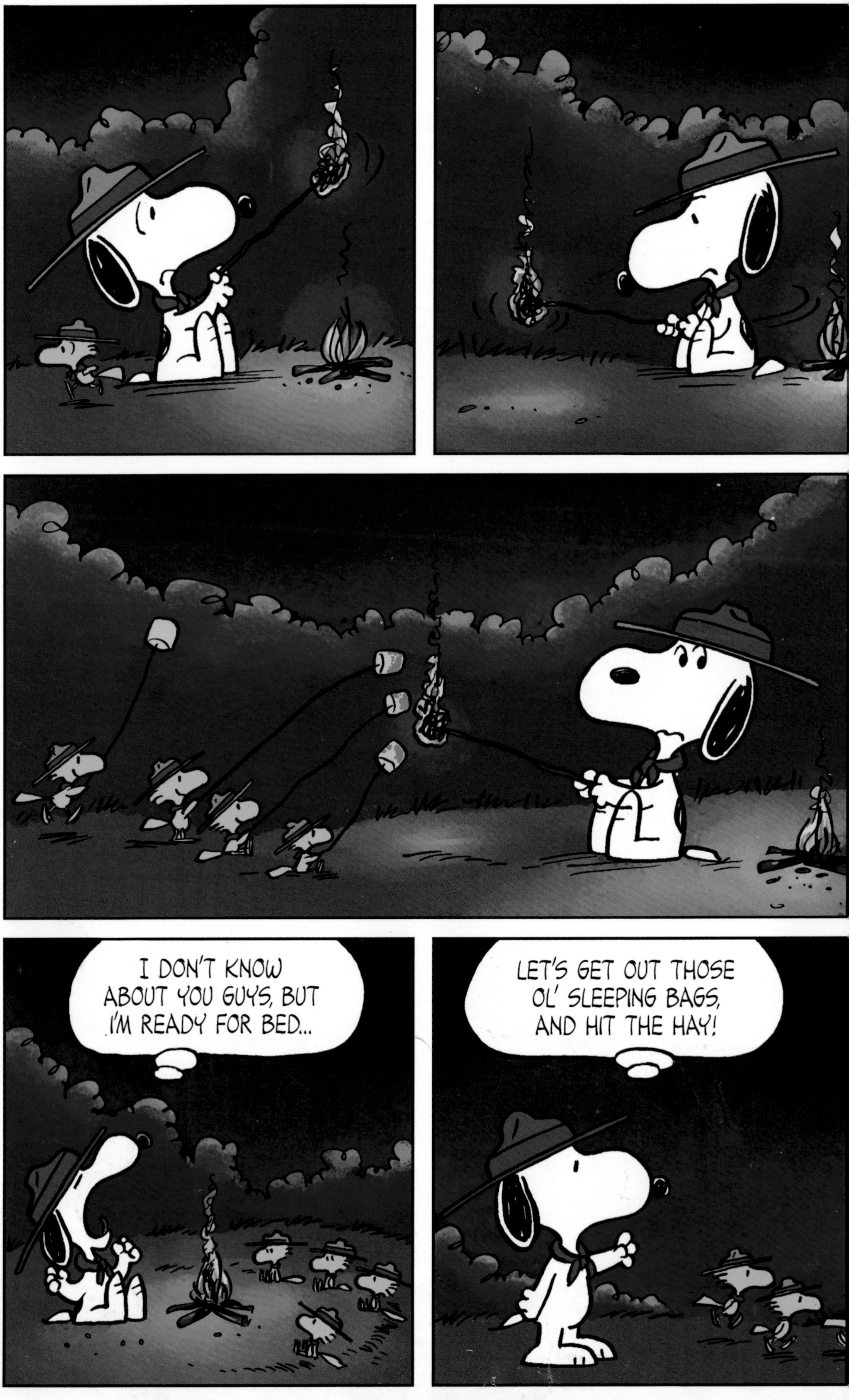
I DON'T KNOW ABOUT YOU GUYS, BUT I'M READY FOR BED...
LET'S GET OUT THOSE OL' SLEEPING BAGS, AND HIT THE HAY!

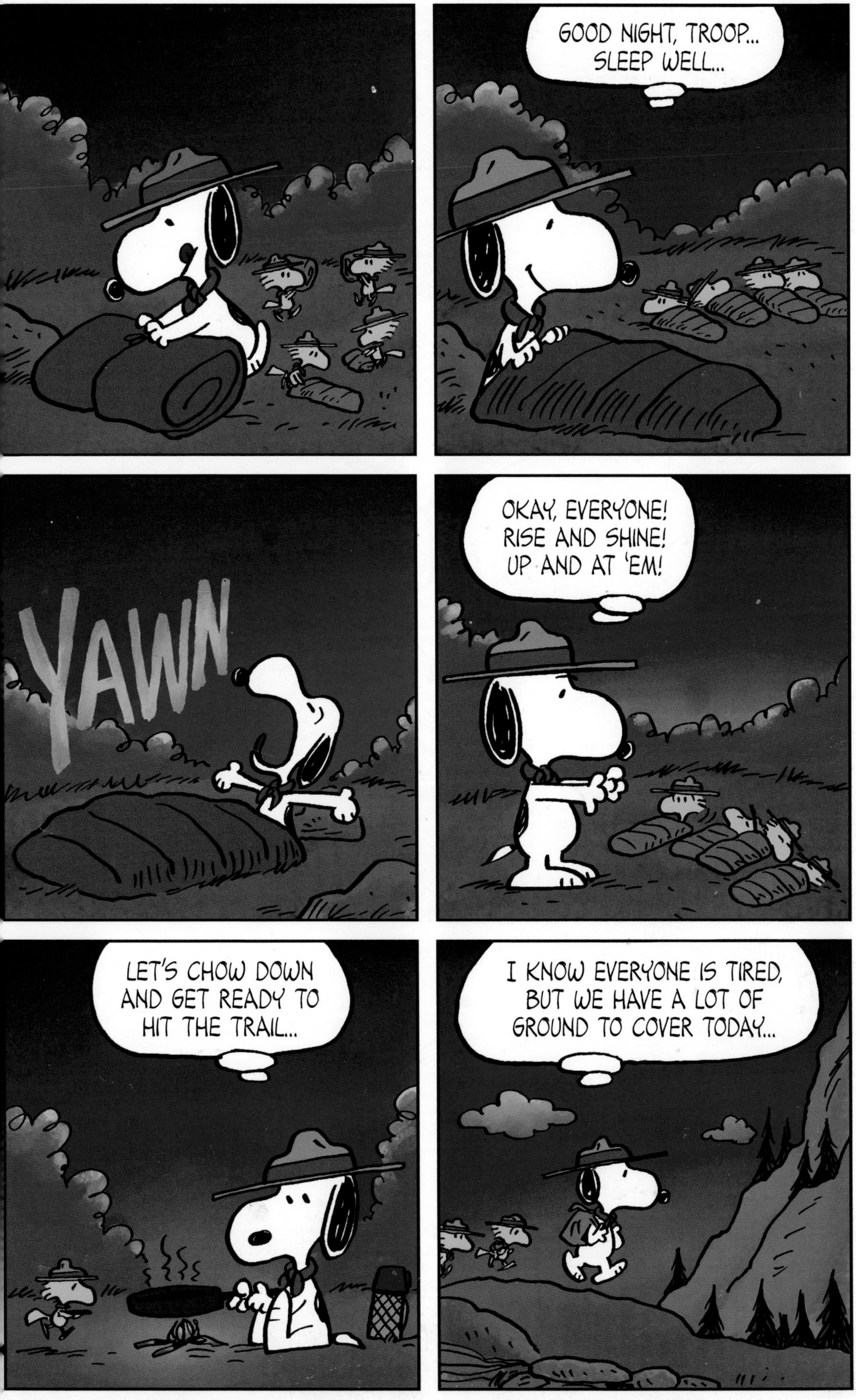
GOOD NIGHT, TROOP... SLEEP WELL...
YAWN
OKAY, EVERYONE! RISE AND SHINE! UP AND AT 'EM!
LET'S CHOW DOWN AND GET READY TO HIT THE TRAIL...
I KNOW EVERYONE IS TIRED, BUT WE HAVE A LOT OF GROUND TO COVER TODAY...

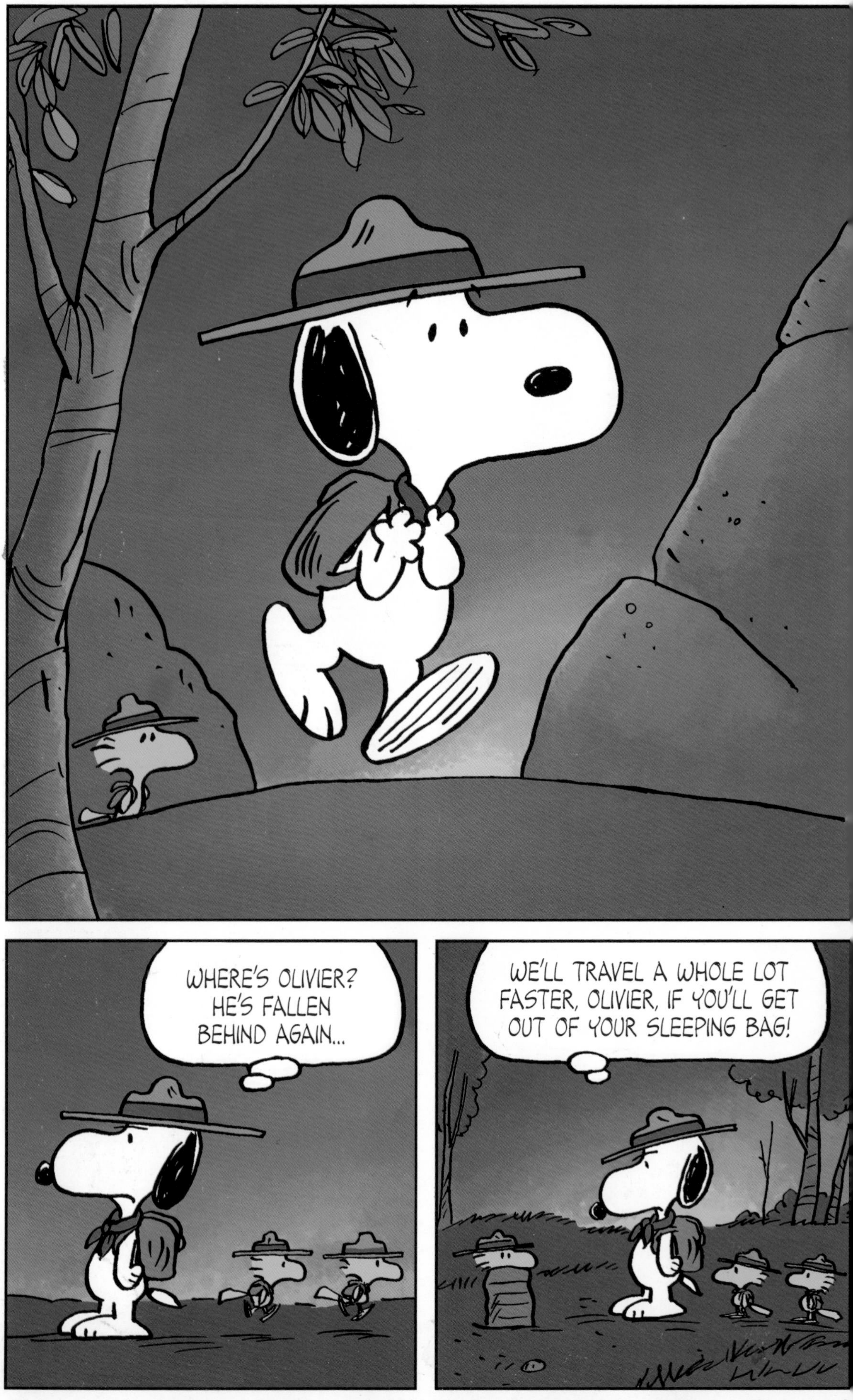
WHERE'S OLIVIER? HE'S FALLEN BEHIND AGAIN...
WE'LL TRAVEL A WHOLE LOT FASTER, OLIVIER, IF YOU'LL GET OUT OF YOUR SLEEPING BAG!

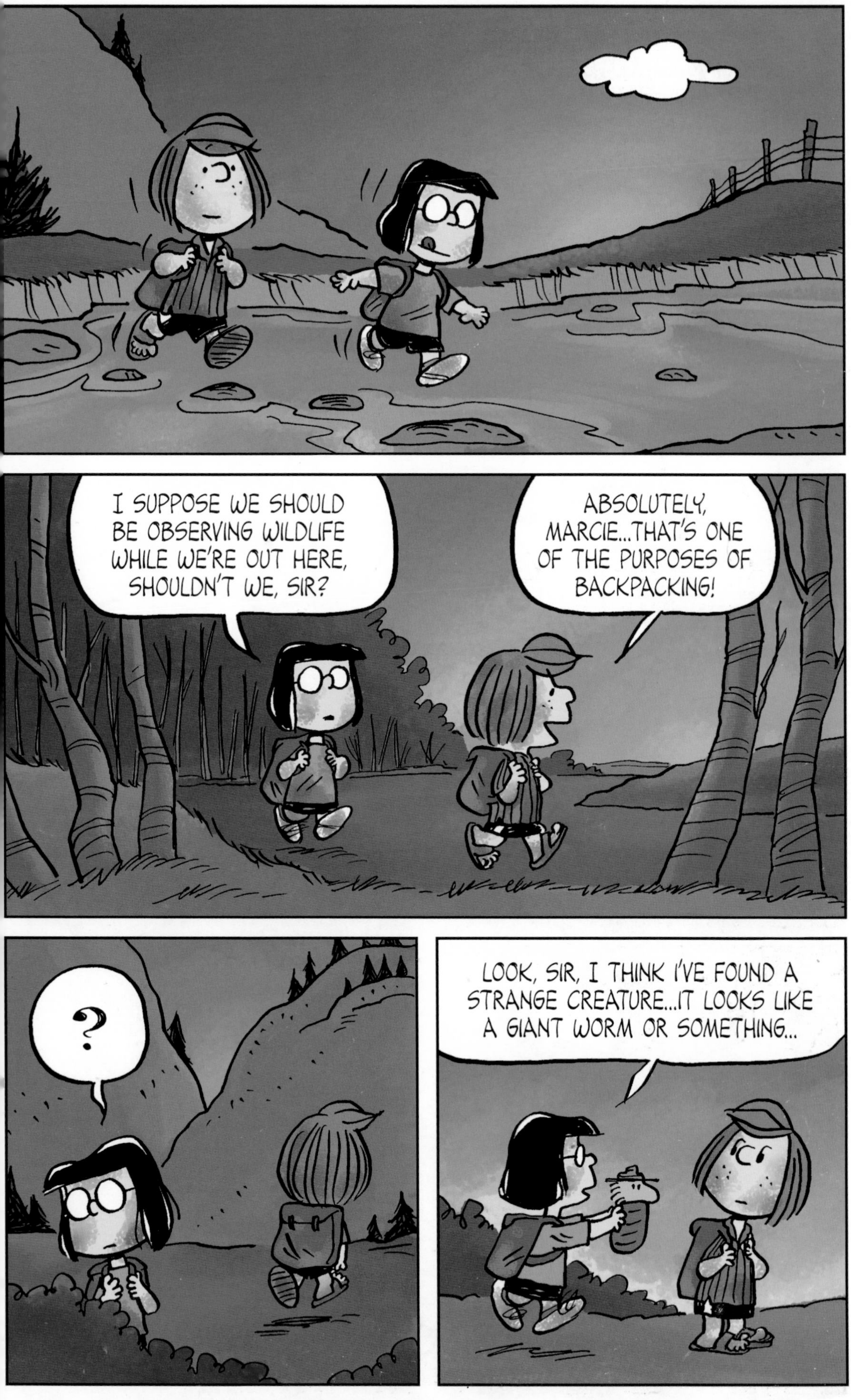
I SUPPOSE WE SHOULD BE OBSERVING WILDLIFE WHILE WE'RE OUT HERE, SHOULDN'T WE, SIR?
ABSOLUTELY, MARCIE...THAT'S ONE OF THE PURPOSES OF BACKPACKING!
?
LOOK, SIR, I THINK I'VE FOUND A STRANGE CREATURE...IT LOOKS LIKE A GIANT WORM OR SOMETHING...

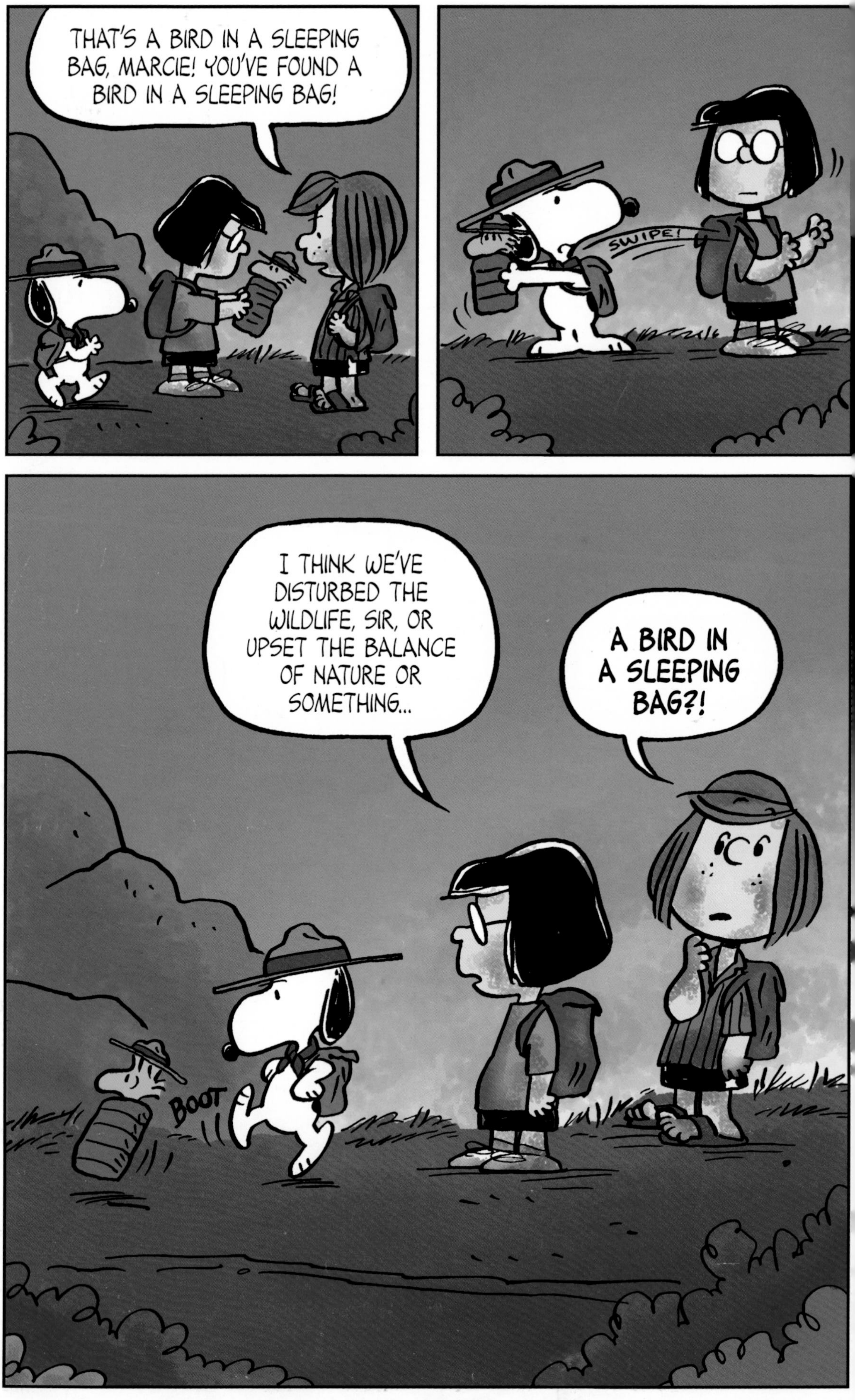
THAT'S A BIRD IN A SLEEPING BAG, MARCIE! YOU'VE FOUND A BIRD IN A SLEEPING BAG!
SWIPE!
I THINK WE'VE DISTURBED THE WILDLIFE, SIR, OR UPSET THE BALANCE OF NATURE OR SOMETHING...
A BIRD IN A SLEEPING BAG?!
BOOT

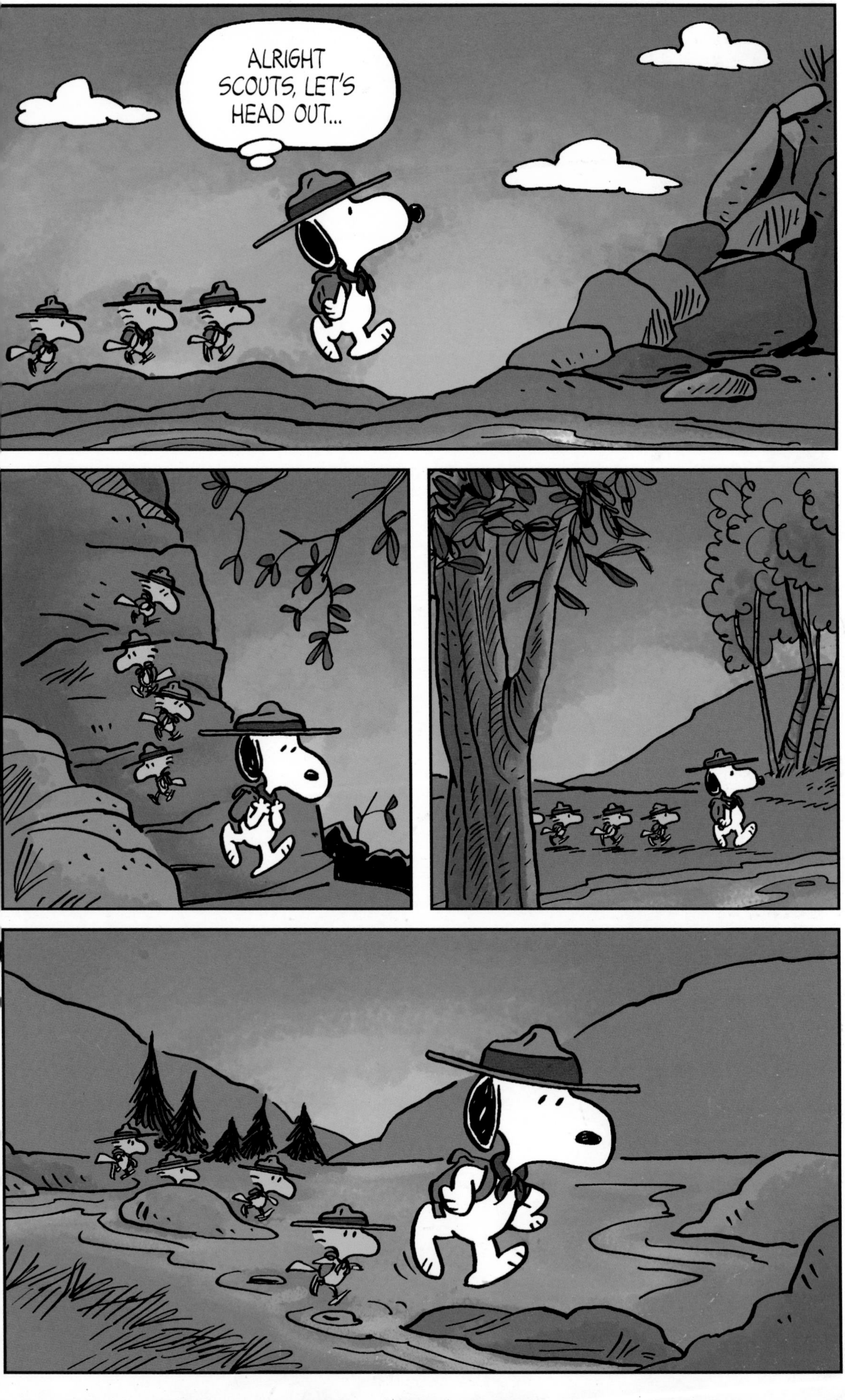
ALRIGHT SCOUTS, LET'S HEAD OUT...

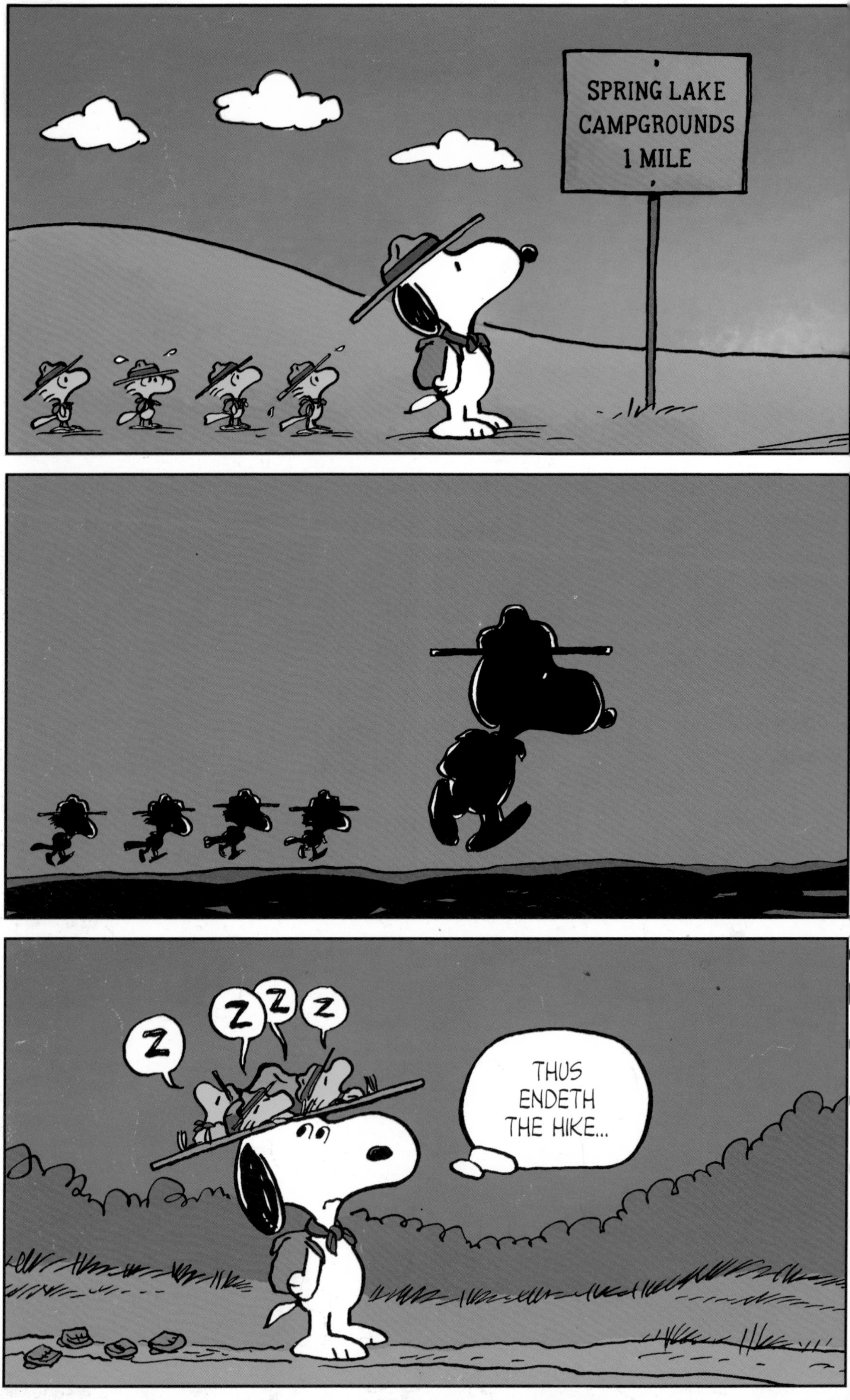
SPRING LAKE CAMPGROUNDS 1 MILE
Z
Z
Z
Z
THUS ENDETH THE HIKE...

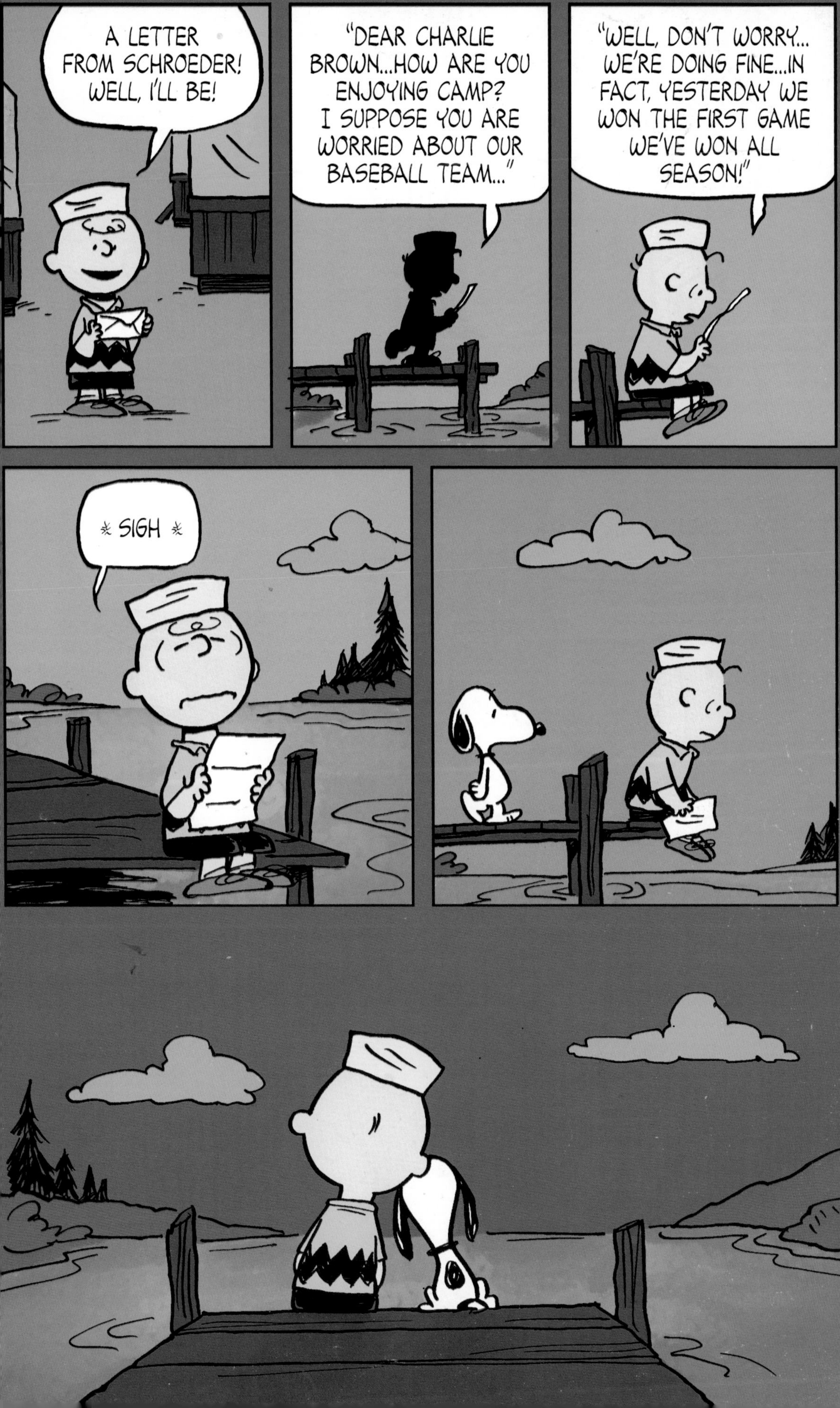
A LETTER FROM SCHROEDER! WELL, I'LL BE!
"DEAR CHARLIE BROWN...HOW ARE YOU ENJOYING CAMP? I SUPPOSE YOU ARE WORRIED ABOUT OUR BASEBALL TEAM..."
"WELL, DON'T WORRY... WE'RE DOING FINE...IN FACT, YESTERDAY WE WON THE FIRST GAME WE'VE WON ALL SEASON!"
SIGH

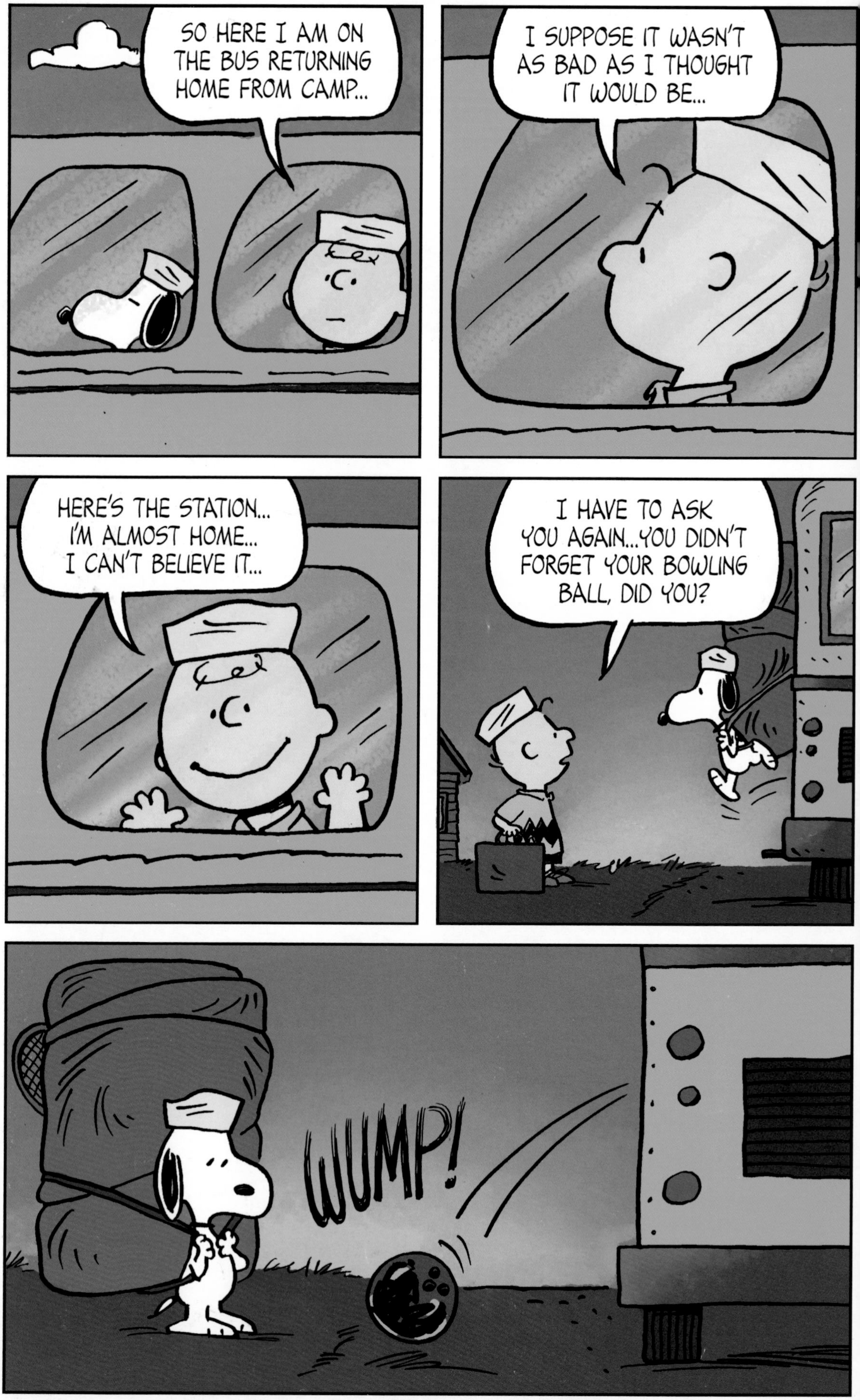
SO HERE I AM ON THE BUS RETURNING HOME FROM CAMP...
I SUPPOSE IT WASN'T AS BAD AS I THOUGHT IT WOULD BE...
HERE'S THE STATION... I'M ALMOST HOME... I CAN'T BELIEVE IT...
I HAVE TO ASK YOU AGAIN...YOU DIDN'T FORGET YOUR BOWLING BALL, DID YOU?
WUMP!

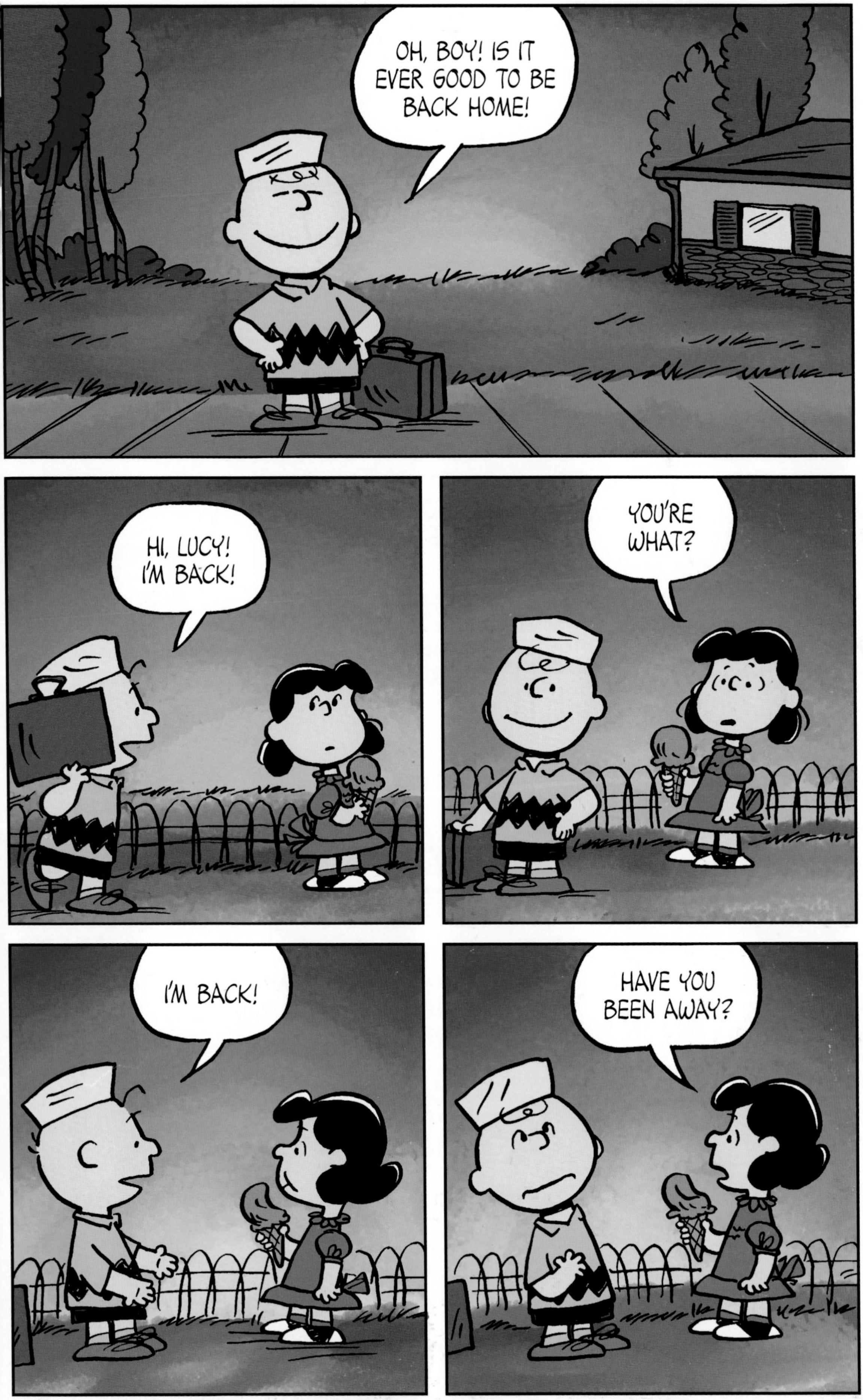
OH, BOY! IS IT EVER GOOD TO BE BACK HOME!
HI, LUCY! I'M BACK!
YOU'RE WHAT?
I'M BACK!
HAVE YOU BEEN AWAY?

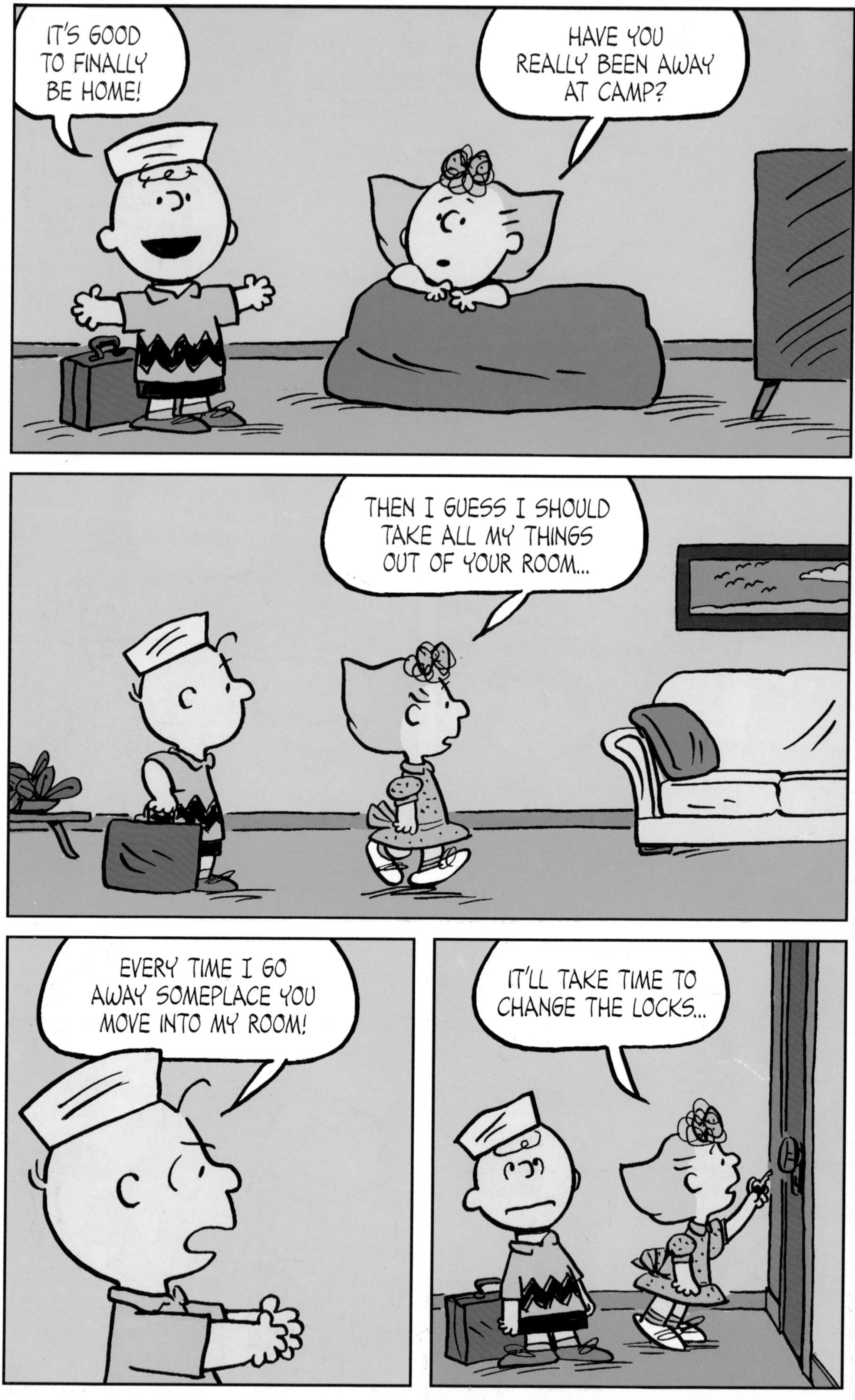
IT'S GOOD TO FINALLY BE HOME!
HAVE YOU REALLY BEEN AWAY AT CAMP?
THEN I GUESS I SHOULD TAKE ALL MY THINGS OUT OF YOUR ROOM...
EVERY TIME I GO AWAY SOMEPLACE YOU MOVE INTO MY ROOM!
IT'LL TAKE TIME TO CHANGE THE LOCKS...

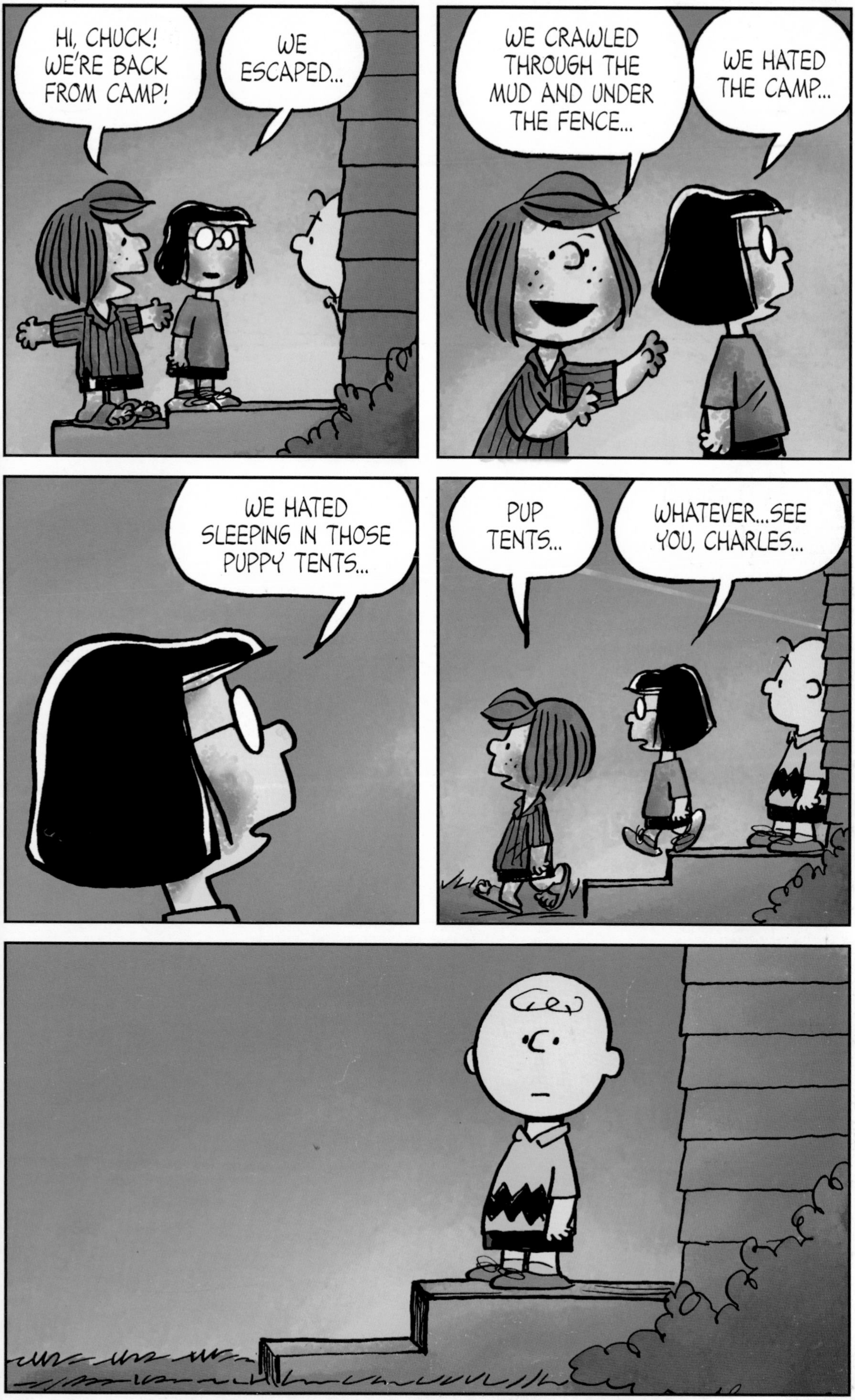
HI, CHUCK! WE'RE BACK FROM CAMP!
WE ESCAPED...
WE CRAWLED THROUGH THE MUD AND UNDER THE FENCE...
WE HATED THE CAMP...
WE HATED SLEEPING IN THOSE PUPPY TENTS...
PUP TENTS...
WHATEVER...SEE YOU, CHARLES...

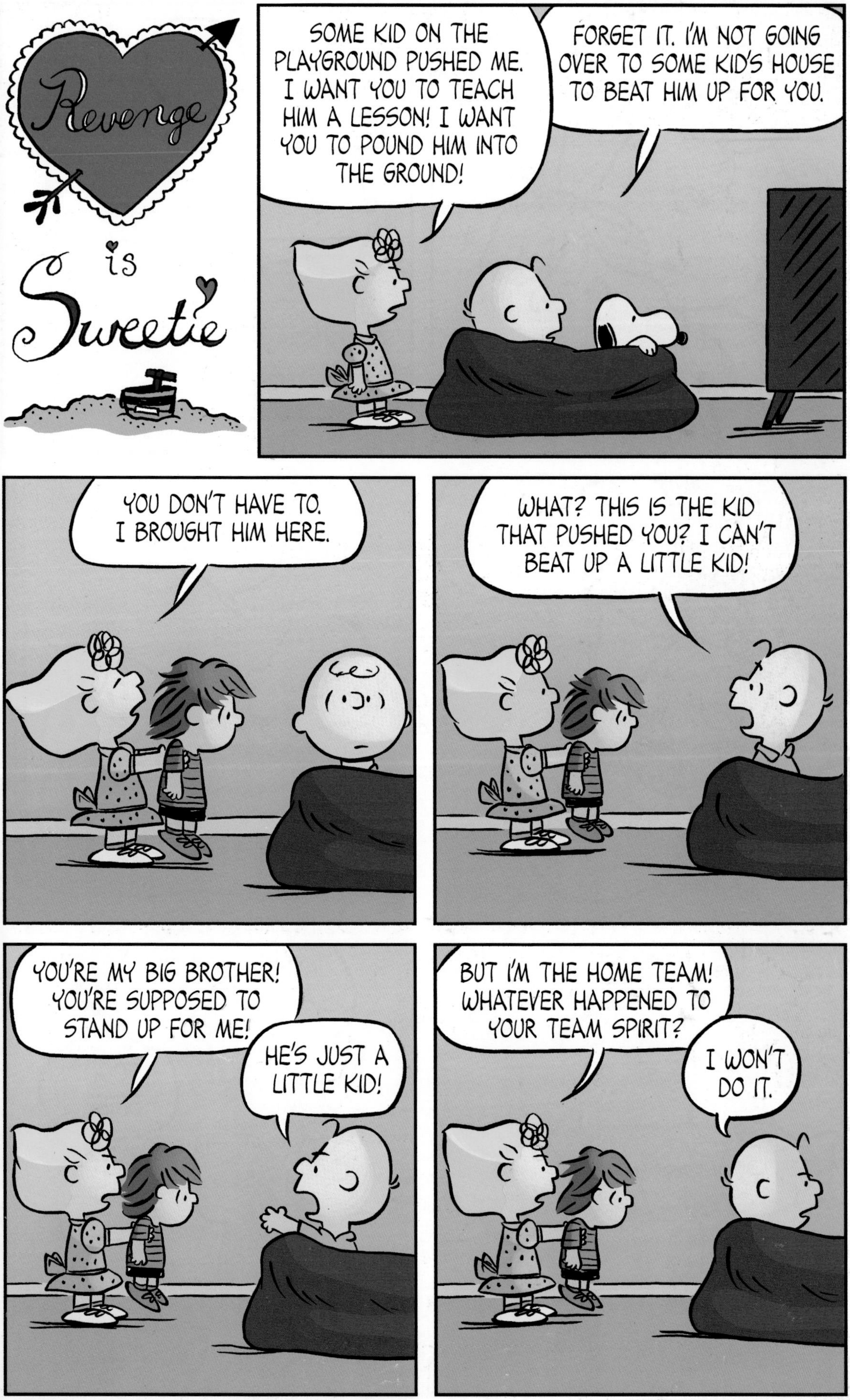
Revenge is Sweetie
SOME KID ON THE PLAYGROUND PUSHED ME. I WANT YOU TO TEACH HIM A LESSON! I WANT YOU TO POUND HIM INTO THE GROUND!
FORGET IT. I'M NOT GOING OVER TO SOME KID'S HOUSE TO BEAT HIM UP FOR YOU.
YOU DON'T HAVE TO. I BROUGHT HIM HERE.
WHAT? THIS IS THE KID THAT PUSHED YOU? I CAN'T BEAT UP A LITTLE KID!
YOU'RE MY BIG BROTHER! YOU'RE SUPPOSED TO STAND UP FOR ME!
HE'S JUST A LITTLE KID!
BUT I'M THE HOME TEAM! WHATEVER HAPPENED TO YOUR TEAM SPIRIT?
I WON'T DO IT.

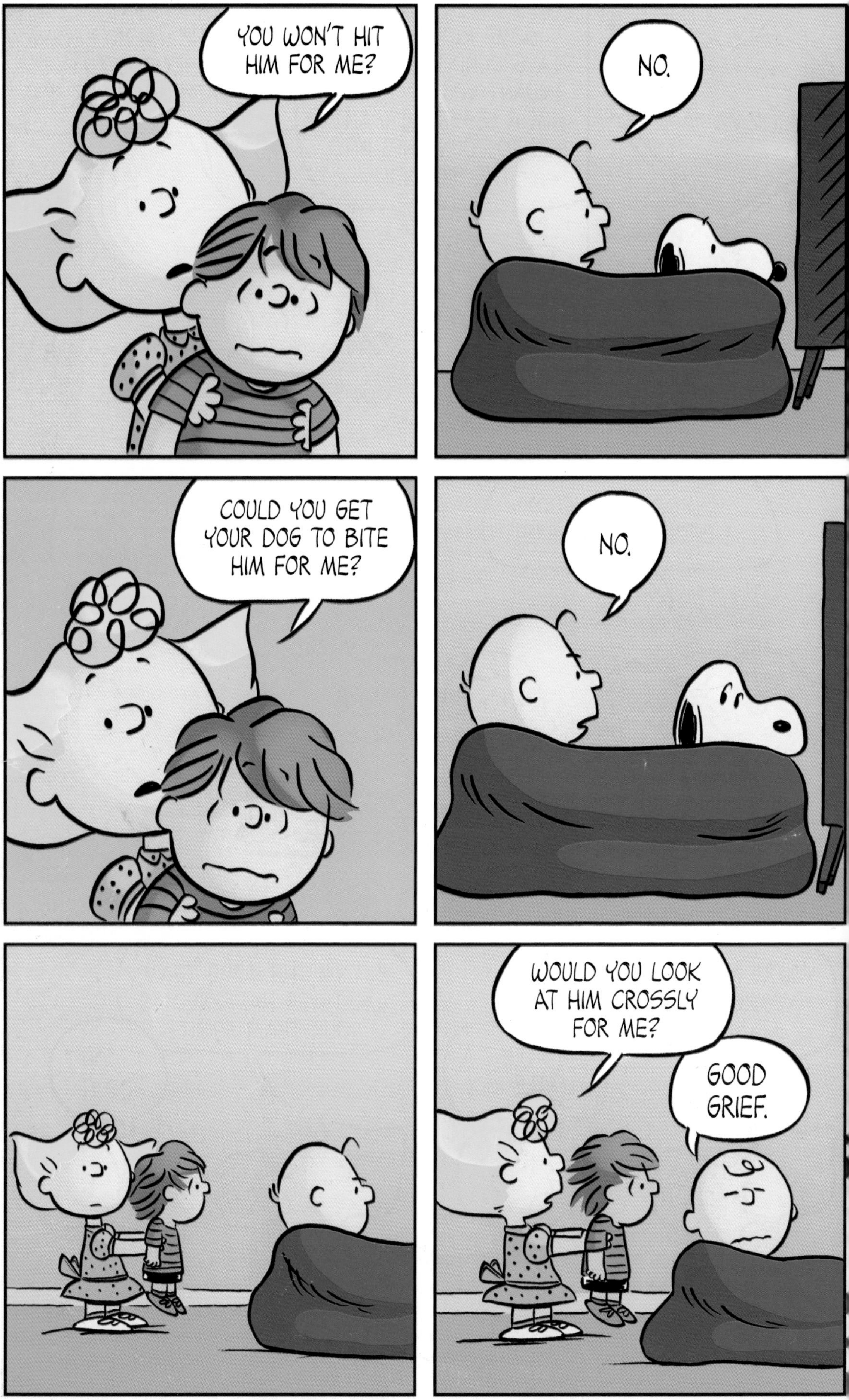
YOU WON'T HIT HIM FOR ME?
NO.
COULD YOU GET YOUR DOG TO BITE HIM FOR ME?
NO.
WOULD YOU LOOK AT HIM CROSSLY FOR ME?
GOOD GRIEF.

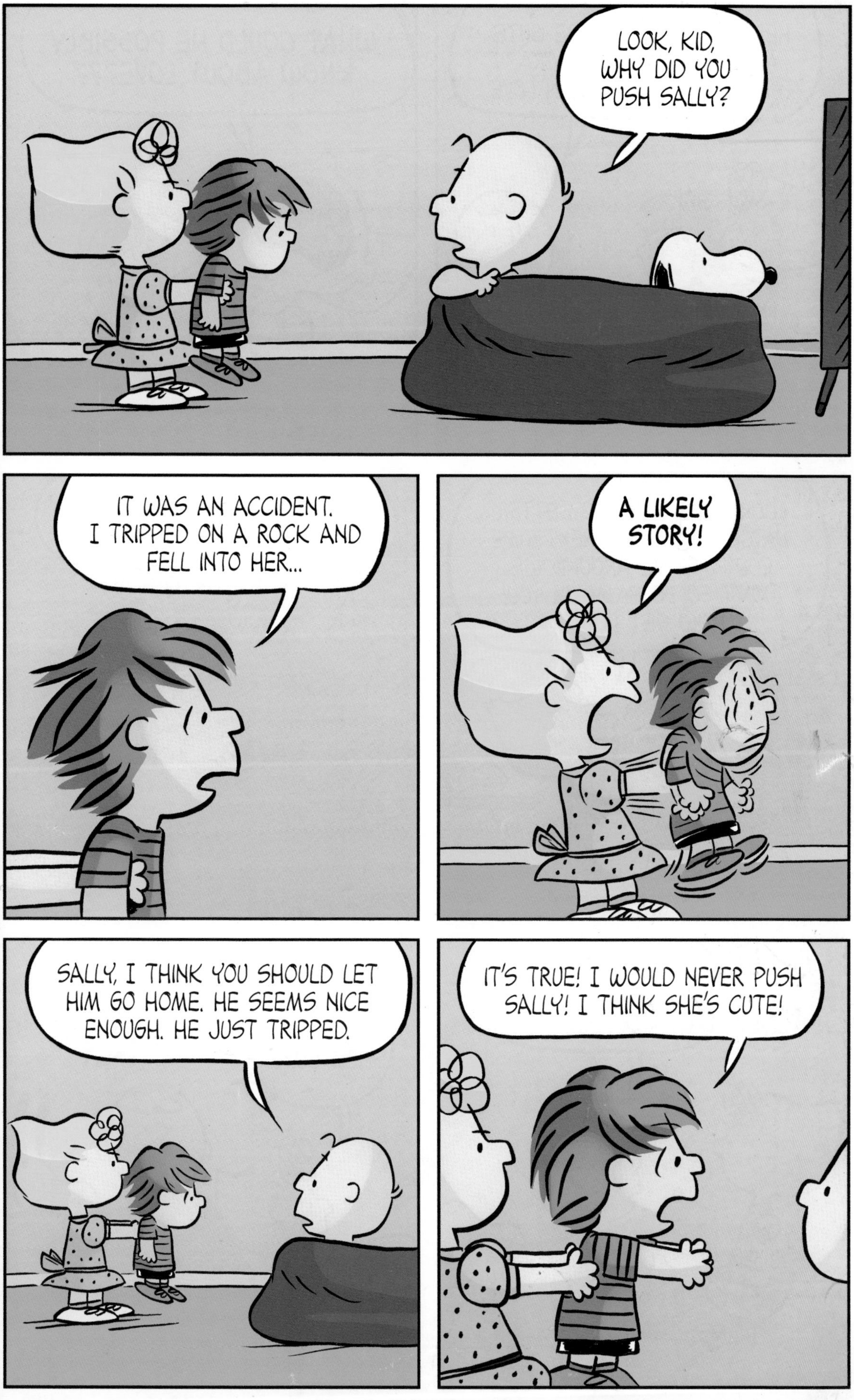
LOOK, KID, WHY DID YOU PUSH SALLY?
IT WAS AN ACCIDENT. I TRIPPED ON A ROCK AND FELL INTO HER...
A LIKELY STORY!
SALLY, I THINK YOU SHOULD LET HIM GO HOME. HE SEEMS NICE ENOUGH. HE JUST TRIPPED.
IT'S TRUE! I WOULD NEVER PUSH SALLY! I THINK SHE'S CUTE!

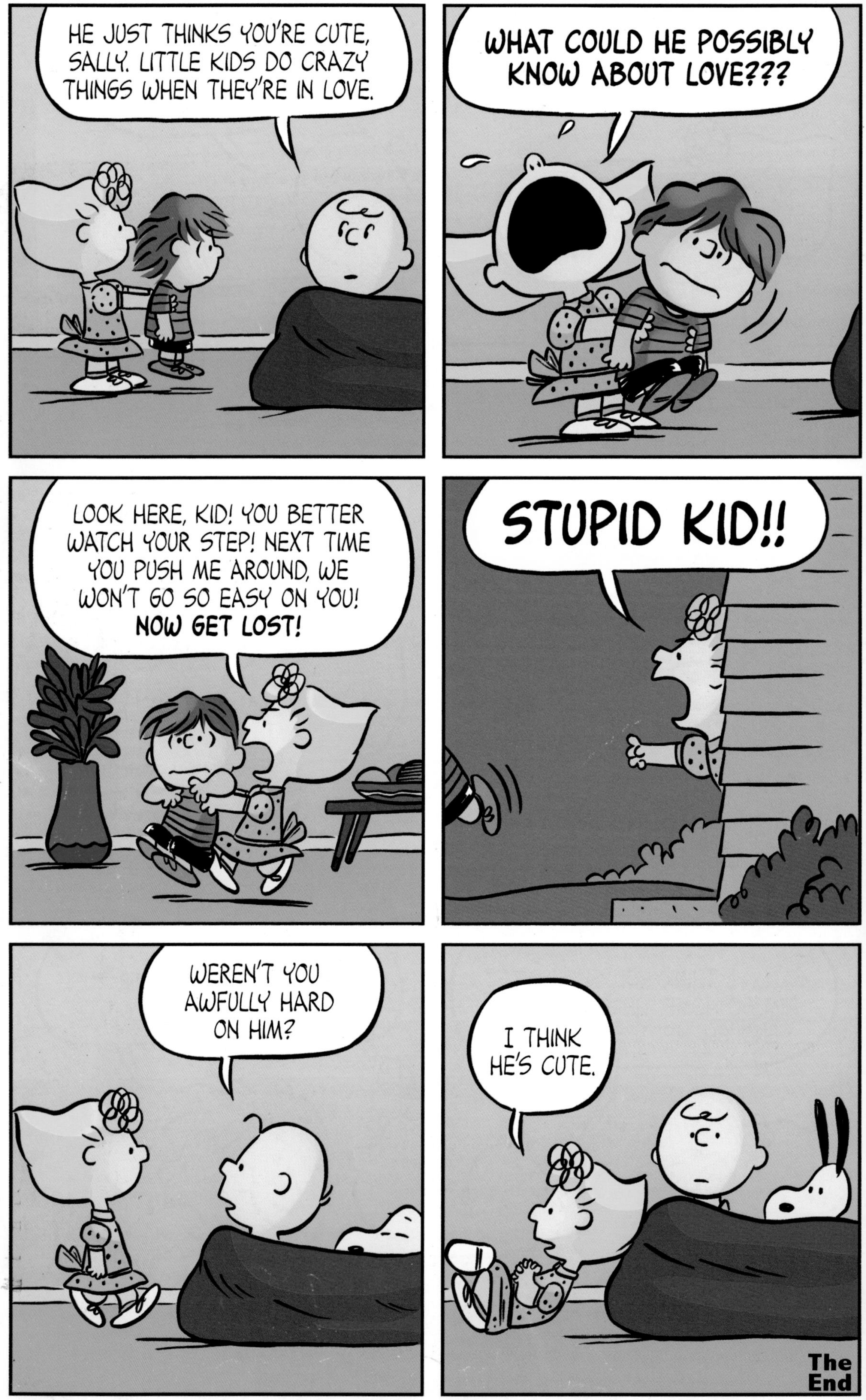
HE JUST THINKS YOU'RE CUTE, SALLY. LITTLE KIDS DO CRAZY THINGS WHEN THEY'RE IN LOVE.
WHAT COULD HE POSSIBLY KNOW ABOUT LOVE???
LOOK HERE, KID! YOU BETTER WATCH YOUR STEP! NEXT TIME YOU PUSH ME AROUND, WE WON'T GO SO EASY ON YOU! NOW GET LOST!
STUPID KID!!
WEREN'T YOU AWFULLY HARD ON HIM?
I THINK HE'S CUTE.
The End

PEANUTS
by SCHULZ

CHOMP CHOMP CHOMP

HERE YOU ARE, SNOOPY... YOU CAN HAVE THE REST OF MY DOUGHNUT...

BIG DEAL!

NOW, I'M SUPPOSED TO BE REAL GRATEFUL...

A CRUMB HERE AND A CRUMB THERE...

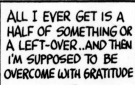

ALL I EVER GET IS A HALF OF SOMETHING OR A LEFT-OVER..AND THEN I'M SUPPOSED TO BE OVERCOME WITH GRATITUDE

A PIECE OF THIS AND A PIECE OF THAT....JUST CRUMBS! I'M ABOUT TENTH-CLASS!

THE MORE I THINK ABOUT IT, THE MADDER I GET...

WHEN I DIE, I'LL PROBABLY GET THE SMALLEST ROOM IN HEAVEN!

HERE YOU ARE, SNOOPY... YOU CAN HAVE PART OF MY CANDY BAR...

BLEAH!

NOW, WHAT WAS **THAT** ALL ABOUT?

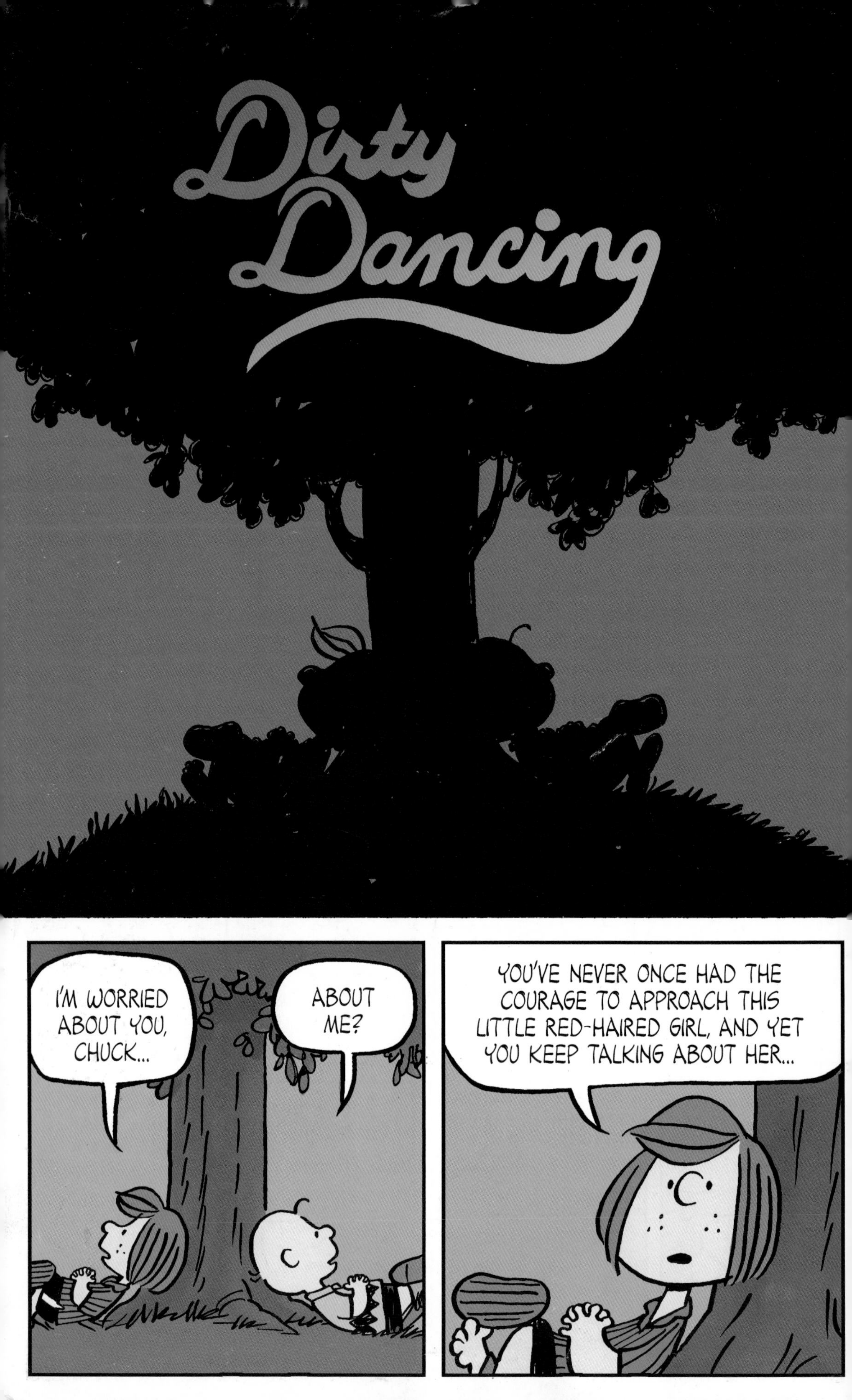
Dirty Dancing
I'M WORRIED ABOUT YOU, CHUCK...
ABOUT ME?
YOU'VE NEVER ONCE HAD THE COURAGE TO APPROACH THIS LITTLE RED-HAIRED GIRL, AND YET YOU KEEP TALKING ABOUT HER...

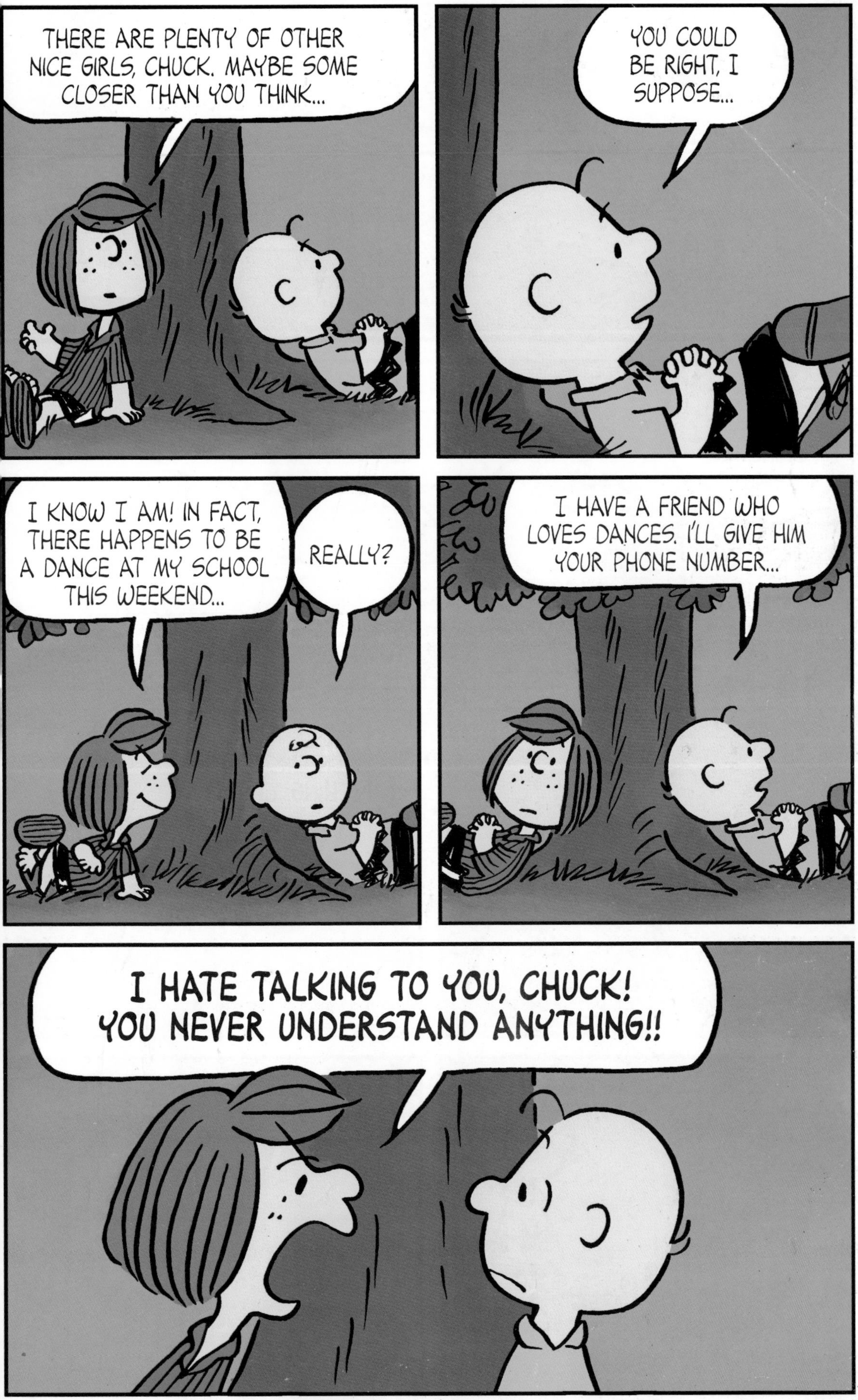
THERE ARE PLENTY OF OTHER NICE GIRLS, CHUCK. MAYBE SOME CLOSER THAN YOU THINK...
YOU COULD BE RIGHT, I SUPPOSE...
I KNOW I AM! IN FACT, THERE HAPPENS TO BE A DANCE AT MY SCHOOL THIS WEEKEND...
REALLY?
I HAVE A FRIEND WHO LOVES DANCES. I'LL GIVE HIM YOUR PHONE NUMBER...
I HATE TALKING TO YOU, CHUCK! YOU NEVER UNDERSTAND ANYTHING!!

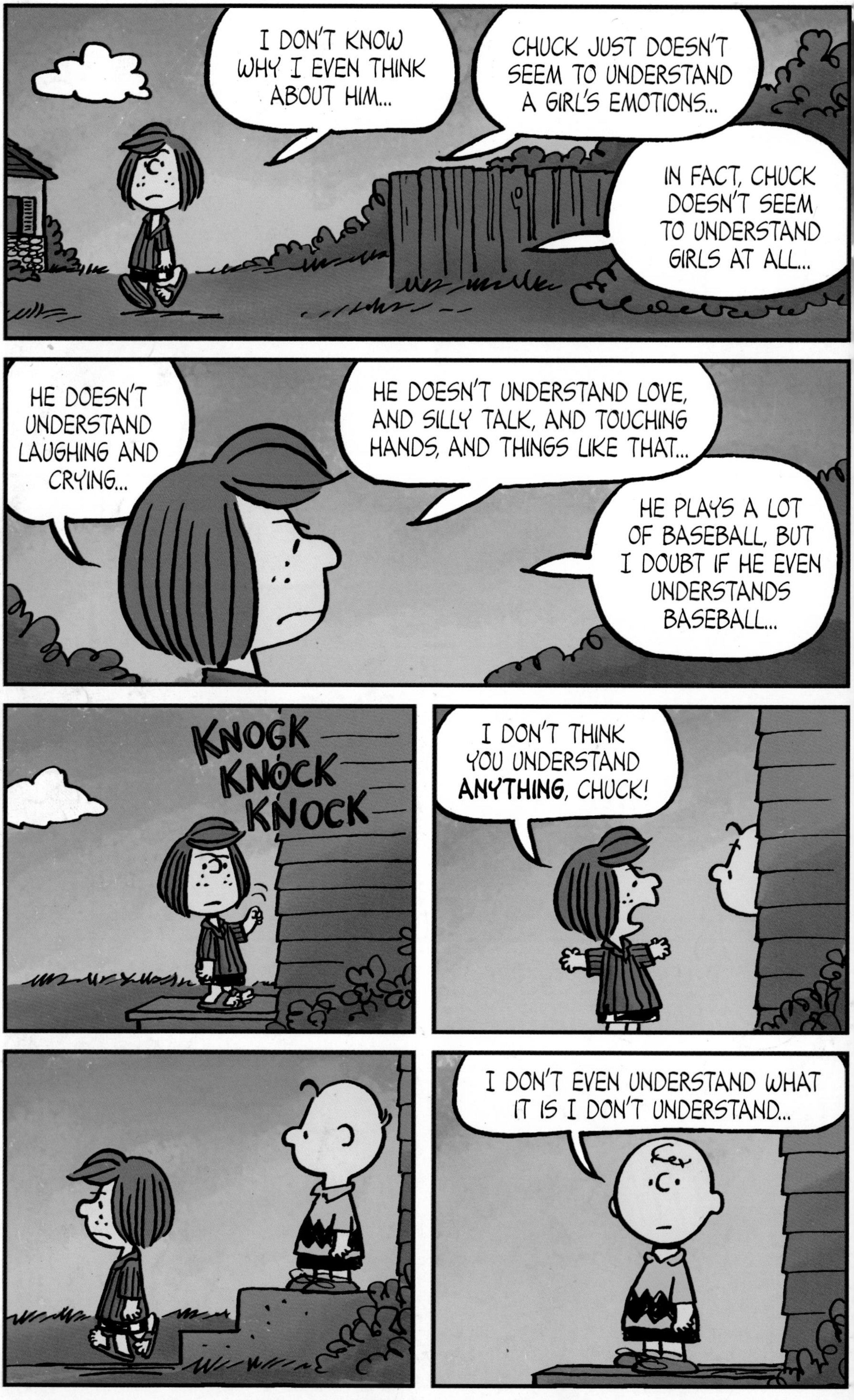
I DON'T KNOW WHY I EVEN THINK ABOUT HIM...
CHUCK JUST DOESN'T SEEM TO UNDERSTAND A GIRL'S EMOTIONS...
IN FACT, CHUCK DOESN'T SEEM TO UNDERSTAND GIRLS AT ALL...
HE DOESN'T UNDERSTAND LAUGHING AND CRYING...
HE DOESN'T UNDERSTAND LOVE, AND SILLY TALK, AND TOUCHING HANDS, AND THINGS LIKE THAT...
HE PLAYS A LOT OF BASEBALL, BUT I DOUBT IF HE EVEN UNDERSTANDS BASEBALL...
KNOCK KNOCK KNOCK
I DON'T THINK YOU UNDERSTAND **ANYTHING**, CHUCK!
I DON'T EVEN UNDERSTAND WHAT IT IS I DON'T UNDERSTAND...

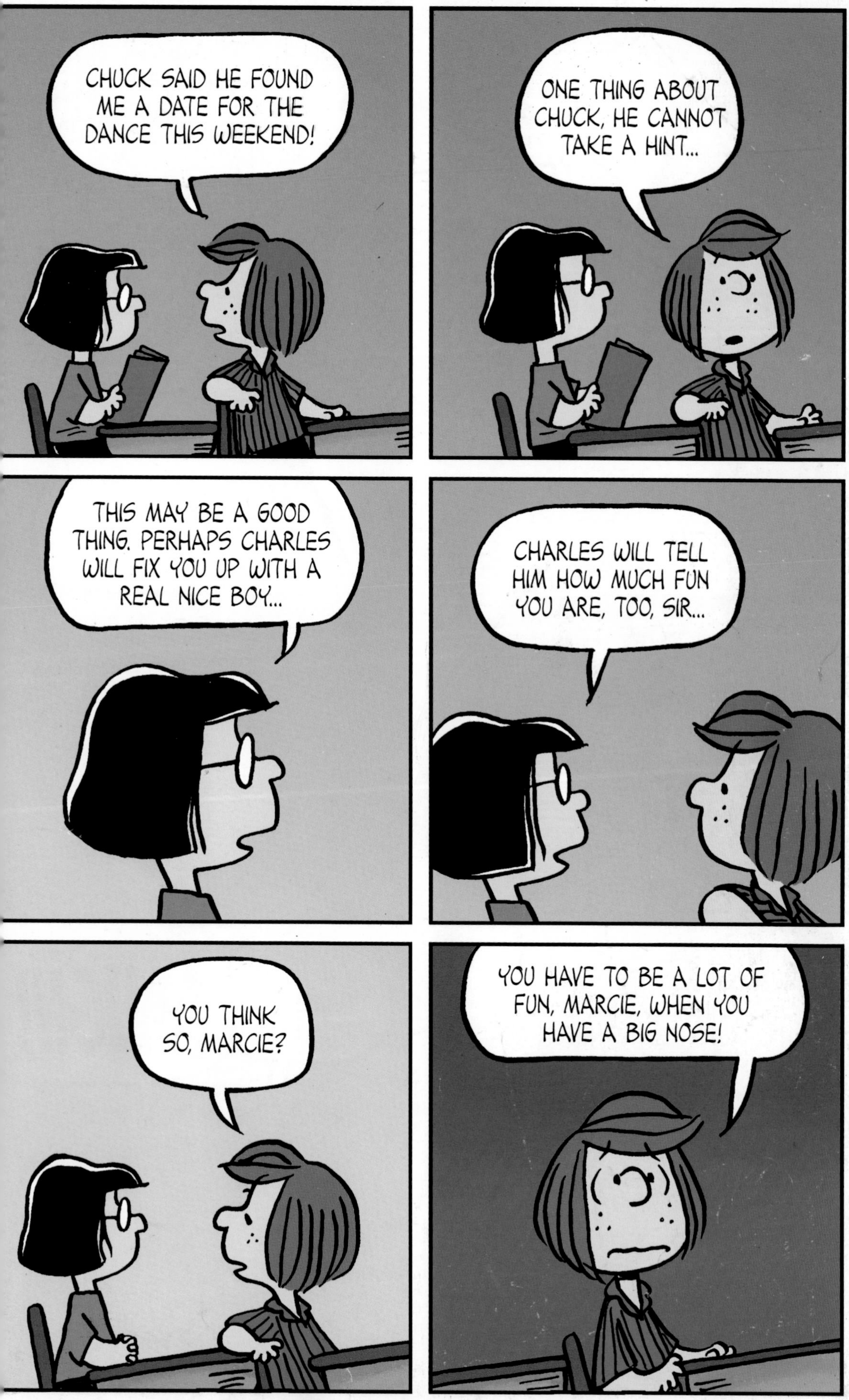
CHUCK SAID HE FOUND ME A DATE FOR THE DANCE THIS WEEKEND!
ONE THING ABOUT CHUCK, HE CANNOT TAKE A HINT...
THIS MAY BE A GOOD THING. PERHAPS CHARLES WILL FIX YOU UP WITH A REAL NICE BOY...
CHARLES WILL TELL HIM HOW MUCH FUN YOU ARE, TOO, SIR...
YOU THINK SO, MARCIE?
YOU HAVE TO BE A LOT OF FUN, MARCIE, WHEN YOU HAVE A BIG NOSE!

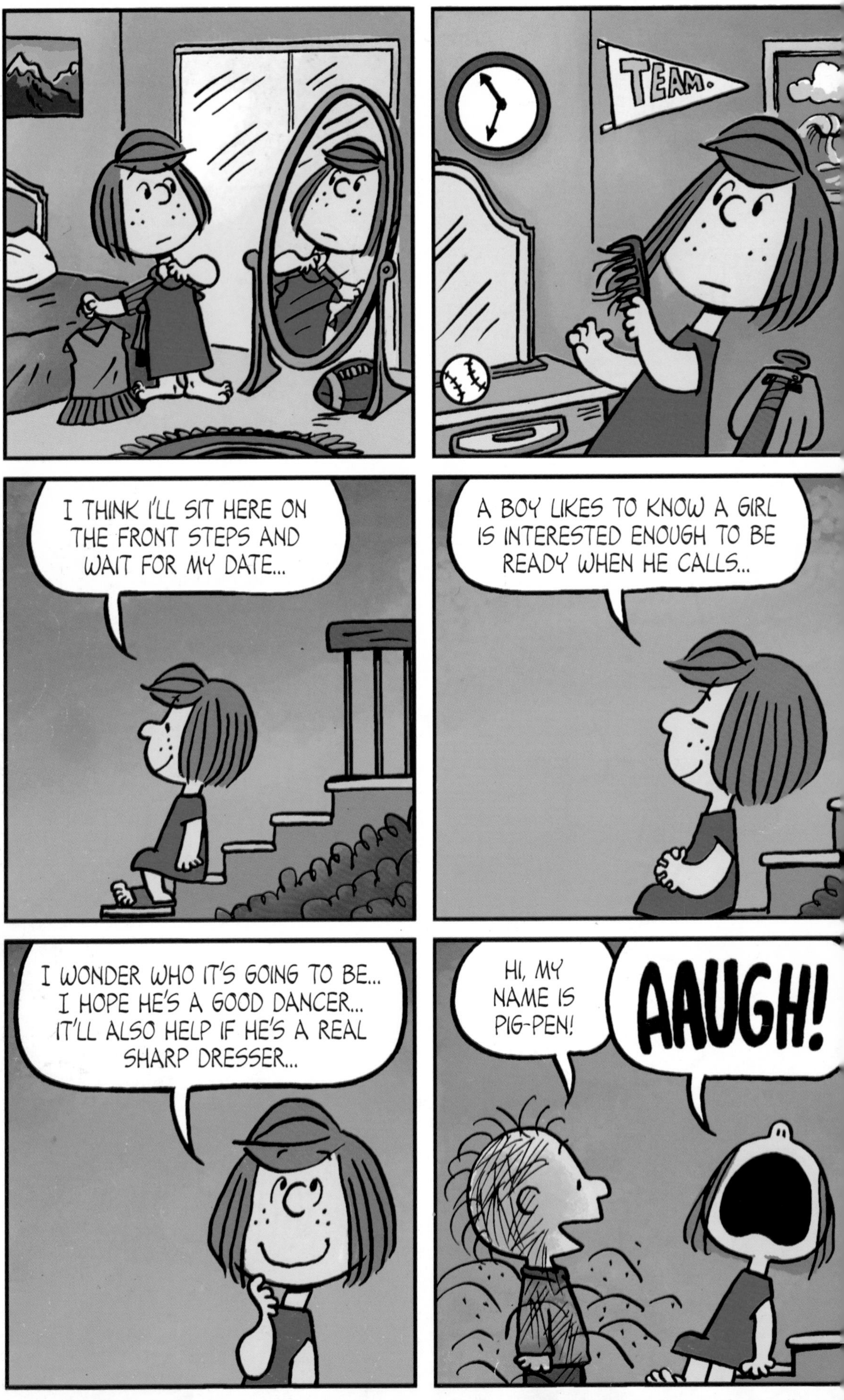
TEAM
I THINK I'LL SIT HERE ON THE FRONT STEPS AND WAIT FOR MY DATE...
A BOY LIKES TO KNOW A GIRL IS INTERESTED ENOUGH TO BE READY WHEN HE CALLS...
I WONDER WHO IT'S GOING TO BE... I HOPE HE'S A GOOD DANCER... IT'LL ALSO HELP IF HE'S A REAL SHARP DRESSER...
HI, MY NAME IS PIG-PEN!
AAUGH!

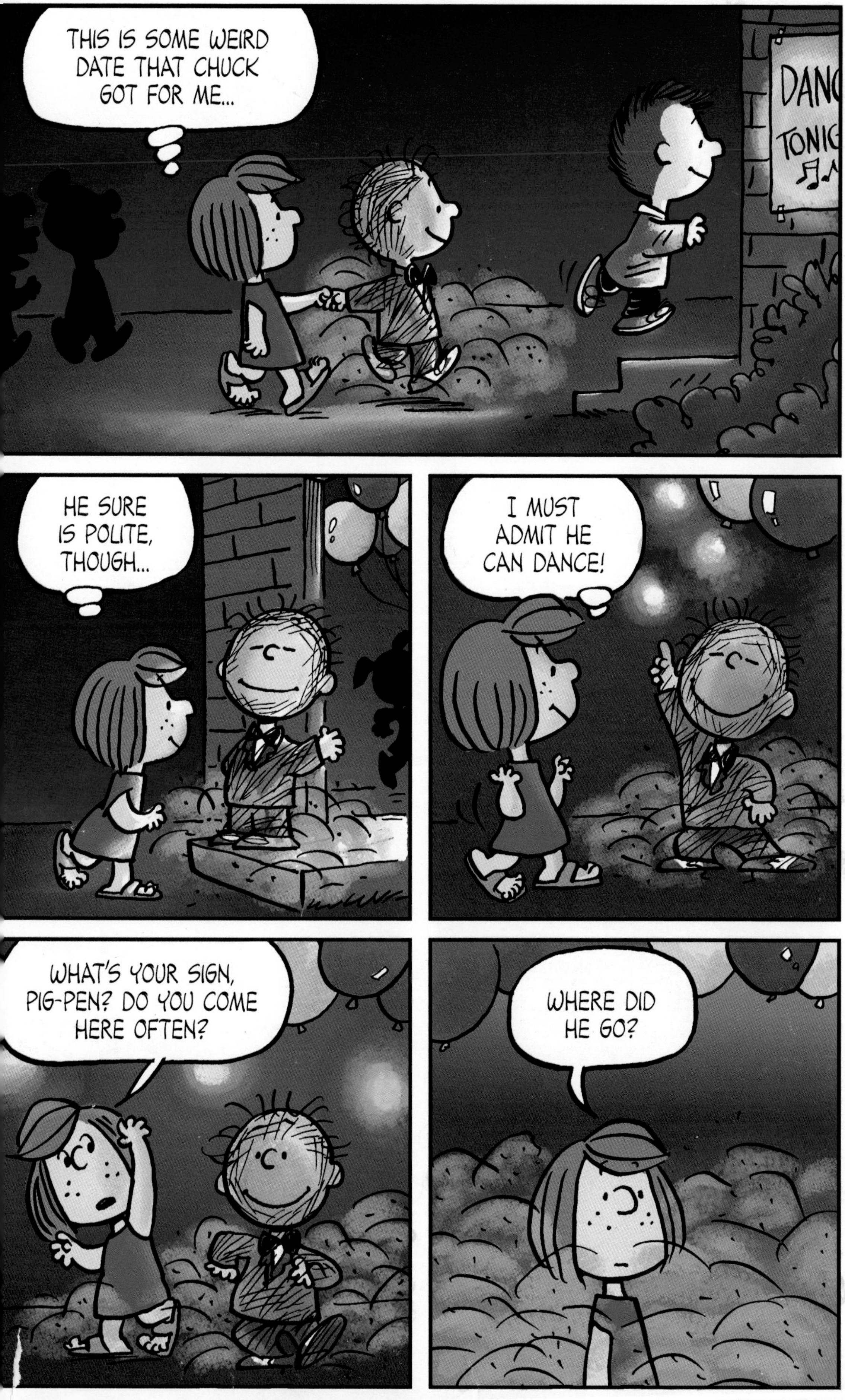
THIS IS SOME WEIRD DATE THAT CHUCK GOT FOR ME...
DANC
TONIG
HE SURE IS POLITE, THOUGH...
I MUST ADMIT HE CAN DANCE!
WHAT'S YOUR SIGN, PIG-PEN? DO YOU COME HERE OFTEN?
WHERE DID HE GO?

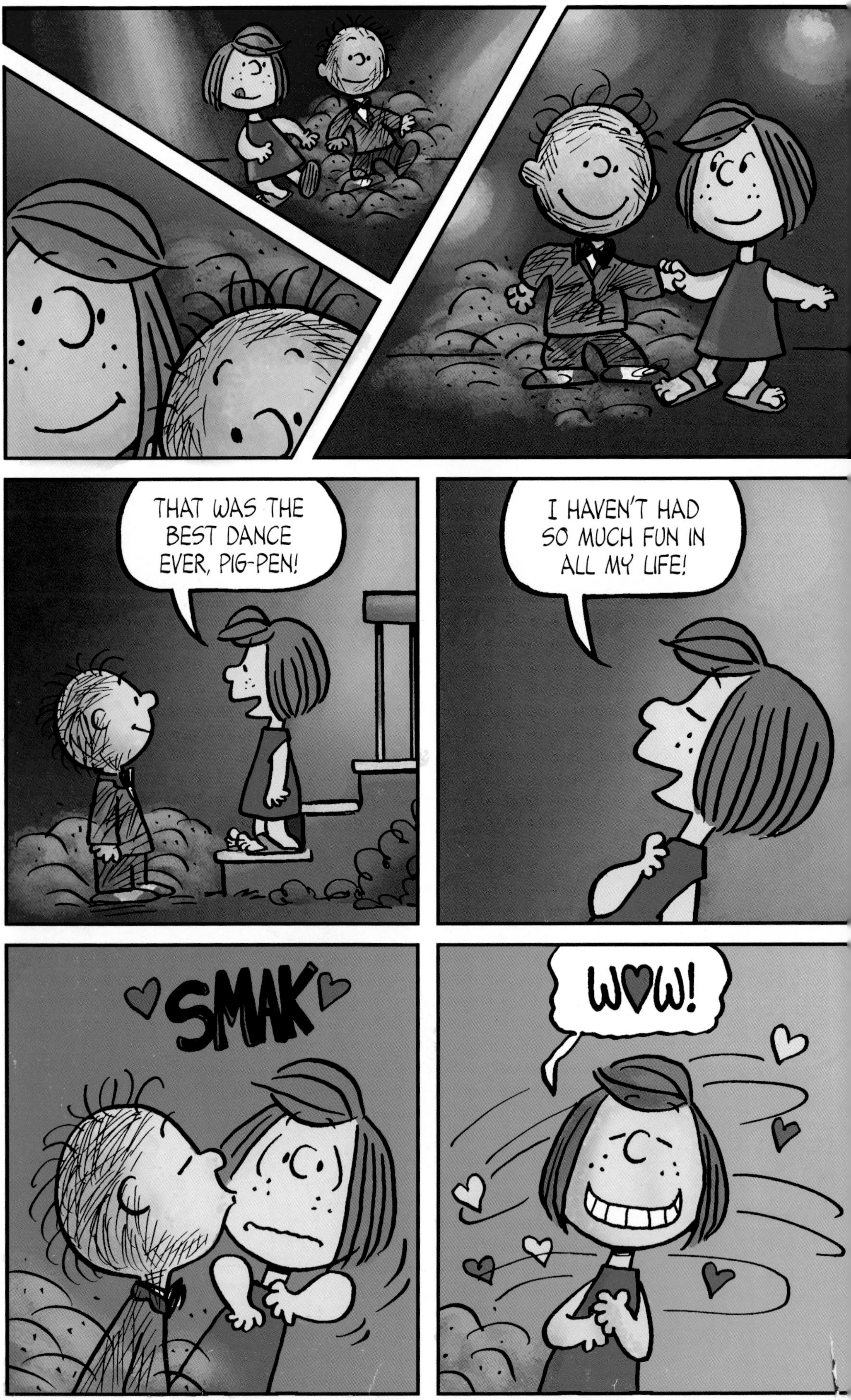
THAT WAS THE BEST DANCE EVER, PIG-PEN!
I HAVEN'T HAD SO MUCH FUN IN ALL MY LIFE!
SMAK
WOW!

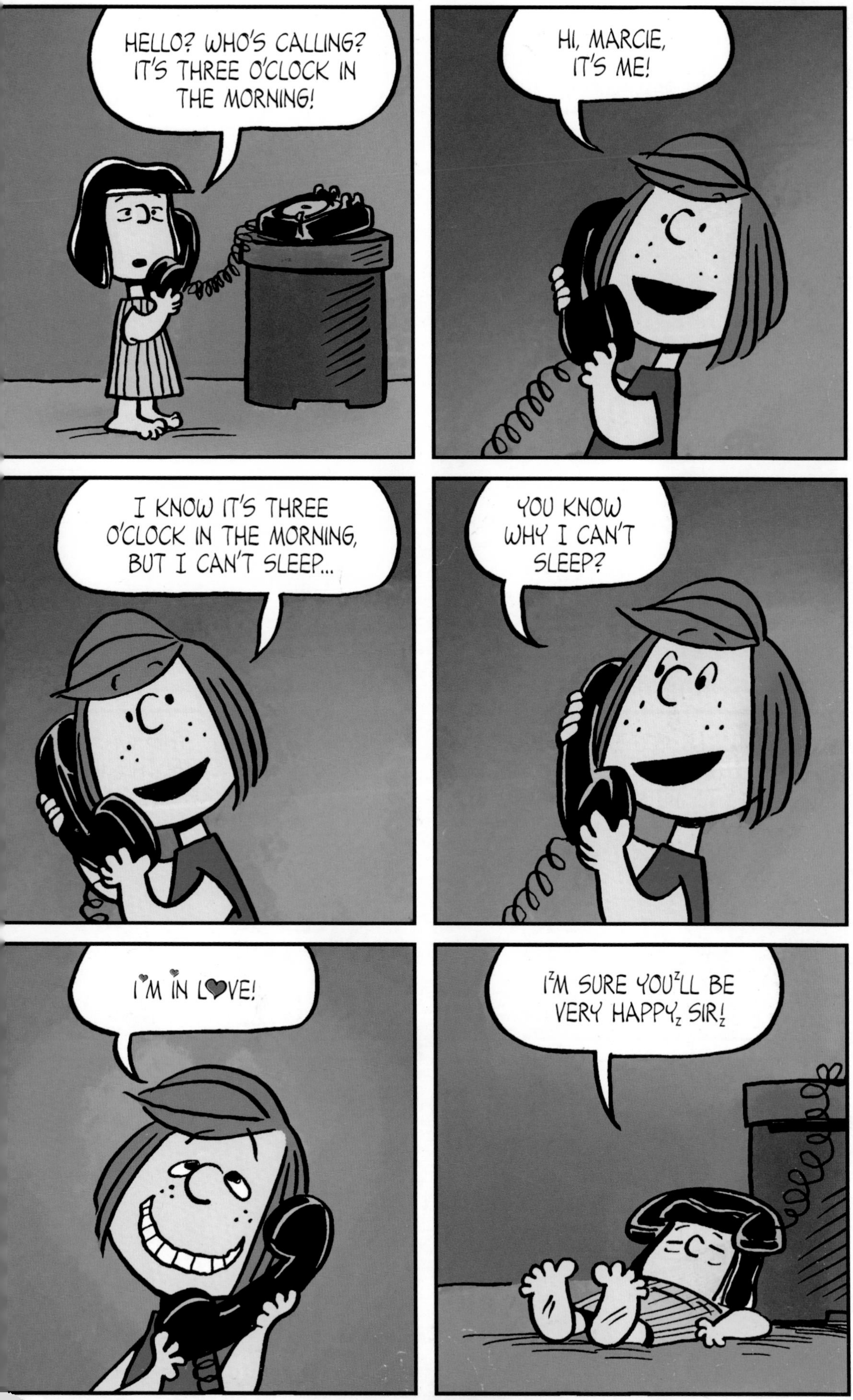
HELLO? WHO'S CALLING? IT'S THREE O'CLOCK IN THE MORNING!
HI, MARCIE, IT'S ME!
I KNOW IT'S THREE O'CLOCK IN THE MORNING, BUT I CAN'T SLEEP...
YOU KNOW WHY I CAN'T SLEEP?
I'M IN LOVE!
I'M SURE YOU'LL BE VERY HAPPY, SIR!

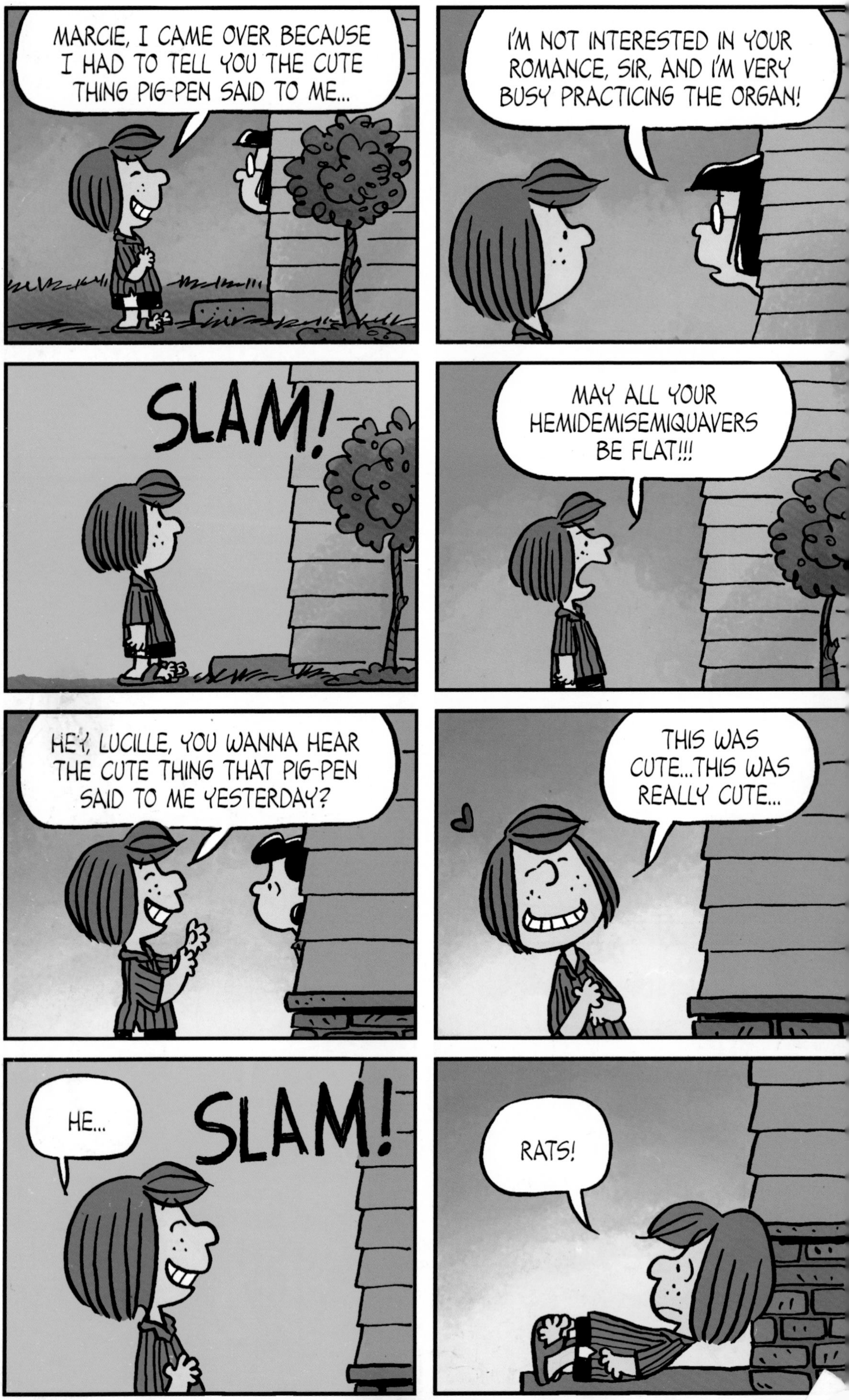
MARCIE, I CAME OVER BECAUSE I HAD TO TELL YOU THE CUTE THING PIG-PEN SAID TO ME...
I'M NOT INTERESTED IN YOUR ROMANCE, SIR, AND I'M VERY BUSY PRACTICING THE ORGAN!
SLAM!
MAY ALL YOUR HEMIDEMISEMIQUAVERS BE FLAT!!!
HEY, LUCILLE, YOU WANNA HEAR THE CUTE THING THAT PIG-PEN SAID TO ME YESTERDAY?
THIS WAS CUTE...THIS WAS REALLY CUTE...
HE...
SLAM!
RATS!

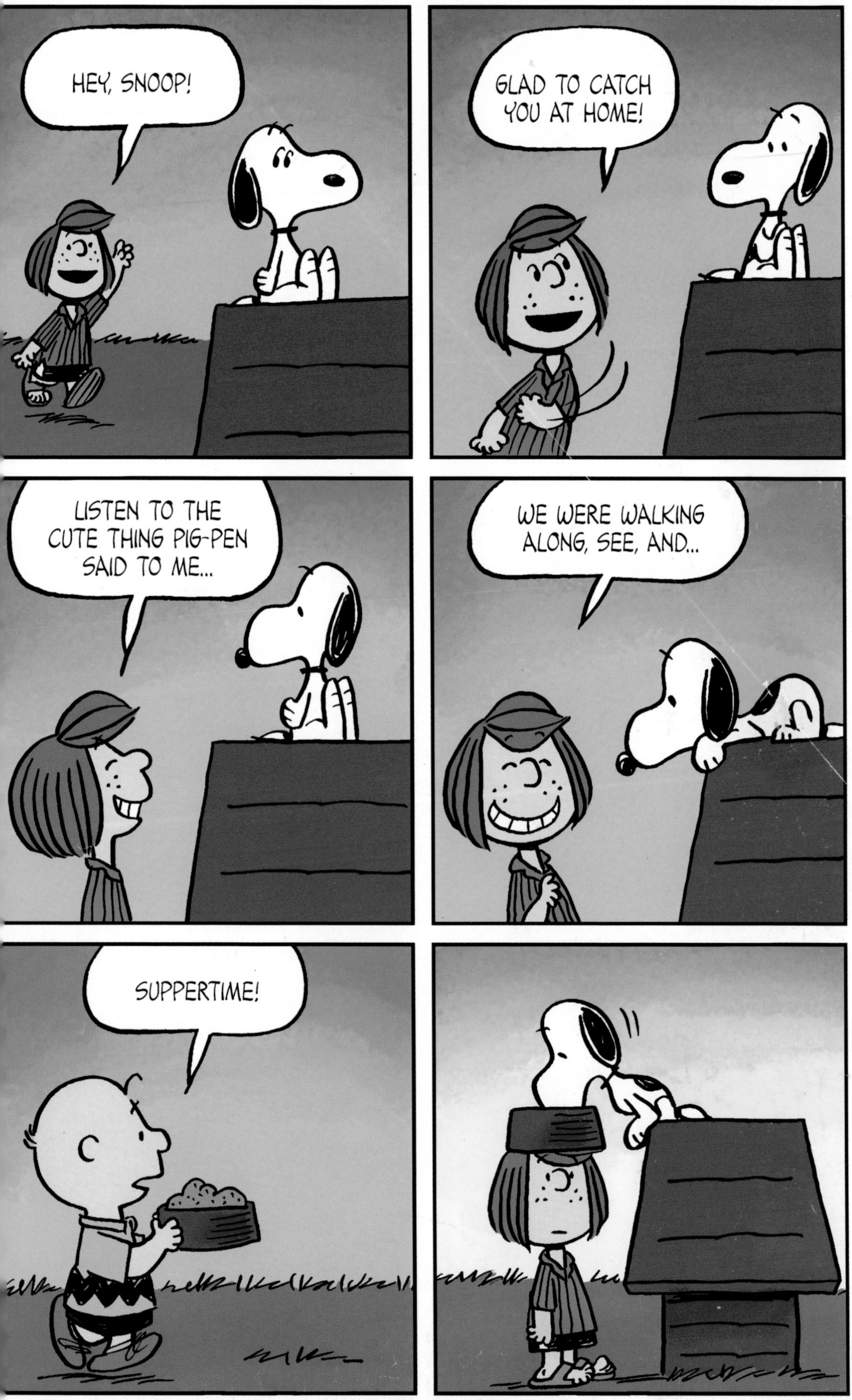
HEY, SNOOP!
GLAD TO CATCH YOU AT HOME!
LISTEN TO THE CUTE THING PIG-PEN SAID TO ME...
WE WERE WALKING ALONG, SEE, AND...
SUPPERTIME!

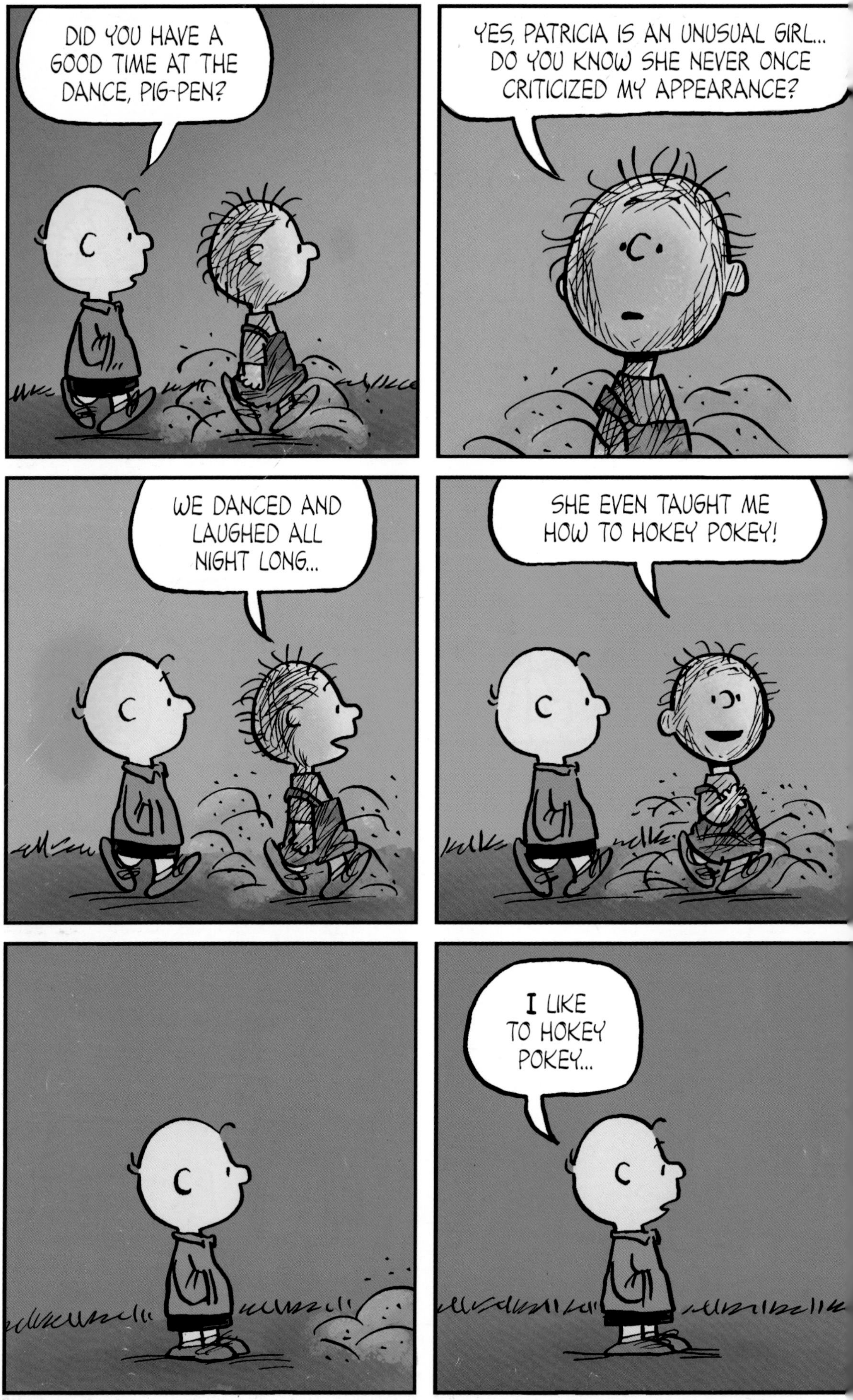
DID YOU HAVE A GOOD TIME AT THE DANCE, PIG-PEN?
YES, PATRICIA IS AN UNUSUAL GIRL... DO YOU KNOW SHE NEVER ONCE CRITICIZED MY APPEARANCE?
WE DANCED AND LAUGHED ALL NIGHT LONG...
SHE EVEN TAUGHT ME HOW TO HOKEY POKEY!
I LIKE TO HOKEY POKEY...

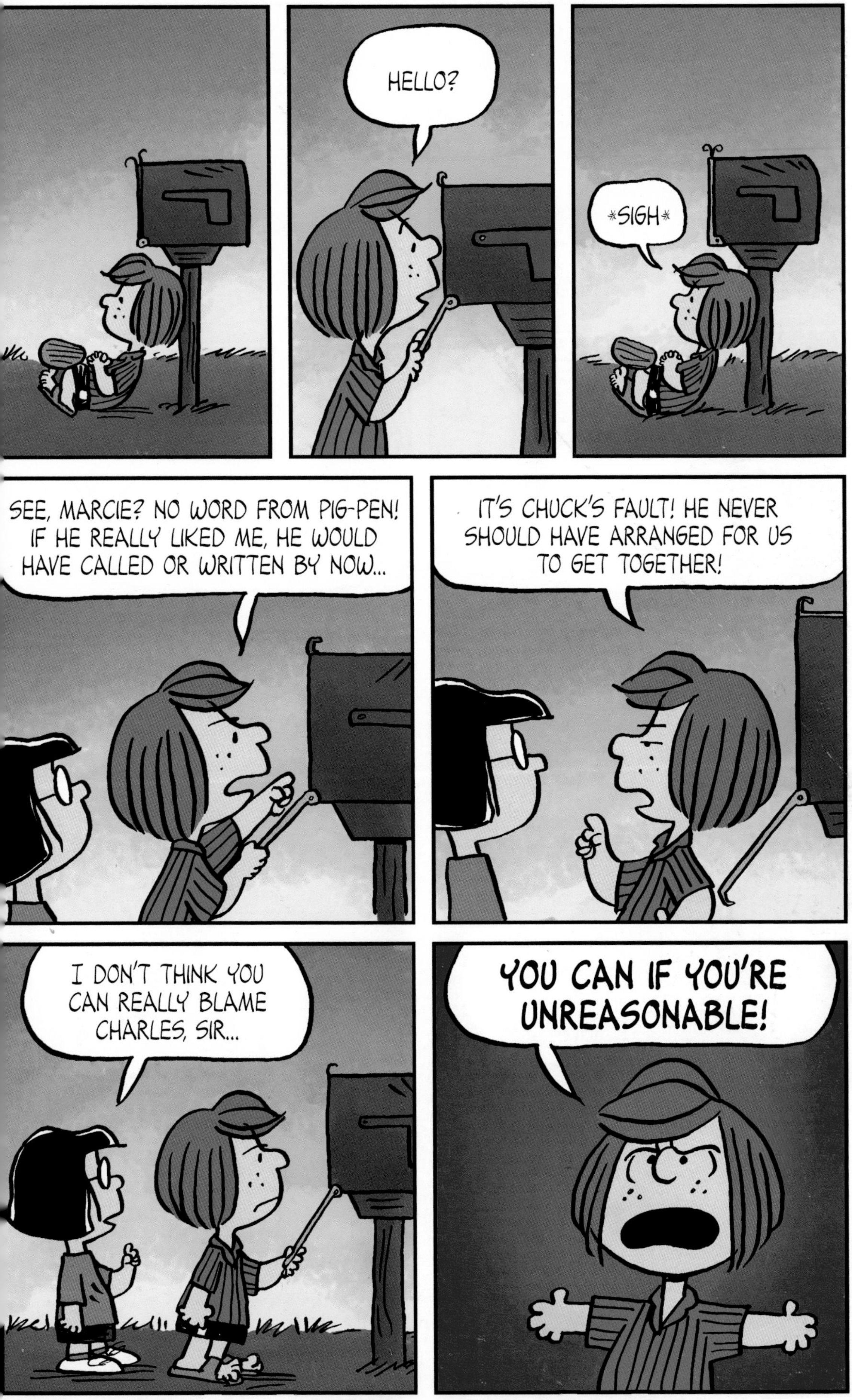
HELLO?
SIGH
SEE, MARCIE? NO WORD FROM PIG-PEN! IF HE REALLY LIKED ME, HE WOULD HAVE CALLED OR WRITTEN BY NOW...
IT'S CHUCK'S FAULT! HE NEVER SHOULD HAVE ARRANGED FOR US TO GET TOGETHER!
I DON'T THINK YOU CAN REALLY BLAME CHARLES, SIR...
YOU CAN IF YOU'RE UNREASONABLE!

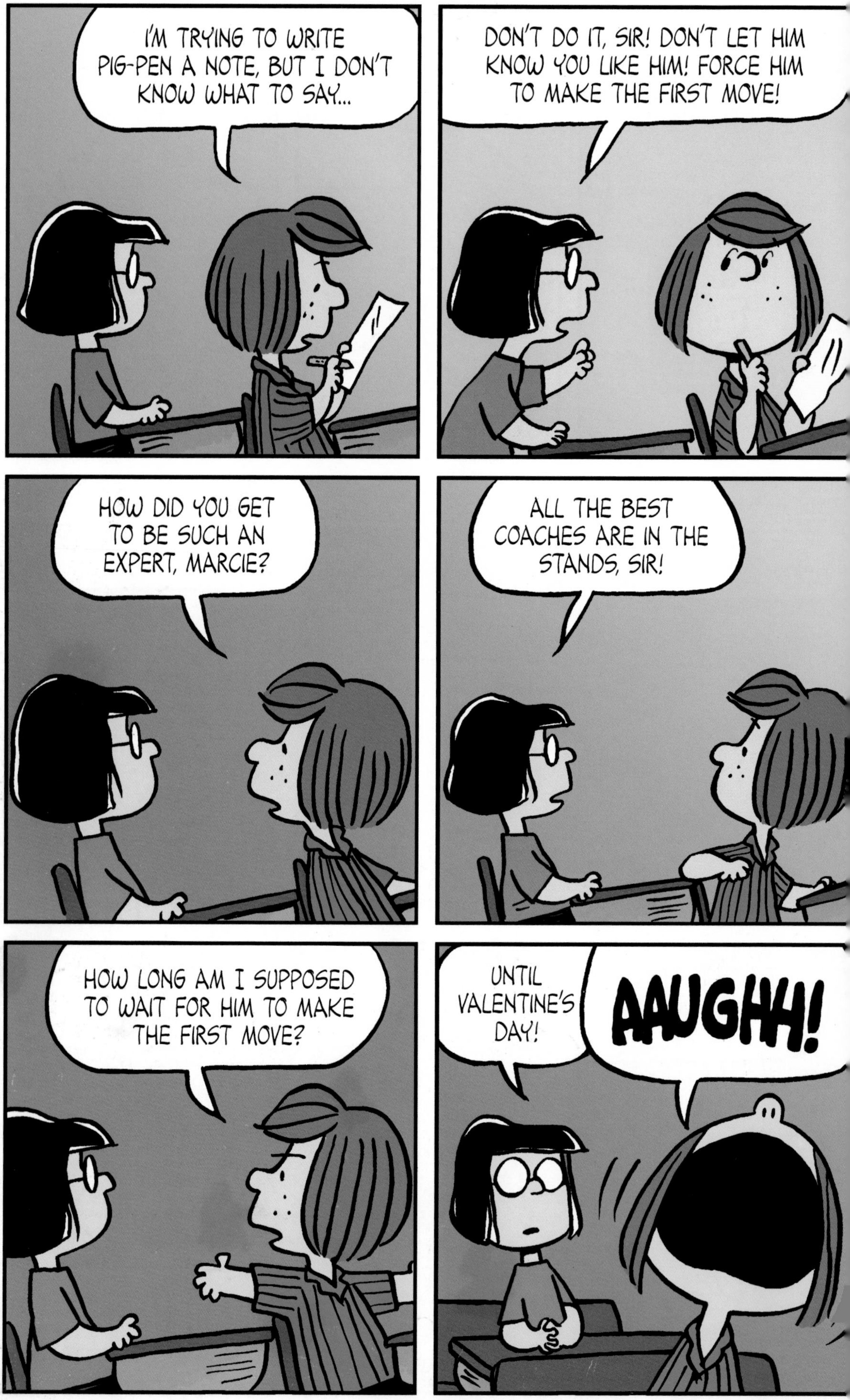

I'M TRYING TO WRITE PIG-PEN A NOTE, BUT I DON'T KNOW WHAT TO SAY...
DON'T DO IT, SIR! DON'T LET HIM KNOW YOU LIKE HIM! FORCE HIM TO MAKE THE FIRST MOVE!
HOW DID YOU GET TO BE SUCH AN EXPERT, MARCIE?
ALL THE BEST COACHES ARE IN THE STANDS, SIR!
HOW LONG AM I SUPPOSED TO WAIT FOR HIM TO MAKE THE FIRST MOVE?
UNTIL VALENTINE'S DAY!
AAUGHH!

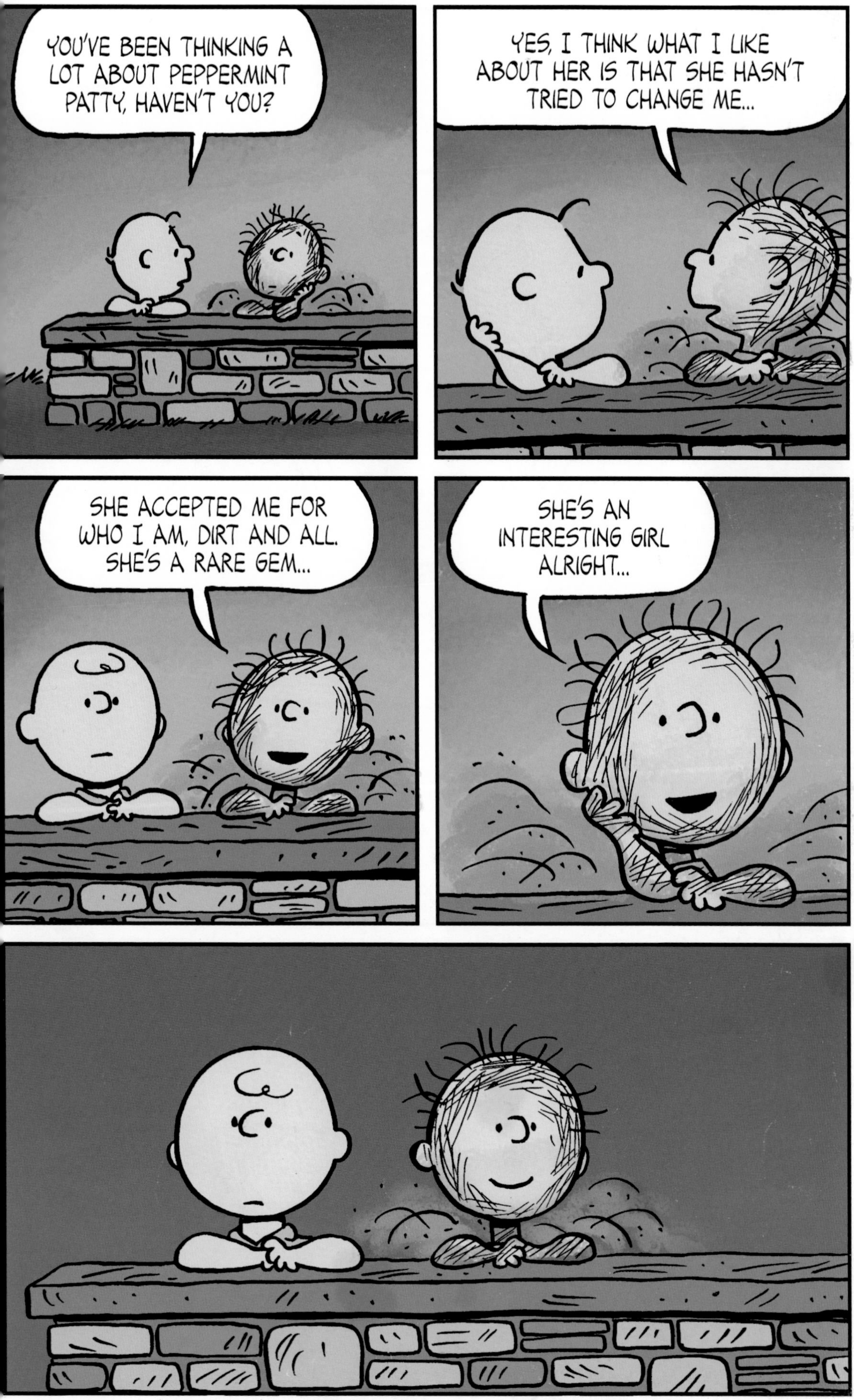
YOU'VE BEEN THINKING A LOT ABOUT PEPPERMINT PATTY, HAVEN'T YOU?
YES, I THINK WHAT I LIKE ABOUT HER IS THAT SHE HASN'T TRIED TO CHANGE ME...
SHE ACCEPTED ME FOR WHO I AM, DIRT AND ALL. SHE'S A RARE GEM...
SHE'S AN INTERESTING GIRL ALRIGHT...

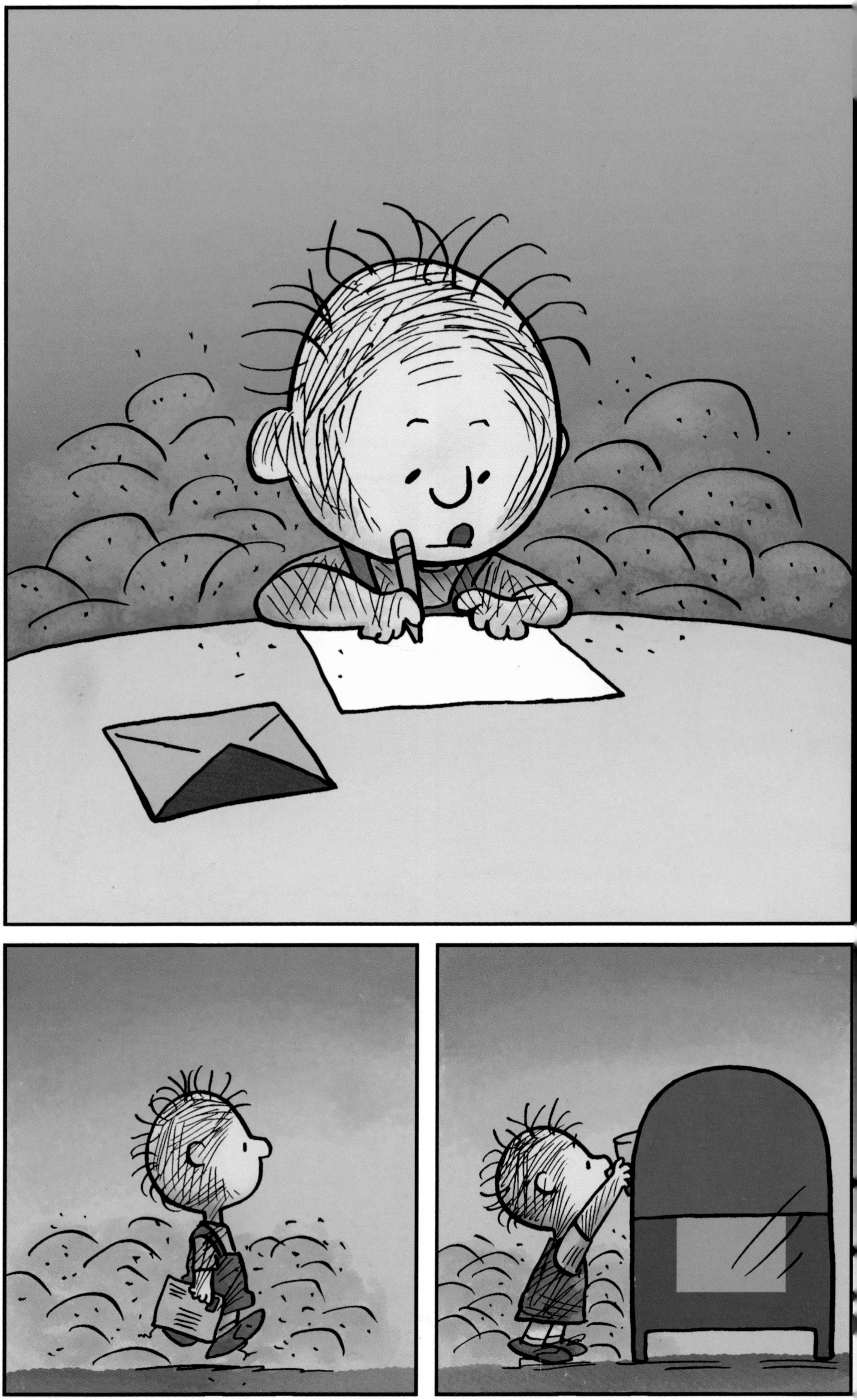

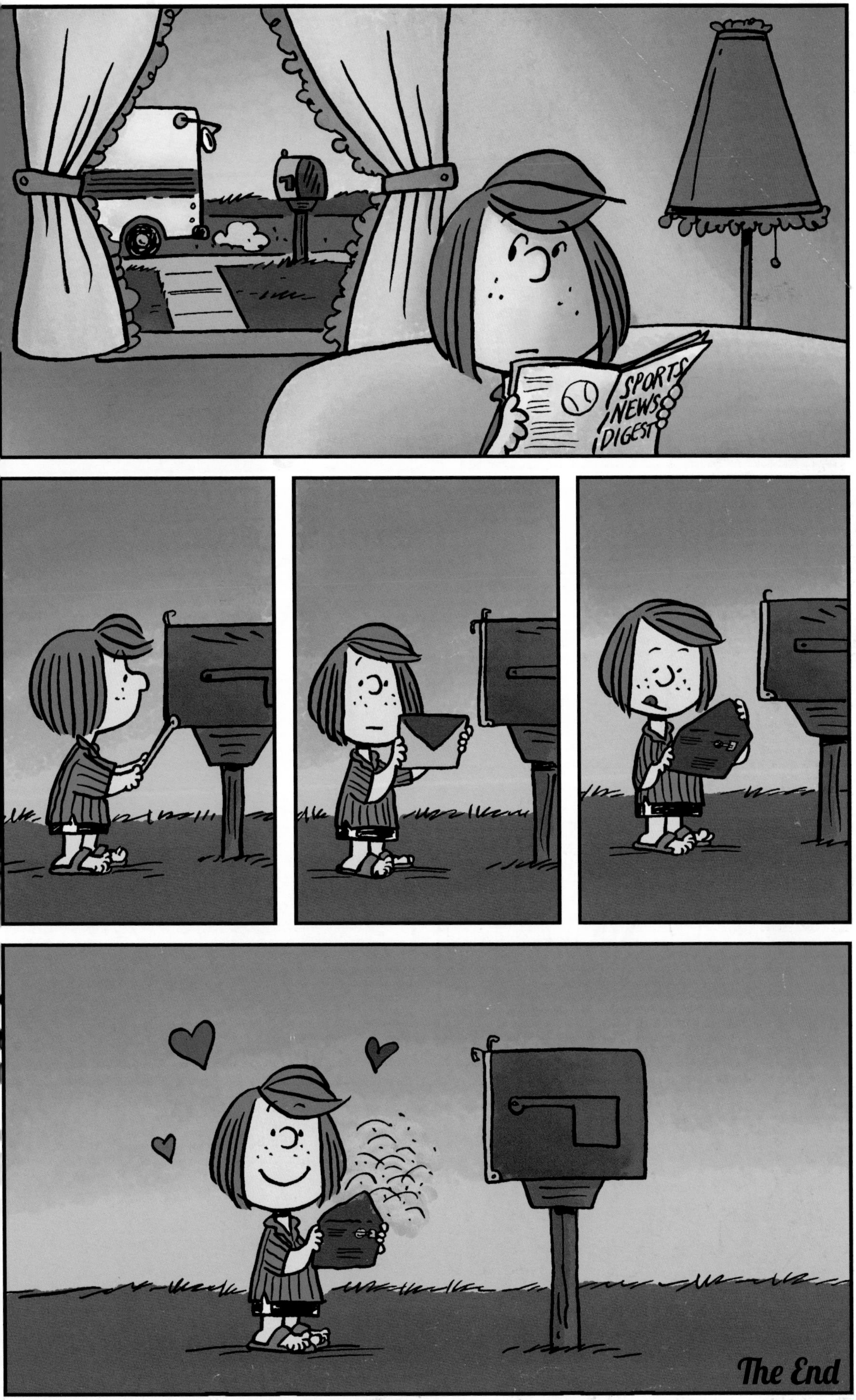
SPORTS NEWS DIGEST
The End

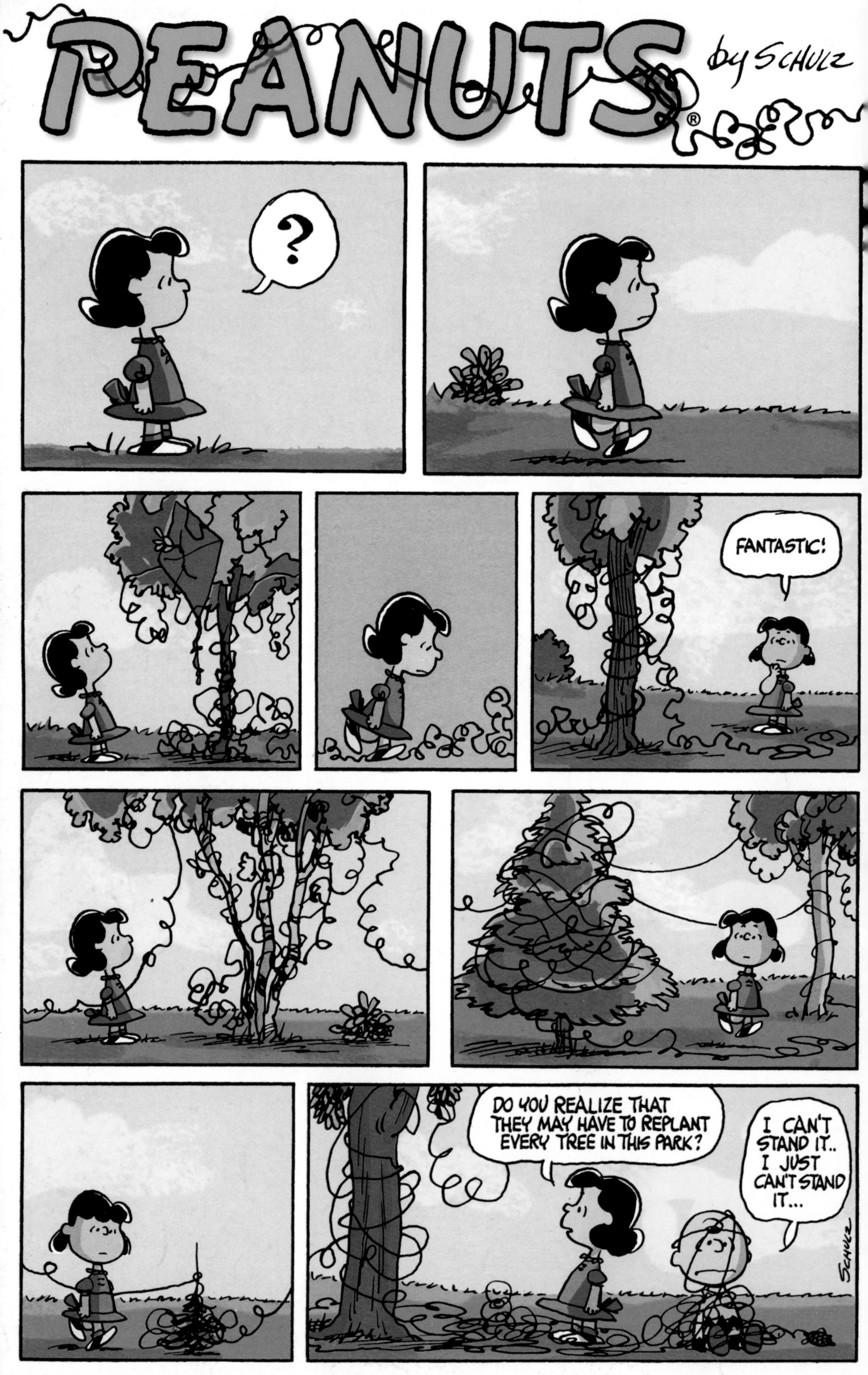
PEANUTS
by SCHULZ
?
FANTASTIC!
DO YOU REALIZE THAT THEY MAY HAVE TO REPLANT EVERY TREE IN THIS PARK?
I CAN'T STAND IT.. I JUST CAN'T STAND IT...
SCHULZ

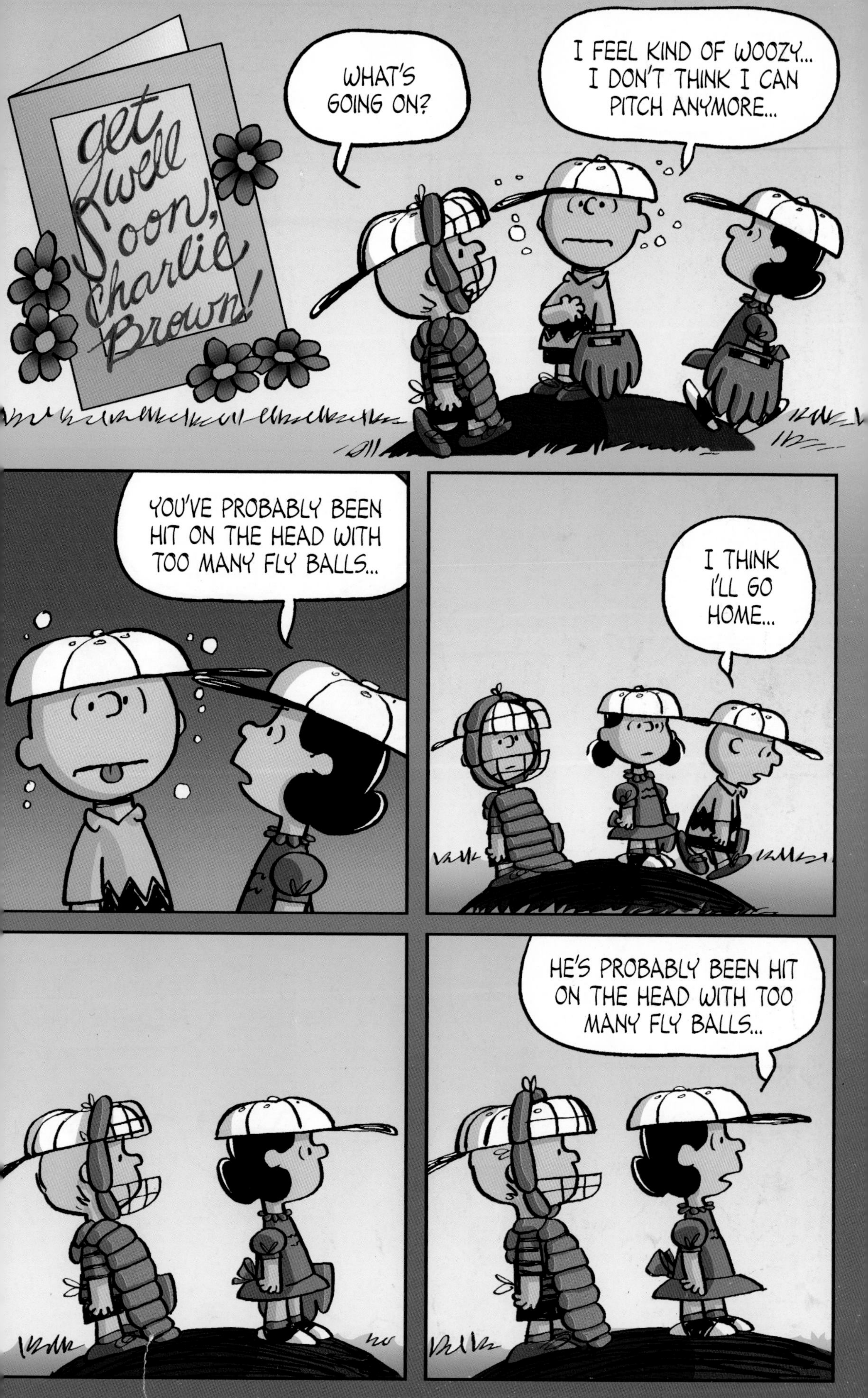
get well soon, Charlie Brown!
WHAT'S GOING ON?
I FEEL KIND OF WOOZY... I DON'T THINK I CAN PITCH ANYMORE...
YOU'VE PROBABLY BEEN HIT ON THE HEAD WITH TOO MANY FLY BALLS...
I THINK I'LL GO HOME...
HE'S PROBABLY BEEN HIT ON THE HEAD WITH TOO MANY FLY BALLS...

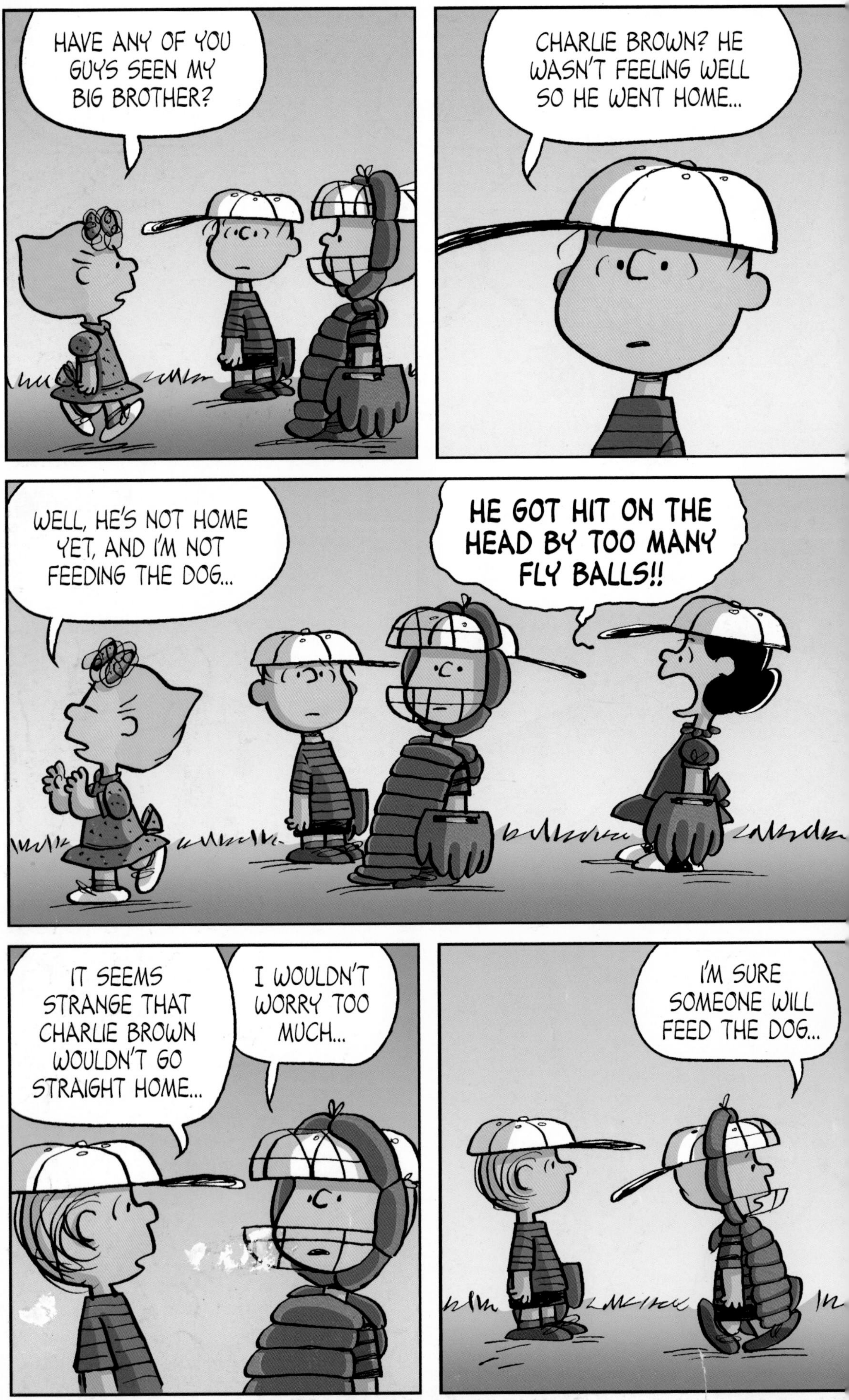

HAVE ANY OF YOU GUYS SEEN MY BIG BROTHER?
CHARLIE BROWN? HE WASN'T FEELING WELL SO HE WENT HOME...
WELL, HE'S NOT HOME YET, AND I'M NOT FEEDING THE DOG...
HE GOT HIT ON THE HEAD BY TOO MANY FLY BALLS!!
IT SEEMS STRANGE THAT CHARLIE BROWN WOULDN'T GO STRAIGHT HOME...
I WOULDN'T WORRY TOO MUCH...
I'M SURE SOMEONE WILL FEED THE DOG...

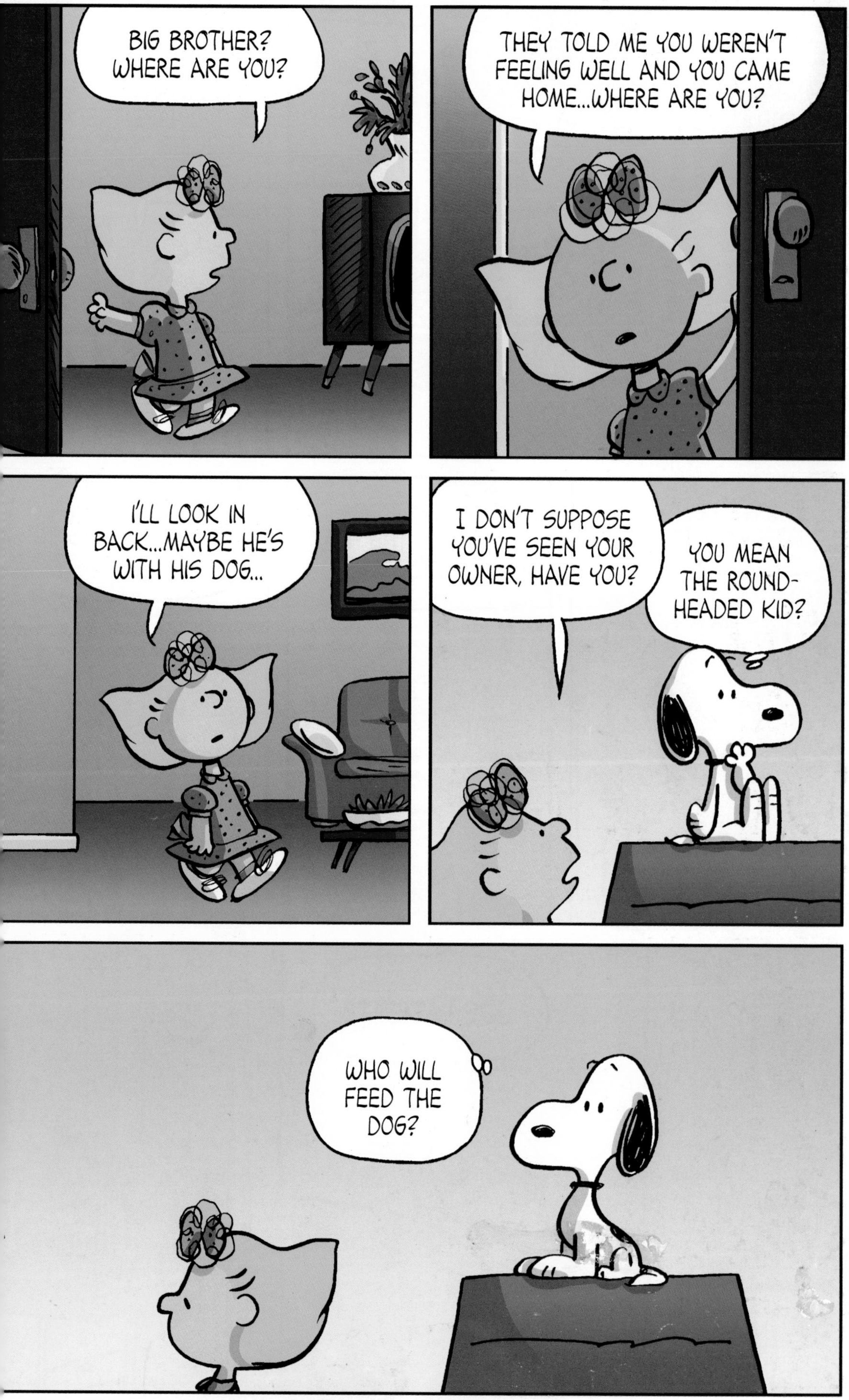
BIG BROTHER? WHERE ARE YOU?
THEY TOLD ME YOU WEREN'T FEELING WELL AND YOU CAME HOME...WHERE ARE YOU?
I'LL LOOK IN BACK...MAYBE HE'S WITH HIS DOG...
I DON'T SUPPOSE YOU'VE SEEN YOUR OWNER, HAVE YOU?
YOU MEAN THE ROUND-HEADED KID?
WHO WILL FEED THE DOG?

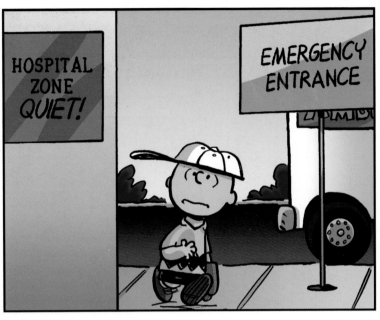

HOSPITAL ZONE QUIET!

EMERGENCY ENTRANCE

GOOD AFTERNOON, MA'AM! I DON'T MEAN TO BE ANY TROUBLE... BUT I HAVE THE AWFUL FEELING THAT I MAY BE AN EMERGENCY!

I DON'T FEEL GOOD... I FEEL KIND OF WOOZY...

NO, MA'AM...I DIDN'T GET HIT ON THE HEAD WITH A FLY BALL...

SO WHAT DO YOU THINK? NOTHING TO WORRY ABOUT?

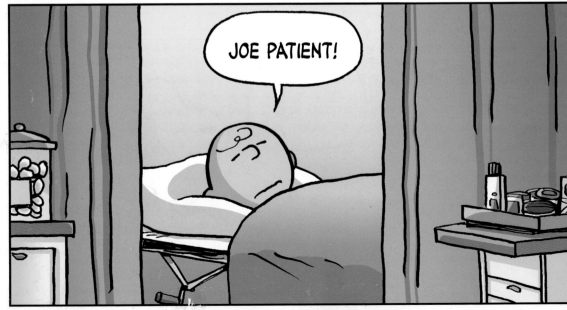

JOE PATIENT!

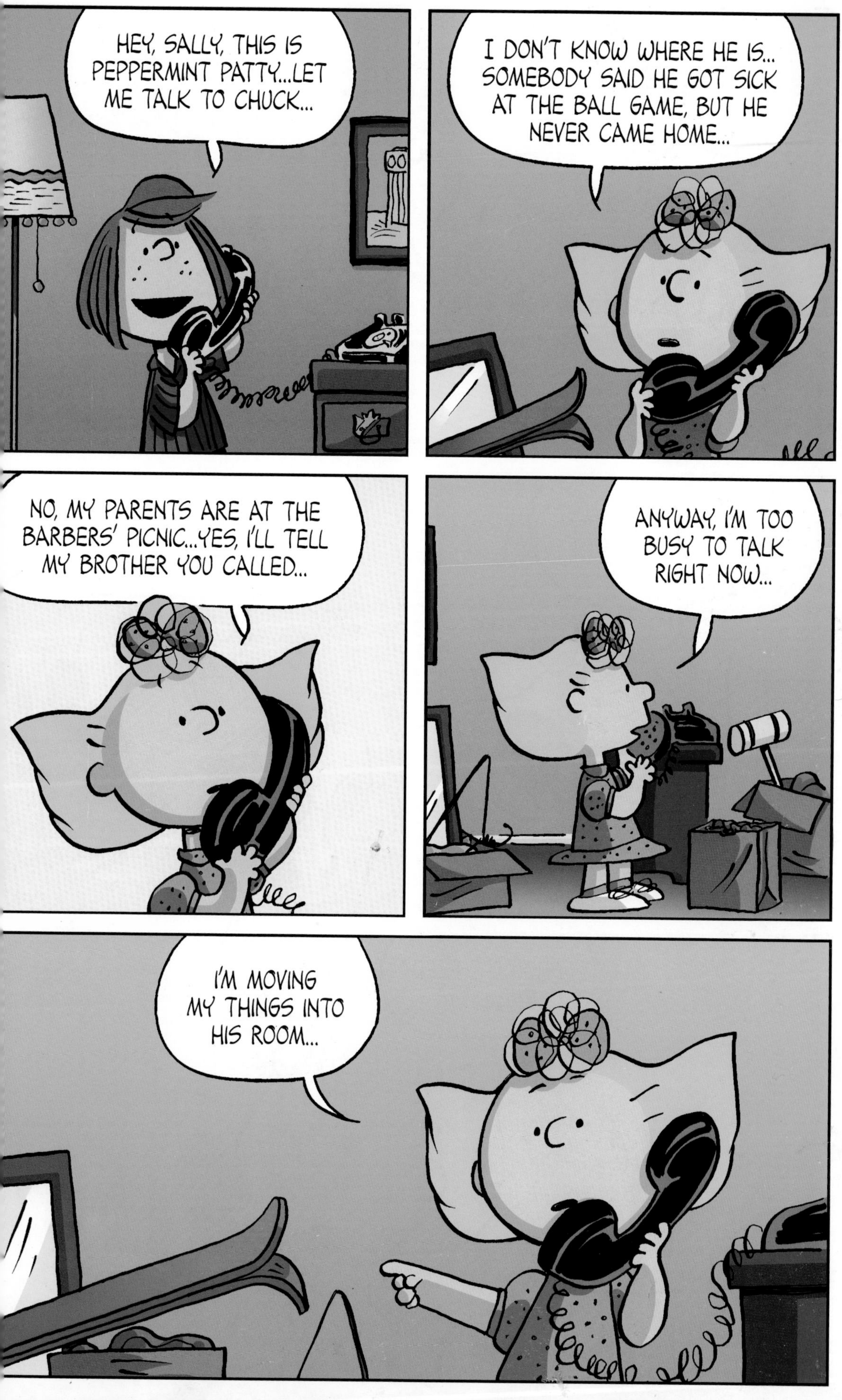
HEY, SALLY, THIS IS PEPPERMINT PATTY...LET ME TALK TO CHUCK...
I DON'T KNOW WHERE HE IS... SOMEBODY SAID HE GOT SICK AT THE BALL GAME, BUT HE NEVER CAME HOME...
NO, MY PARENTS ARE AT THE BARBERS' PICNIC...YES, I'LL TELL MY BROTHER YOU CALLED...
ANYWAY, I'M TOO BUSY TO TALK RIGHT NOW...
I'M MOVING MY THINGS INTO HIS ROOM...

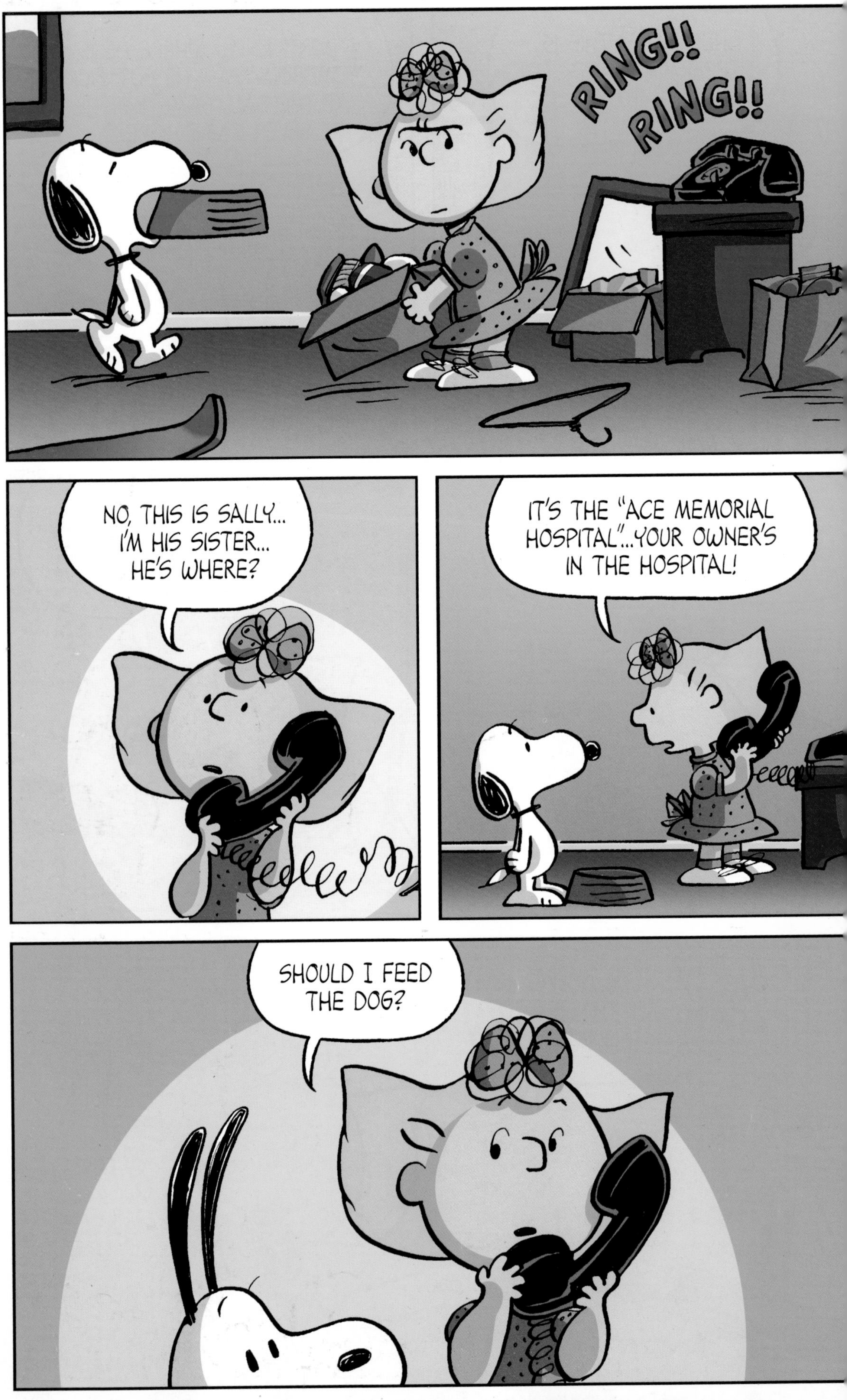
RING!! RING!!
NO, THIS IS SALLY... I'M HIS SISTER... HE'S WHERE?
IT'S THE "ACE MEMORIAL HOSPITAL"...YOUR OWNER'S IN THE HOSPITAL!
SHOULD I FEED THE DOG?

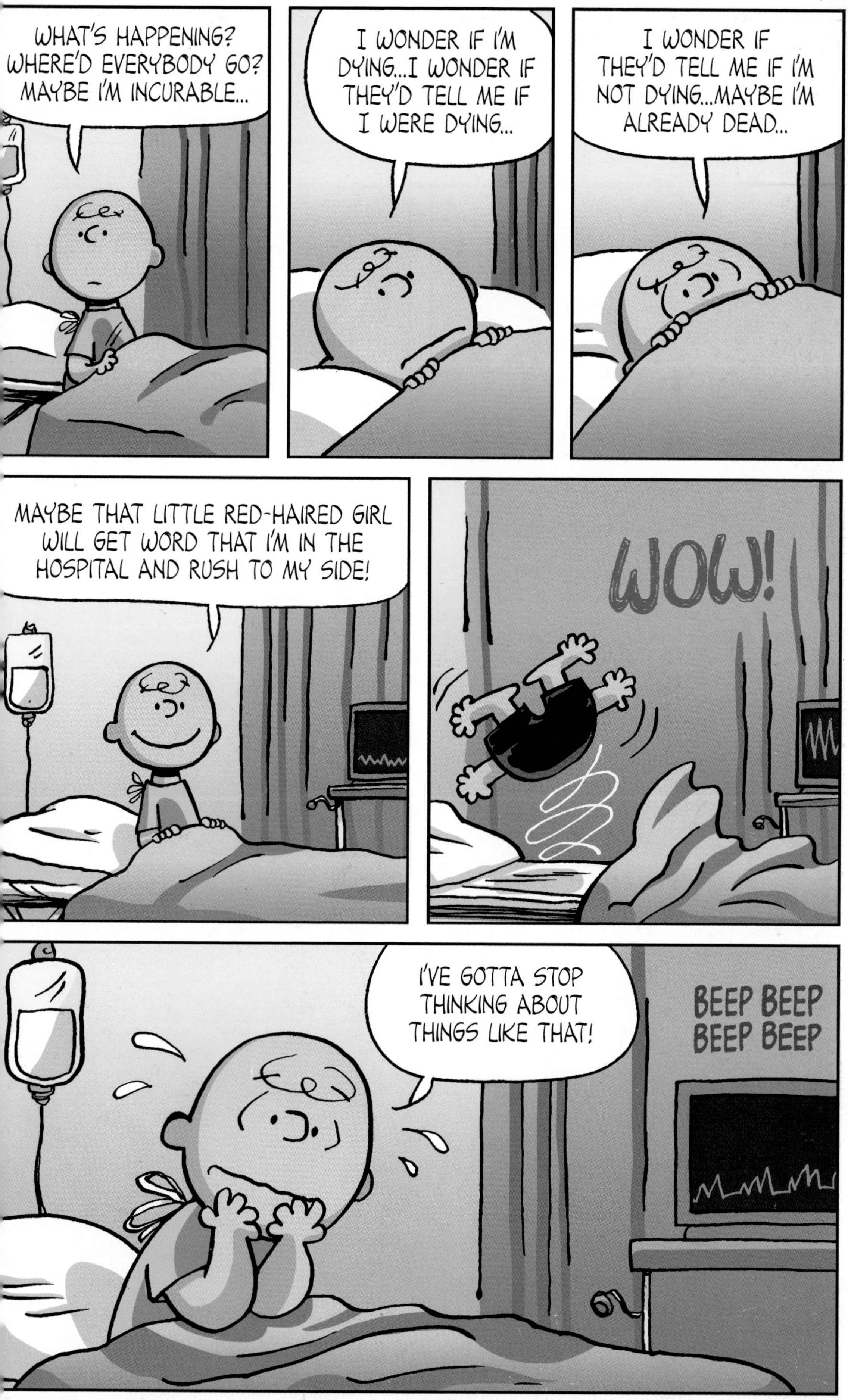
WHAT'S HAPPENING? WHERE'D EVERYBODY GO? MAYBE I'M INCURABLE...
I WONDER IF I'M DYING...I WONDER IF THEY'D TELL ME IF I WERE DYING...
I WONDER IF THEY'D TELL ME IF I'M NOT DYING...MAYBE I'M ALREADY DEAD...
MAYBE THAT LITTLE RED-HAIRED GIRL WILL GET WORD THAT I'M IN THE HOSPITAL AND RUSH TO MY SIDE!
WOW!
I'VE GOTTA STOP THINKING ABOUT THINGS LIKE THAT!
BEEP BEEP BEEP BEEP

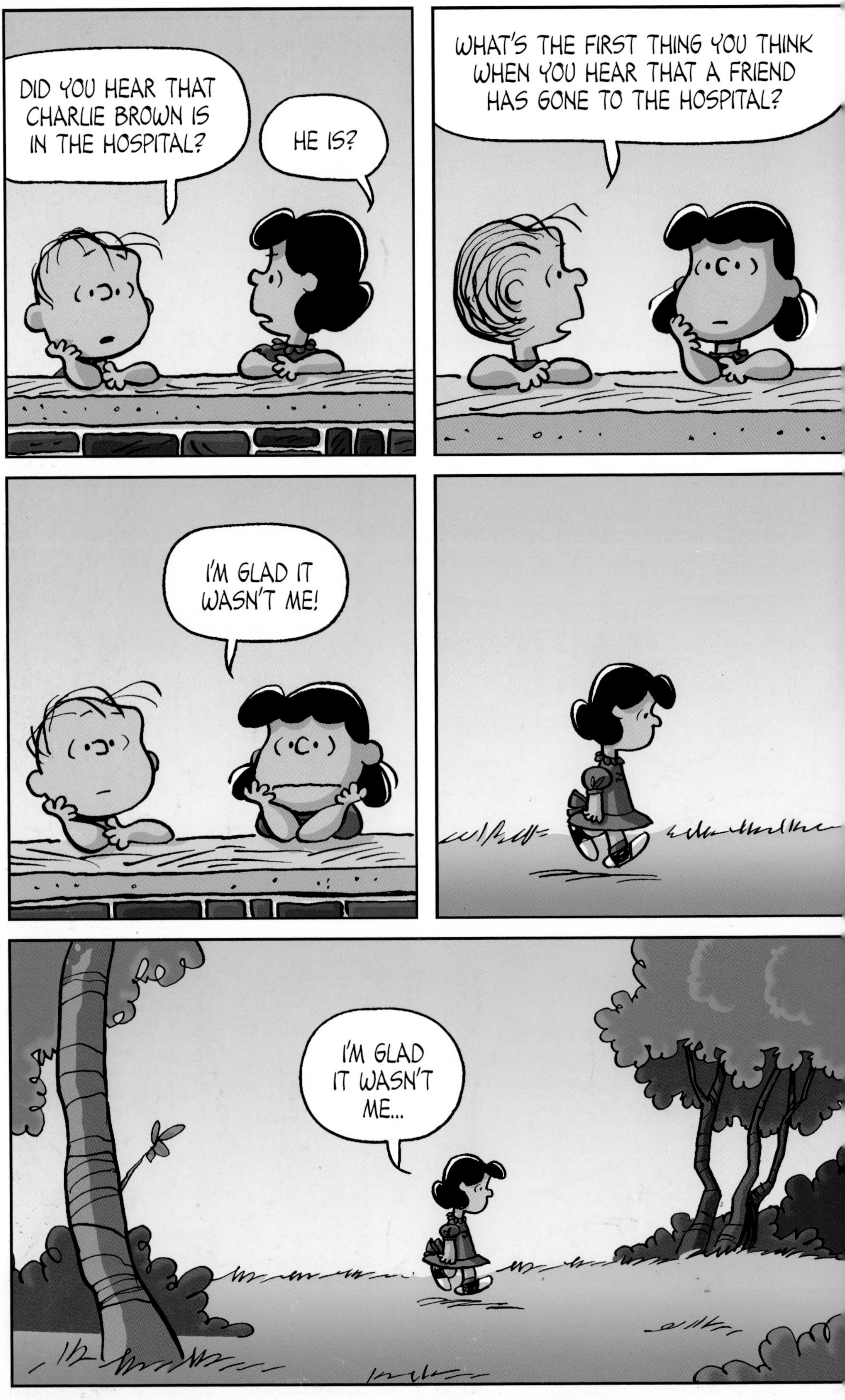
DID YOU HEAR THAT CHARLIE BROWN IS IN THE HOSPITAL?
HE IS?
WHAT'S THE FIRST THING YOU THINK WHEN YOU HEAR THAT A FRIEND HAS GONE TO THE HOSPITAL?
I'M GLAD IT WASN'T ME!
I'M GLAD IT WASN'T ME...

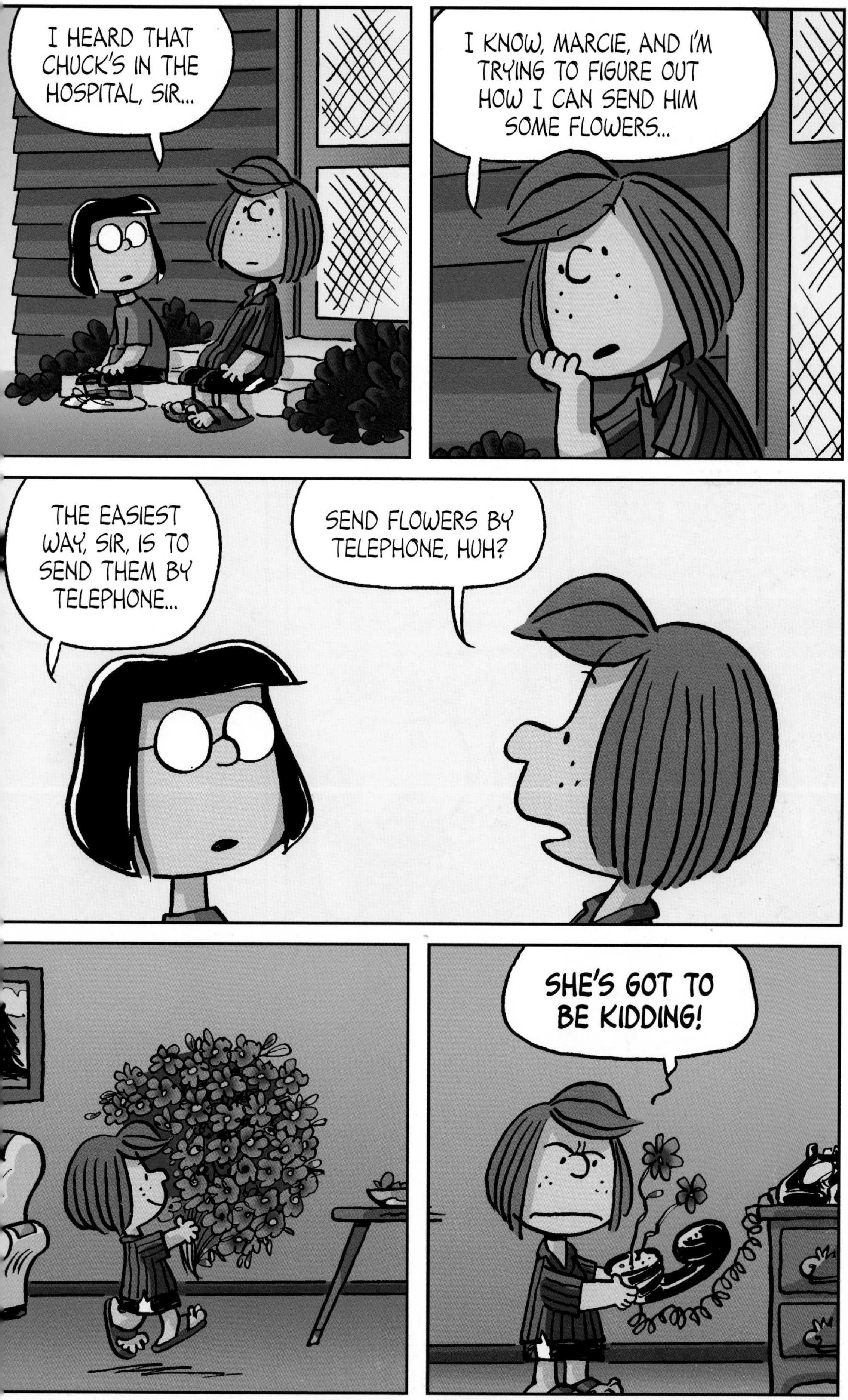
I HEARD THAT CHUCK'S IN THE HOSPITAL, SIR...
I KNOW, MARCIE, AND I'M TRYING TO FIGURE OUT HOW I CAN SEND HIM SOME FLOWERS...
THE EASIEST WAY, SIR, IS TO SEND THEM BY TELEPHONE...
SEND FLOWERS BY TELEPHONE, HUH?
SHE'S GOT TO BE KIDDING!

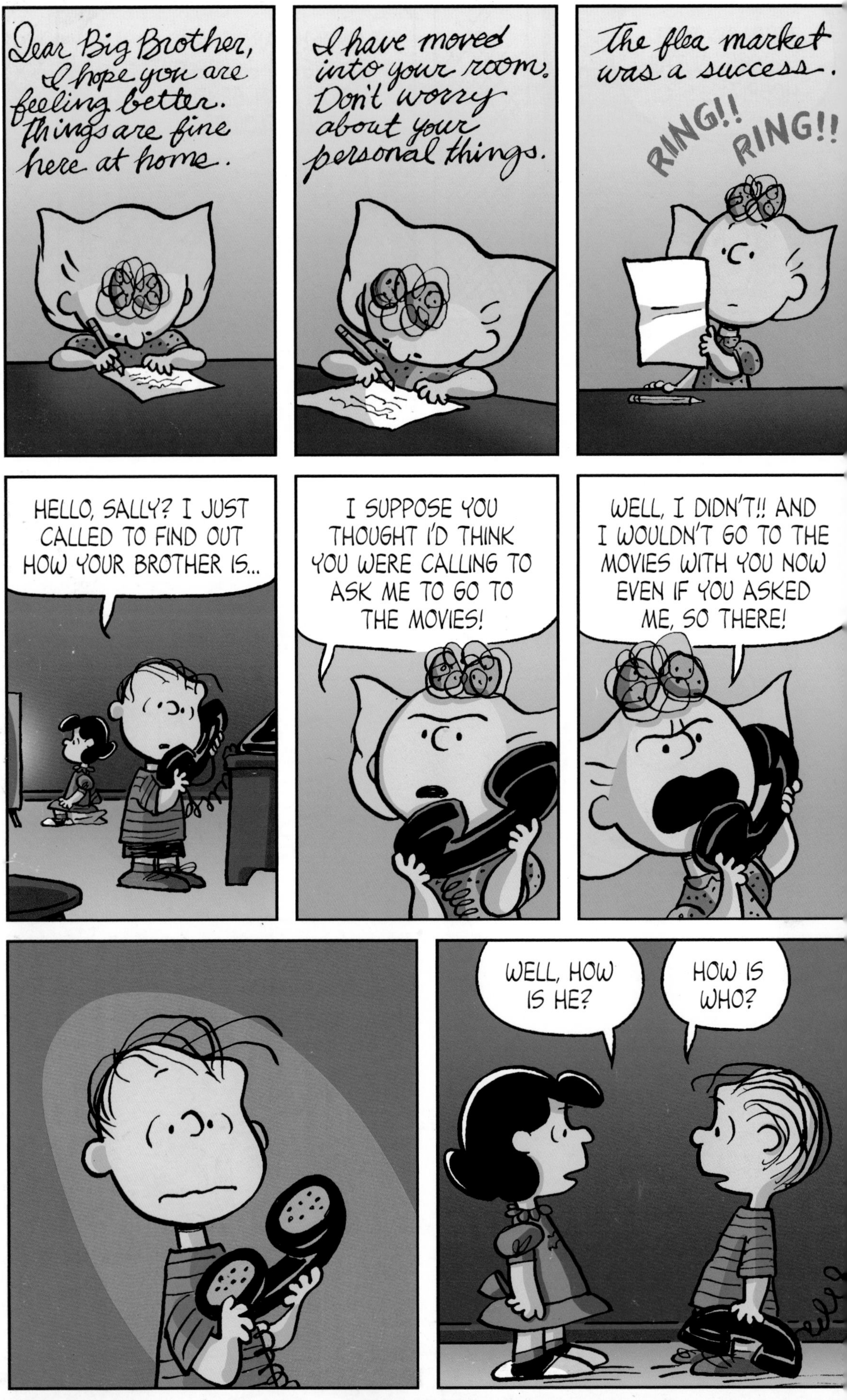
Dear Big Brother,
I hope you are feeling better. Things are fine here at home.
I have moved into your room. Don't worry about your personal things.
The flea market was a success.
RING!!
RING!!
HELLO, SALLY? I JUST CALLED TO FIND OUT HOW YOUR BROTHER IS...
I SUPPOSE YOU THOUGHT I'D THINK YOU WERE CALLING TO ASK ME TO GO TO THE MOVIES!
WELL, I DIDN'T!! AND I WOULDN'T GO TO THE MOVIES WITH YOU NOW EVEN IF YOU ASKED ME, SO THERE!
WELL, HOW IS HE?
HOW IS WHO?

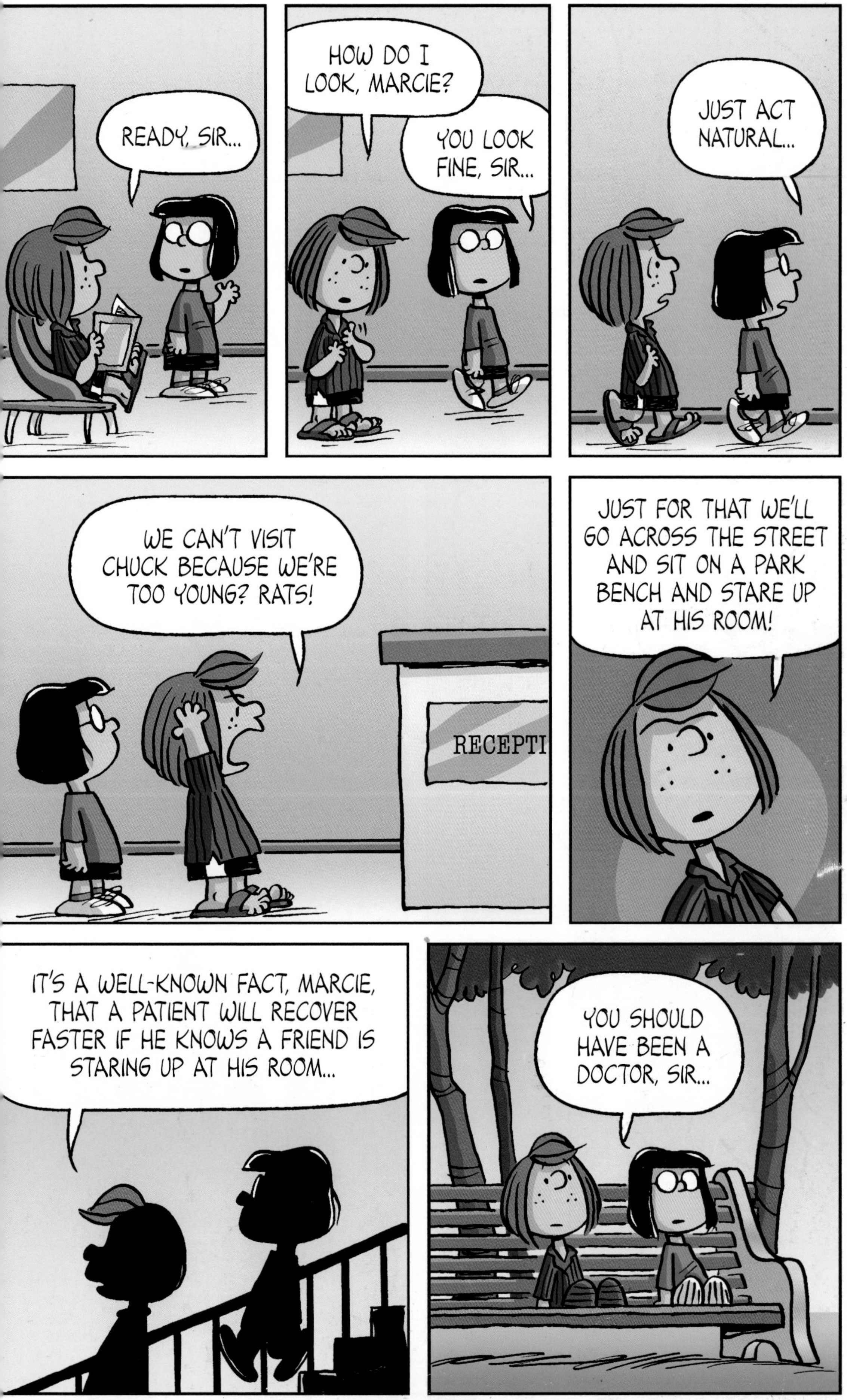
READY, SIR...
HOW DO I LOOK, MARCIE?
YOU LOOK FINE, SIR...
JUST ACT NATURAL...
WE CAN'T VISIT CHUCK BECAUSE WE'RE TOO YOUNG? RATS!
RECEPTI
JUST FOR THAT WE'LL GO ACROSS THE STREET AND SIT ON A PARK BENCH AND STARE UP AT HIS ROOM!
IT'S A WELL-KNOWN FACT, MARCIE, THAT A PATIENT WILL RECOVER FASTER IF HE KNOWS A FRIEND IS STARING UP AT HIS ROOM...
YOU SHOULD HAVE BEEN A DOCTOR, SIR...

FIRST I WAS SURROUNDED BY DOCTORS AND NURSES... NOW EVERYBODY'S GONE...

NOBODY LIKES ME... I DON'T HAVE A SINGLE FRIEND IN THE WHOLE WORLD!

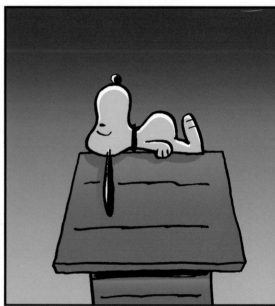

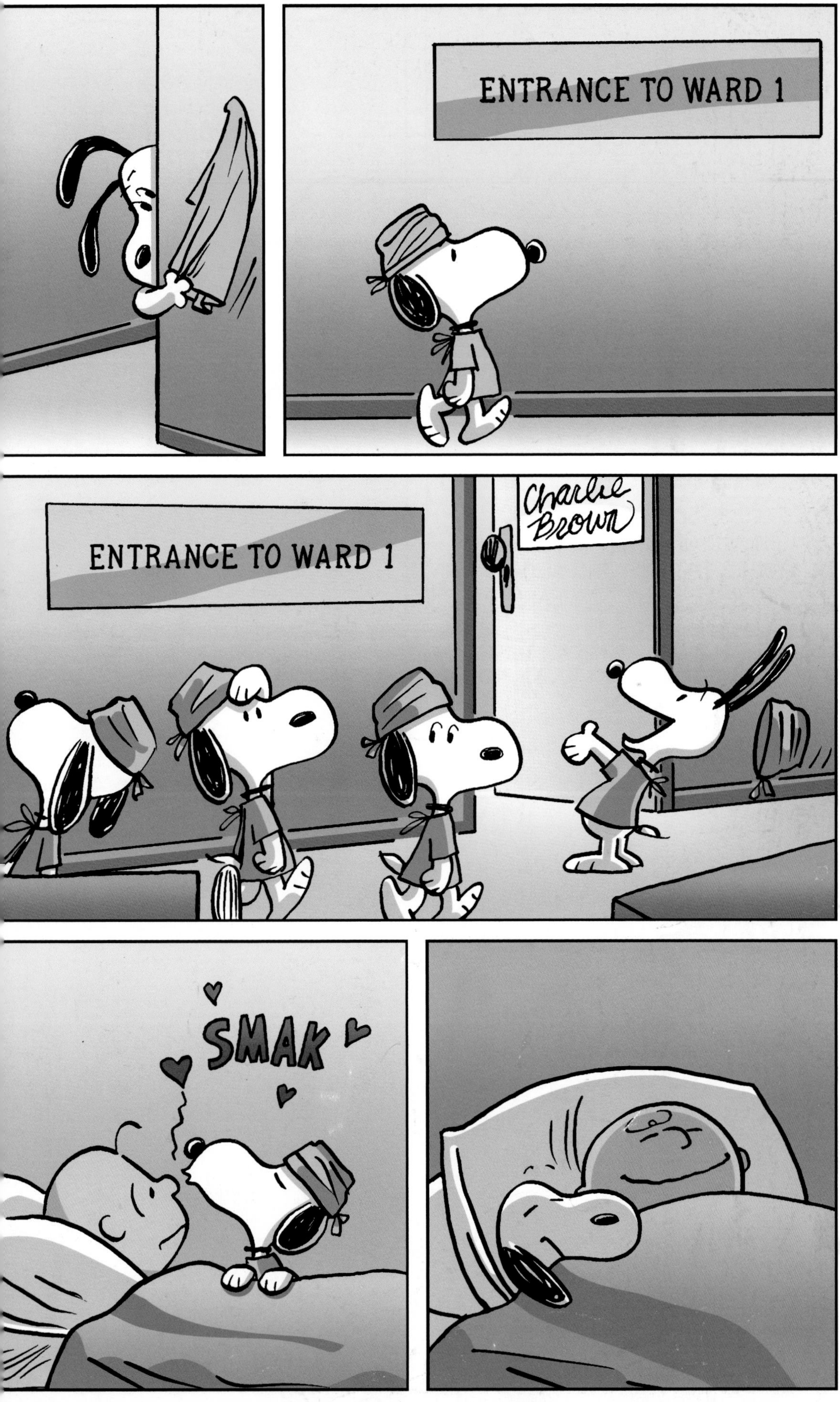
ENTRANCE TO WARD 1
ENTRANCE TO WARD 1
Charlie Brown
SMAK

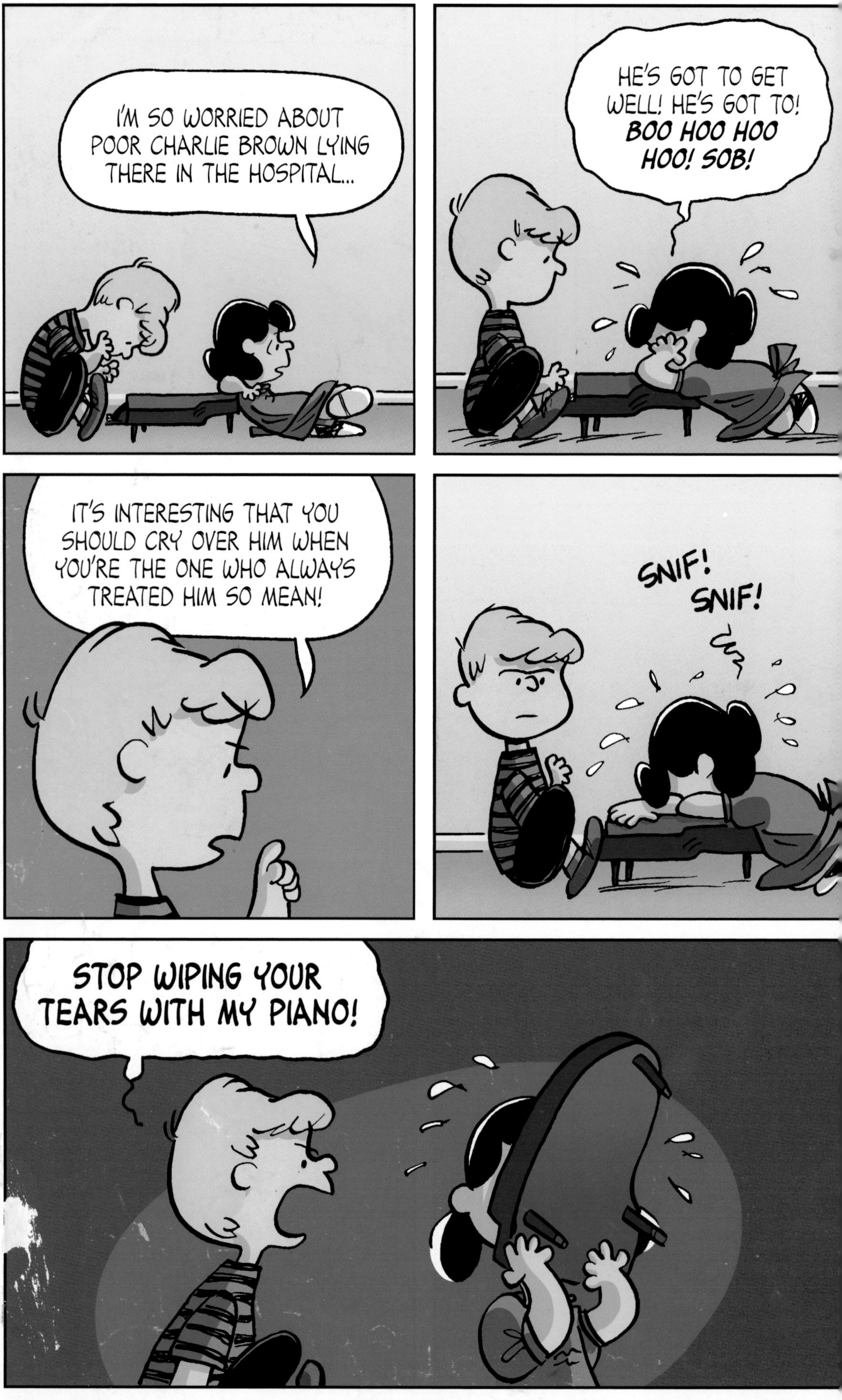
I'M SO WORRIED ABOUT POOR CHARLIE BROWN LYING THERE IN THE HOSPITAL...
HE'S GOT TO GET WELL! HE'S GOT TO! BOO HOO HOO HOO! SOB!
IT'S INTERESTING THAT YOU SHOULD CRY OVER HIM WHEN YOU'RE THE ONE WHO ALWAYS TREATED HIM SO MEAN!
SNIF! SNIF!
STOP WIPING YOUR TEARS WITH MY PIANO!

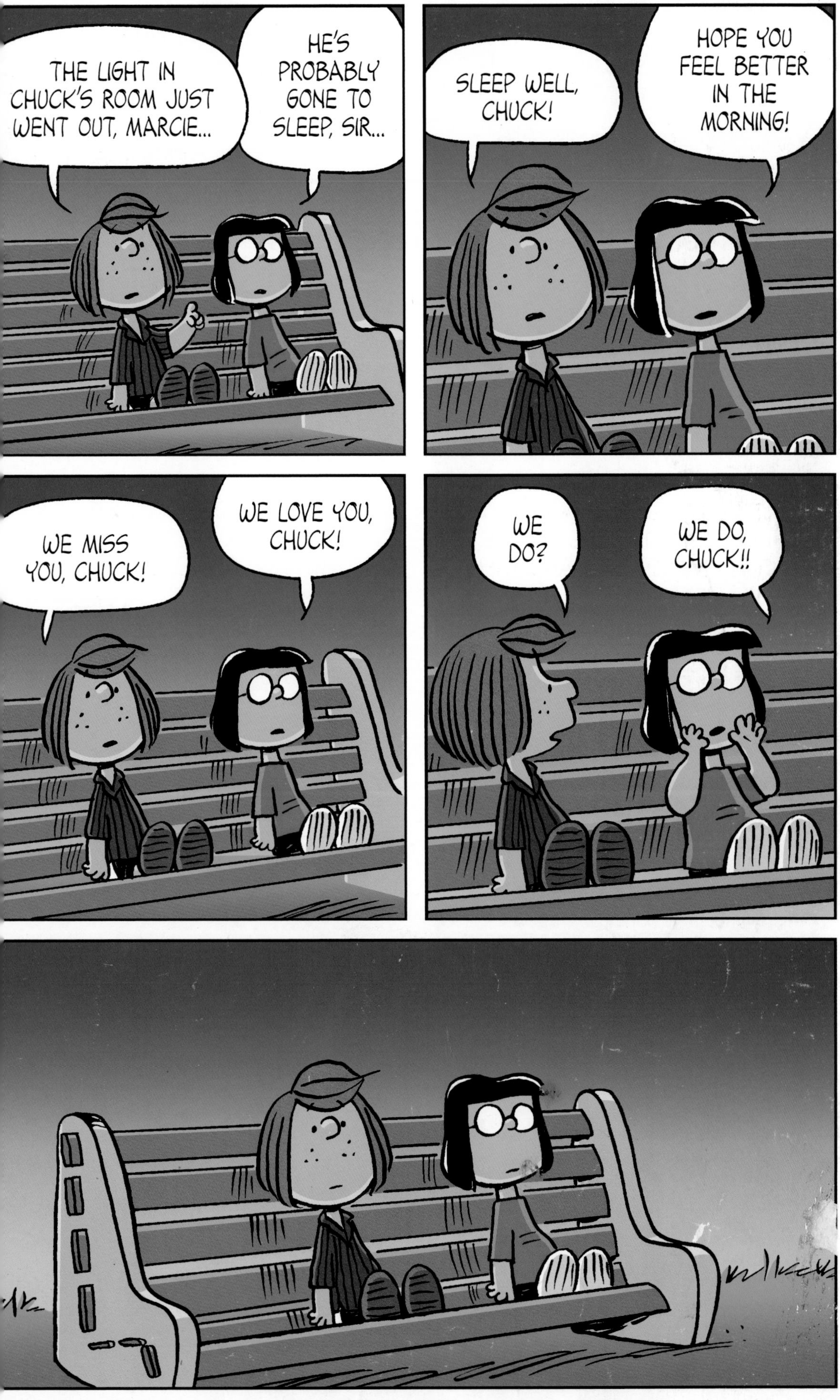
THE LIGHT IN CHUCK'S ROOM JUST WENT OUT, MARCIE...
HE'S PROBABLY GONE TO SLEEP, SIR...
SLEEP WELL, CHUCK!
HOPE YOU FEEL BETTER IN THE MORNING!
WE MISS YOU, CHUCK!
WE LOVE YOU, CHUCK!
WE DO?
WE DO, CHUCK!!

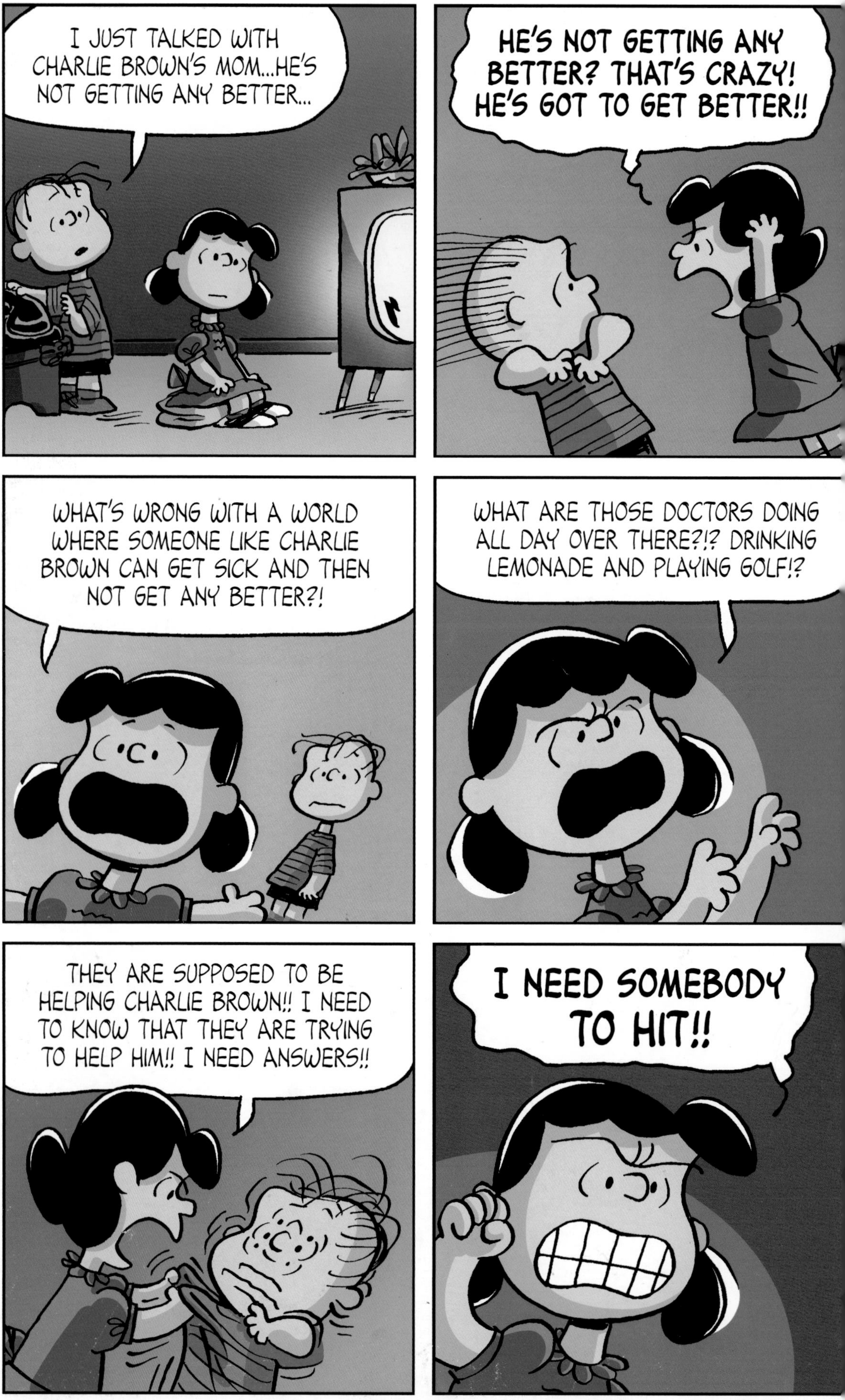
I JUST TALKED WITH CHARLIE BROWN'S MOM...HE'S NOT GETTING ANY BETTER...
HE'S NOT GETTING ANY BETTER? THAT'S CRAZY! HE'S GOT TO GET BETTER!!
WHAT'S WRONG WITH A WORLD WHERE SOMEONE LIKE CHARLIE BROWN CAN GET SICK AND THEN NOT GET ANY BETTER?!
WHAT ARE THOSE DOCTORS DOING ALL DAY OVER THERE?!? DRINKING LEMONADE AND PLAYING GOLF!?
THEY ARE SUPPOSED TO BE HELPING CHARLIE BROWN!! I NEED TO KNOW THAT THEY ARE TRYING TO HELP HIM!! I NEED ANSWERS!!
I NEED SOMEBODY TO HIT!!

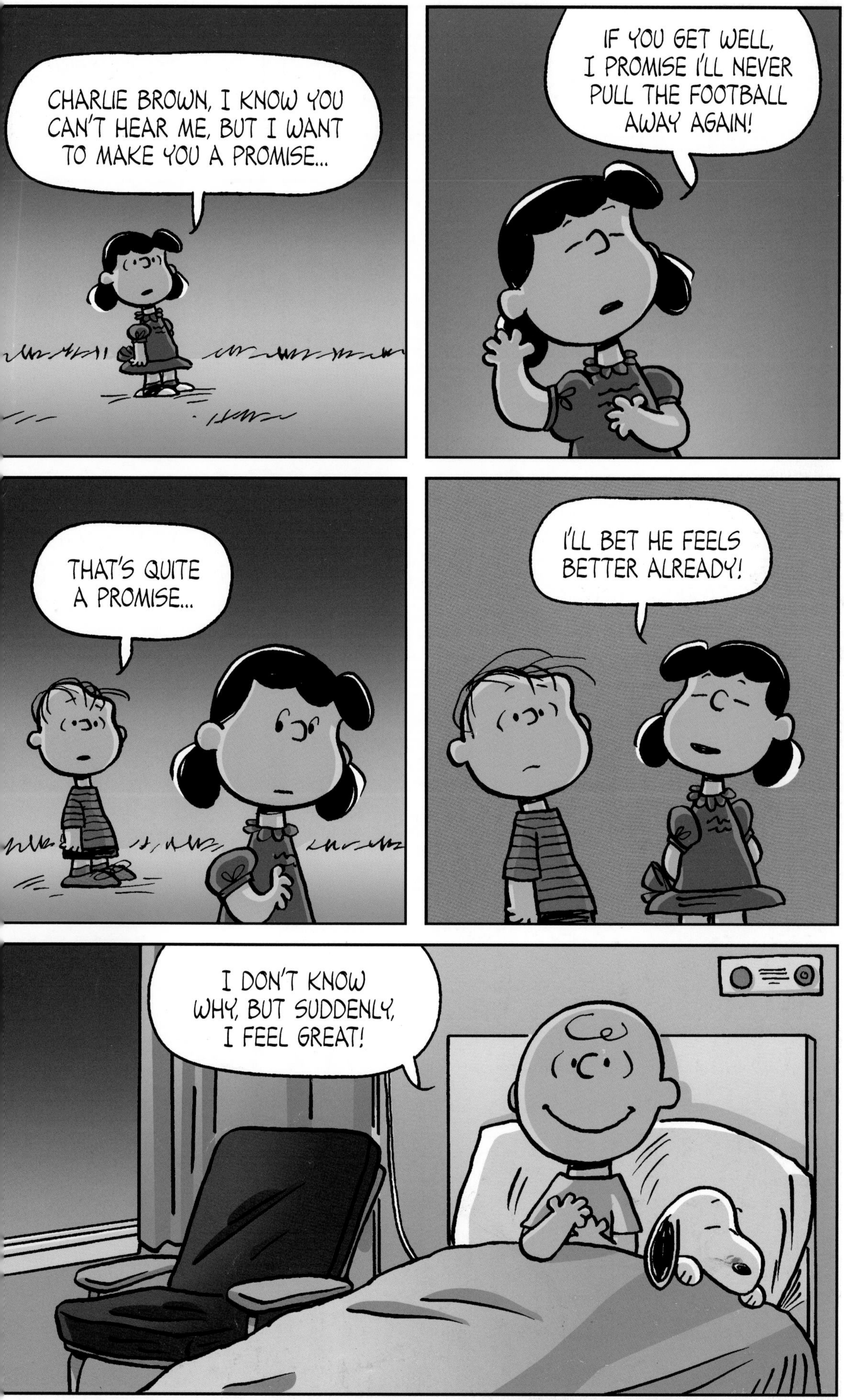
CHARLIE BROWN, I KNOW YOU CAN'T HEAR ME, BUT I WANT TO MAKE YOU A PROMISE...
IF YOU GET WELL, I PROMISE I'LL NEVER PULL THE FOOTBALL AWAY AGAIN!
THAT'S QUITE A PROMISE...
I'LL BET HE FEELS BETTER ALREADY!
I DON'T KNOW WHY, BUT SUDDENLY, I FEEL GREAT!

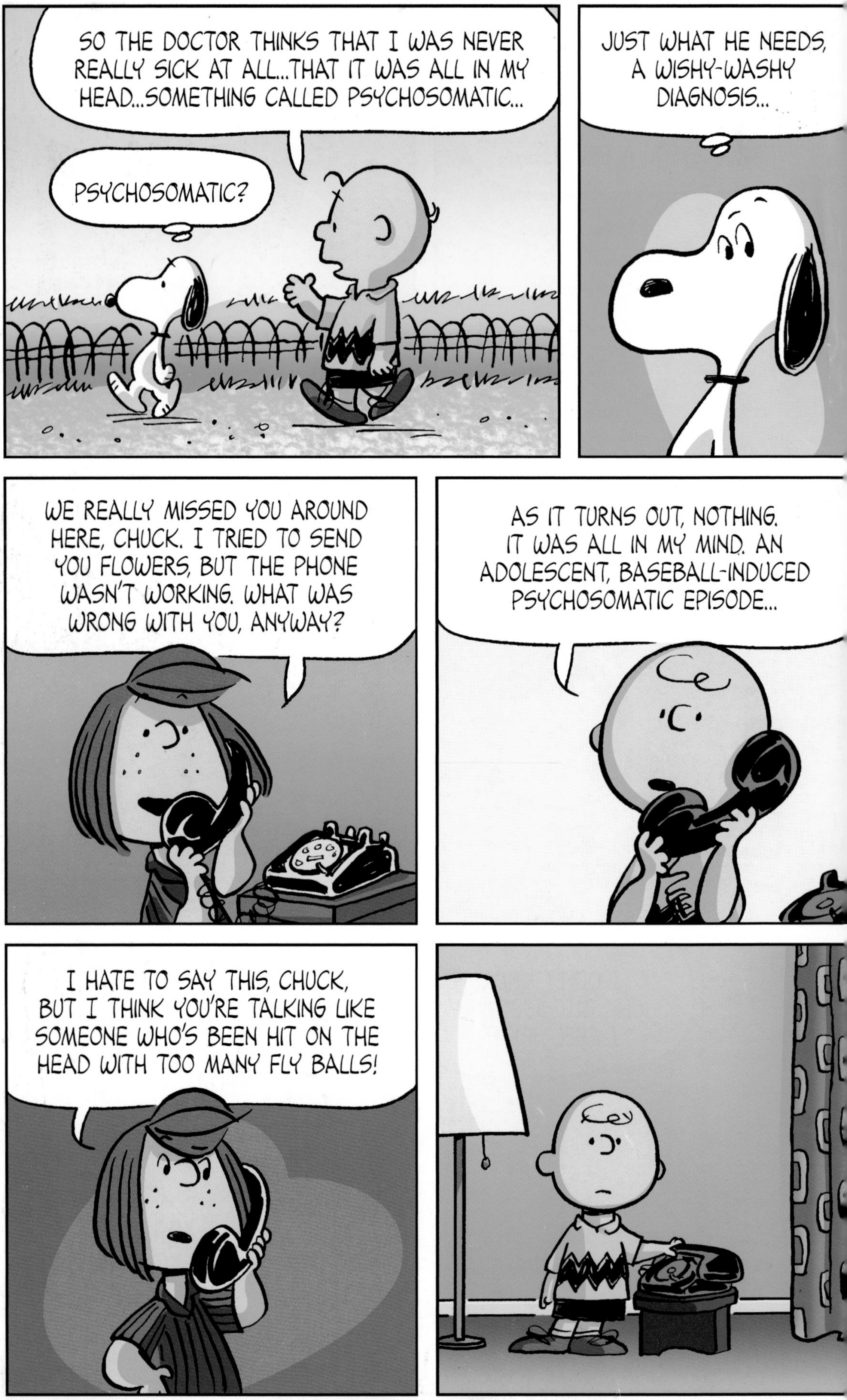
SO THE DOCTOR THINKS THAT I WAS NEVER REALLY SICK AT ALL...THAT IT WAS ALL IN MY HEAD...SOMETHING CALLED PSYCHOSOMATIC...
PSYCHOSOMATIC?
JUST WHAT HE NEEDS, A WISHY-WASHY DIAGNOSIS...
WE REALLY MISSED YOU AROUND HERE, CHUCK. I TRIED TO SEND YOU FLOWERS, BUT THE PHONE WASN'T WORKING. WHAT WAS WRONG WITH YOU, ANYWAY?
AS IT TURNS OUT, NOTHING. IT WAS ALL IN MY MIND. AN ADOLESCENT, BASEBALL-INDUCED PSYCHOSOMATIC EPISODE...
I HATE TO SAY THIS, CHUCK, BUT I THINK YOU'RE TALKING LIKE SOMEONE WHO'S BEEN HIT ON THE HEAD WITH TOO MANY FLY BALLS!

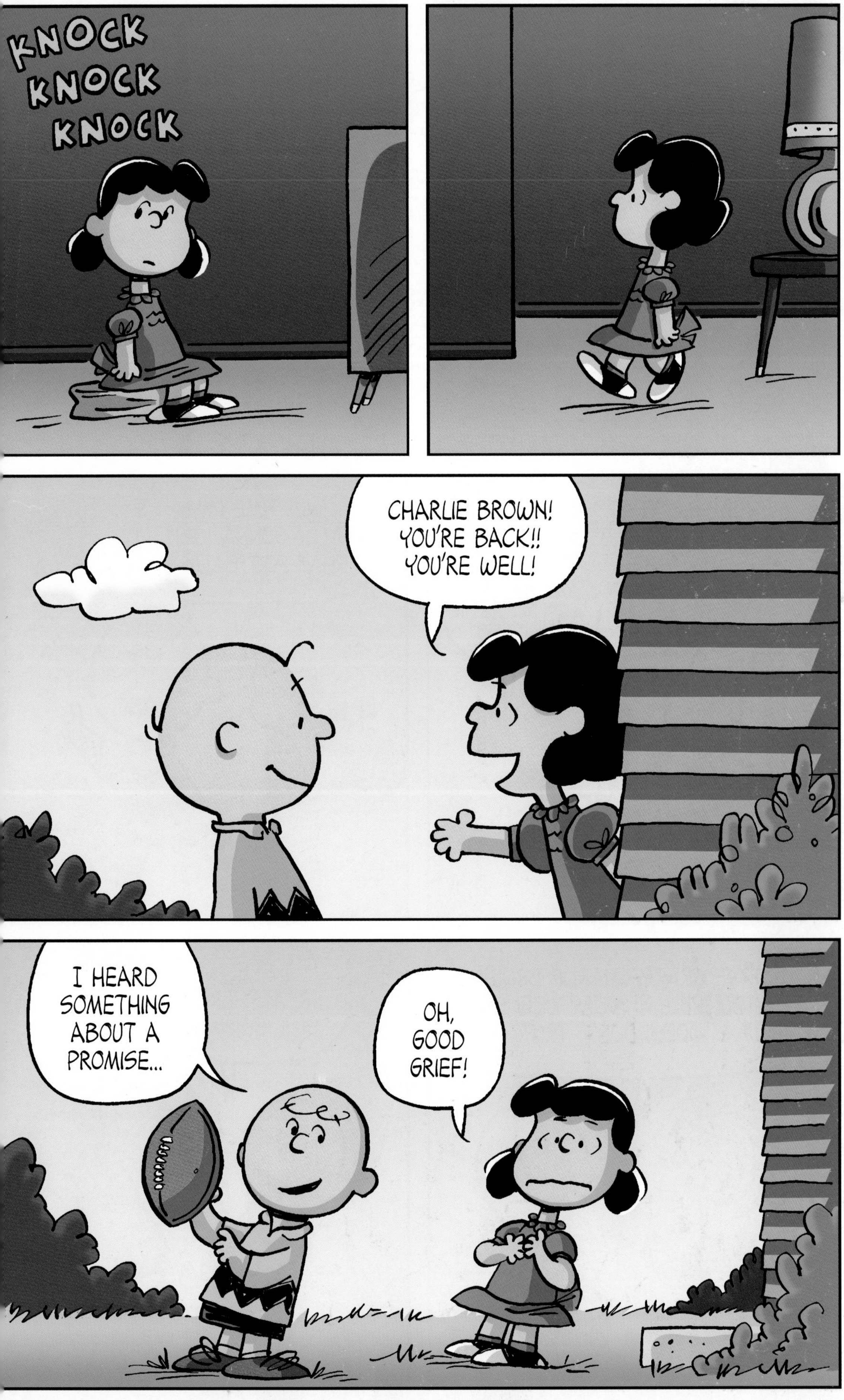
KNOCK KNOCK KNOCK
CHARLIE BROWN! YOU'RE BACK!! YOU'RE WELL!
I HEARD SOMETHING ABOUT A PROMISE...
OH, GOOD GRIEF!

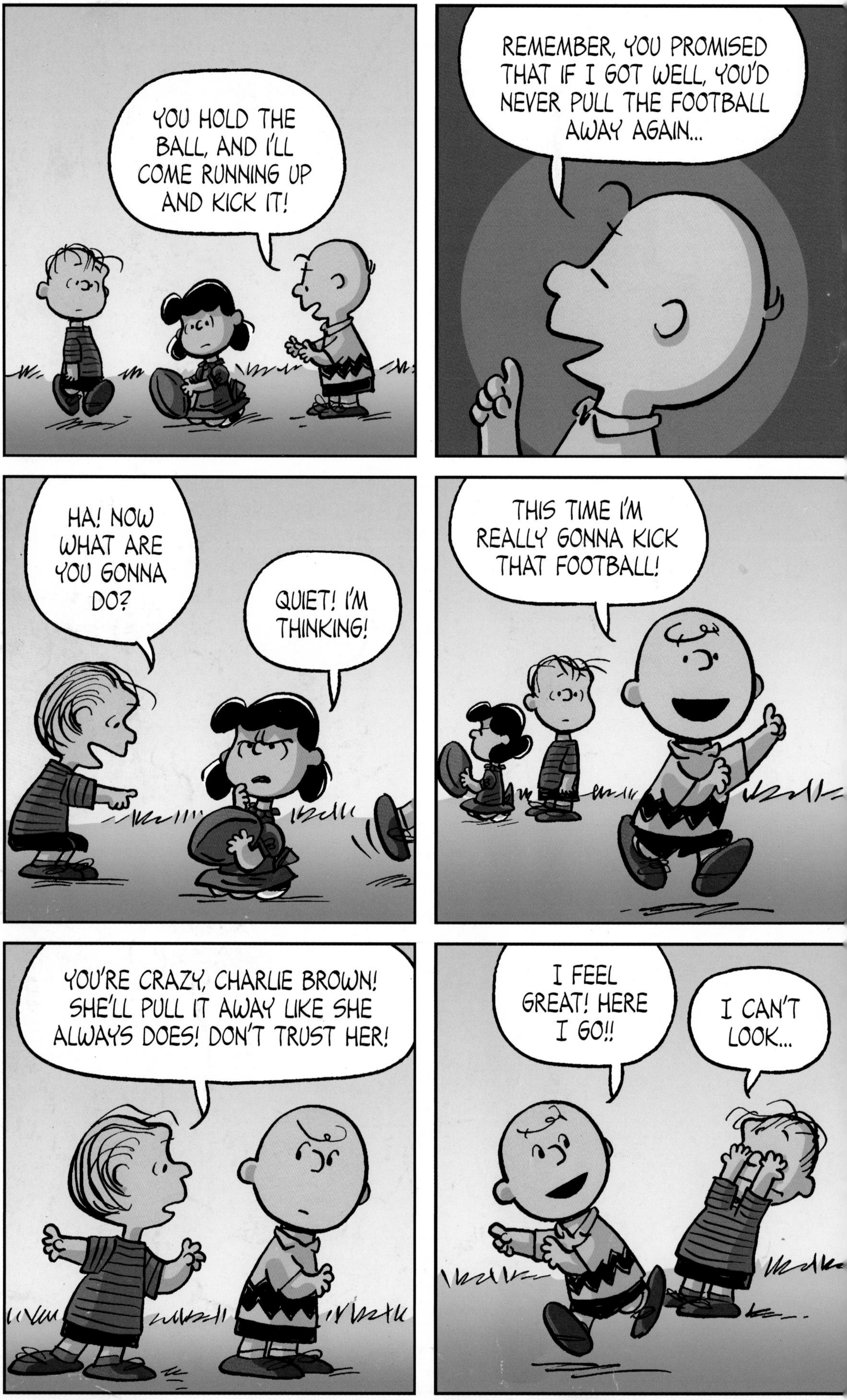
YOU HOLD THE BALL, AND I'LL COME RUNNING UP AND KICK IT!
REMEMBER, YOU PROMISED THAT IF I GOT WELL, YOU'D NEVER PULL THE FOOTBALL AWAY AGAIN...
HA! NOW WHAT ARE YOU GONNA DO?
QUIET! I'M THINKING!
THIS TIME I'M REALLY GONNA KICK THAT FOOTBALL!
YOU'RE CRAZY, CHARLIE BROWN! SHE'LL PULL IT AWAY LIKE SHE ALWAYS DOES! DON'T TRUST HER!
I FEEL GREAT! HERE I GO!!
I CAN'T LOOK...

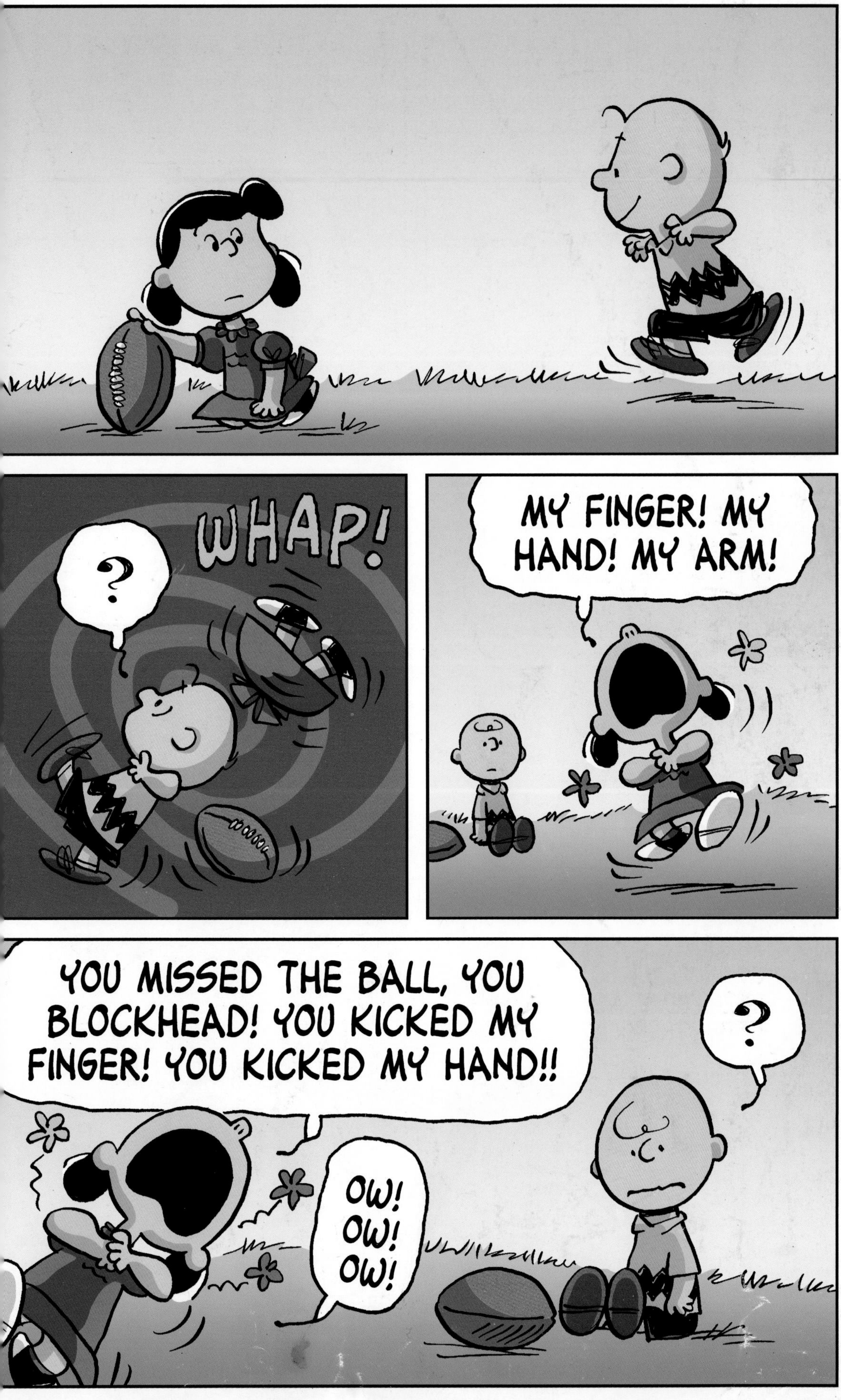
WHAP!
?
MY FINGER! MY HAND! MY ARM!
YOU MISSED THE BALL, YOU BLOCKHEAD! YOU KICKED MY FINGER! YOU KICKED MY HAND!!
OW! OW! OW!
?

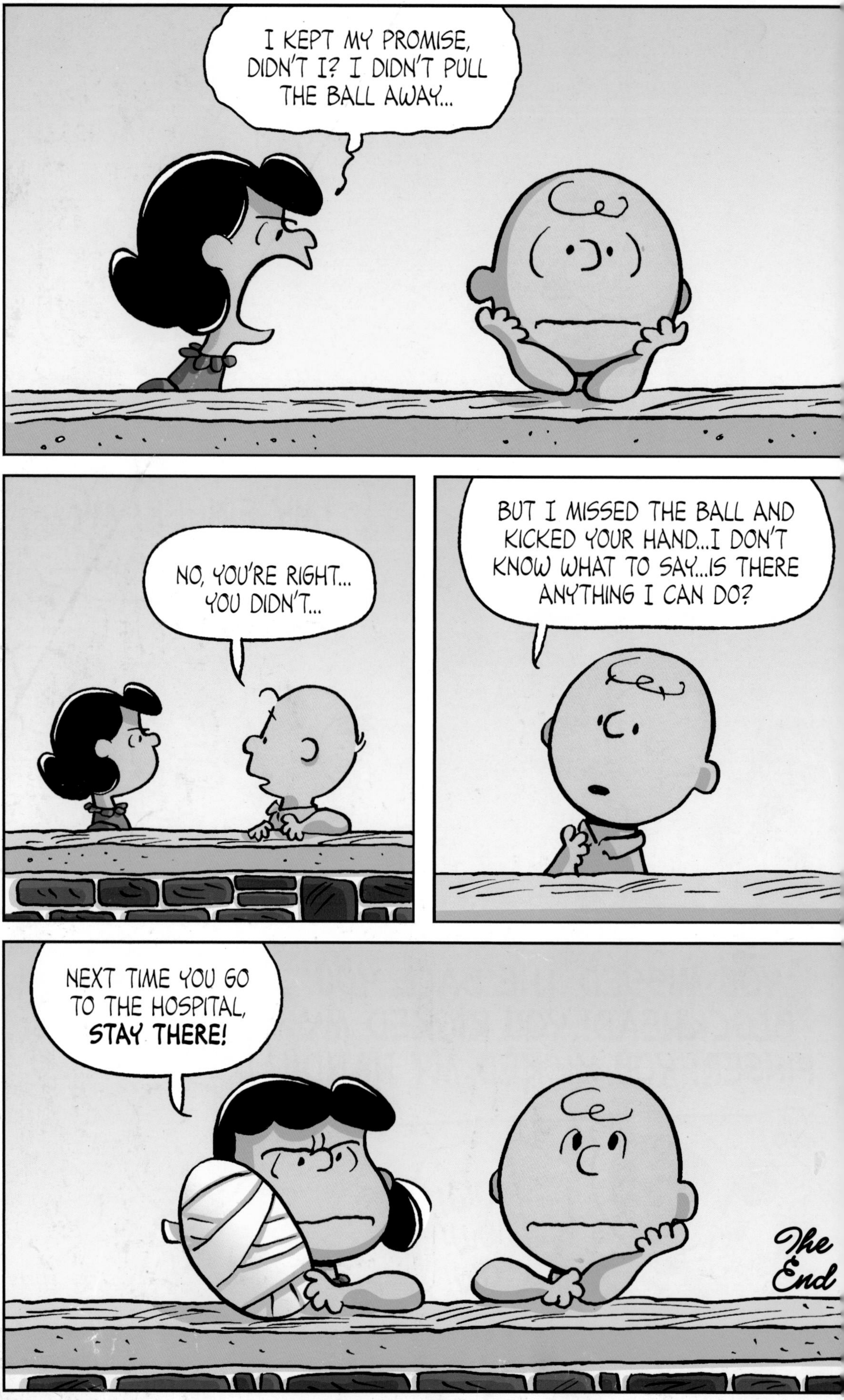

I KEPT MY PROMISE, DIDN'T I? I DIDN'T PULL THE BALL AWAY...
NO, YOU'RE RIGHT... YOU DIDN'T...
BUT I MISSED THE BALL AND KICKED YOUR HAND...I DON'T KNOW WHAT TO SAY...IS THERE ANYTHING I CAN DO?
NEXT TIME YOU GO TO THE HOSPITAL, **STAY THERE!**
The End

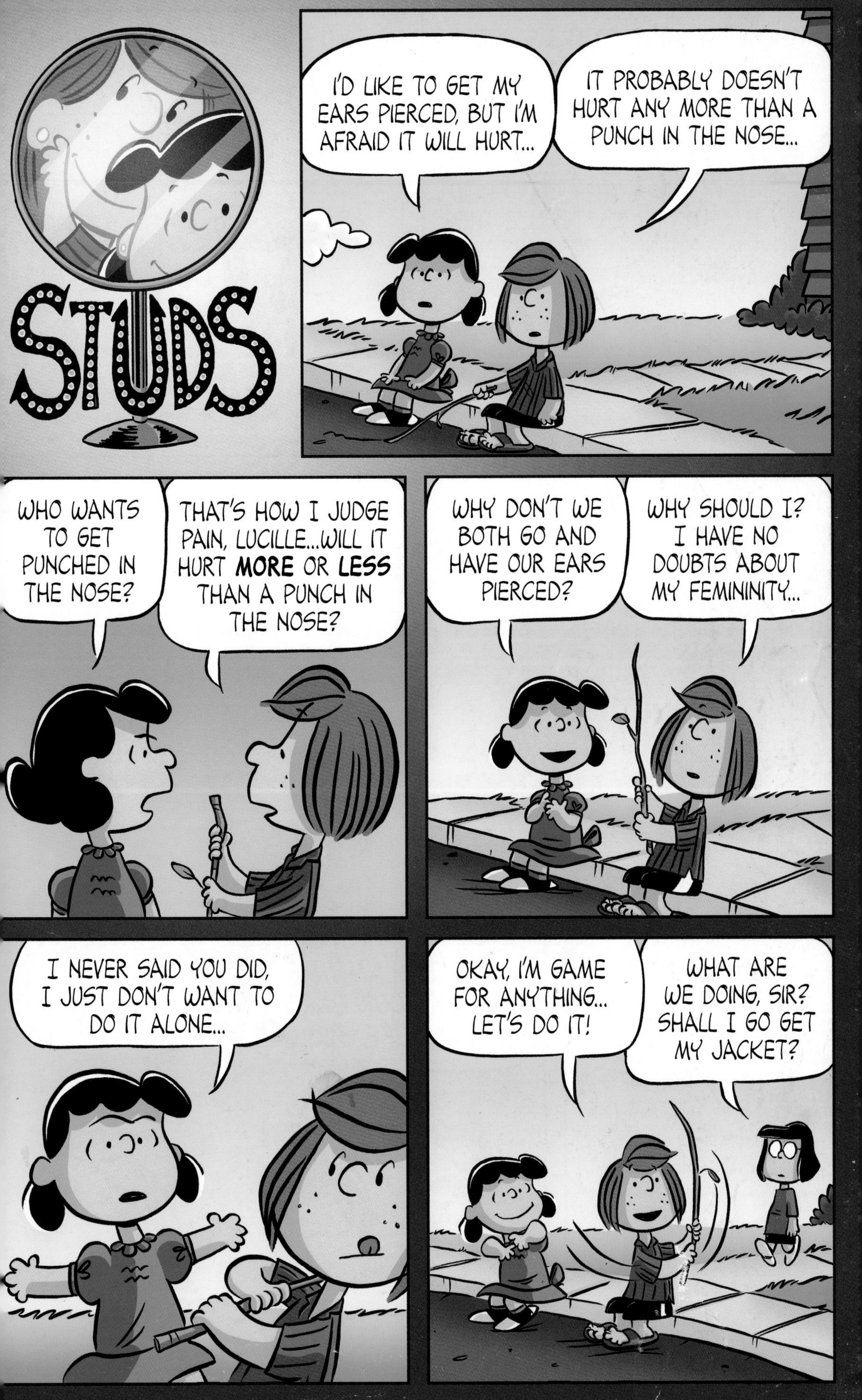
STUDS
I'D LIKE TO GET MY EARS PIERCED, BUT I'M AFRAID IT WILL HURT...
IT PROBABLY DOESN'T HURT ANY MORE THAN A PUNCH IN THE NOSE...
WHO WANTS TO GET PUNCHED IN THE NOSE?
THAT'S HOW I JUDGE PAIN, LUCILLE...WILL IT HURT **MORE** OR **LESS** THAN A PUNCH IN THE NOSE?
WHY DON'T WE BOTH GO AND HAVE OUR EARS PIERCED?
WHY SHOULD I? I HAVE NO DOUBTS ABOUT MY FEMININITY...
I NEVER SAID YOU DID, I JUST DON'T WANT TO DO IT ALONE...
OKAY, I'M GAME FOR ANYTHING... LET'S DO IT!
WHAT ARE WE DOING, SIR? SHALL I GO GET MY JACKET?

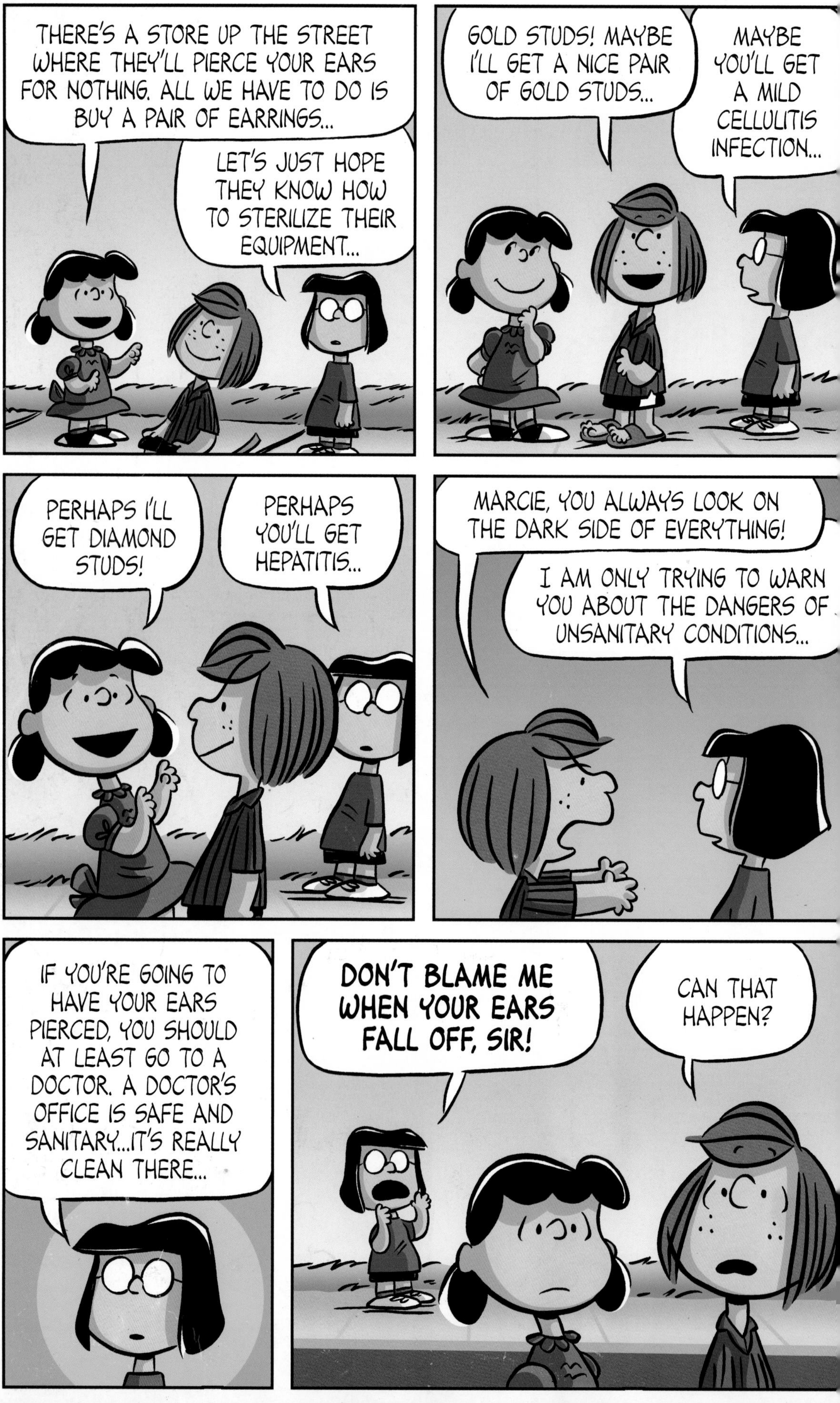
THERE'S A STORE UP THE STREET WHERE THEY'LL PIERCE YOUR EARS FOR NOTHING. ALL WE HAVE TO DO IS BUY A PAIR OF EARRINGS...
LET'S JUST HOPE THEY KNOW HOW TO STERILIZE THEIR EQUIPMENT...
GOLD STUDS! MAYBE I'LL GET A NICE PAIR OF GOLD STUDS...
MAYBE YOU'LL GET A MILD CELLULITIS INFECTION...
PERHAPS I'LL GET DIAMOND STUDS!
PERHAPS YOU'LL GET HEPATITIS...
MARCIE, YOU ALWAYS LOOK ON THE DARK SIDE OF EVERYTHING!
I AM ONLY TRYING TO WARN YOU ABOUT THE DANGERS OF UNSANITARY CONDITIONS...
IF YOU'RE GOING TO HAVE YOUR EARS PIERCED, YOU SHOULD AT LEAST GO TO A DOCTOR. A DOCTOR'S OFFICE IS SAFE AND SANITARY...IT'S REALLY CLEAN THERE...
DON'T BLAME ME WHEN YOUR EARS FALL OFF, SIR!
CAN THAT HAPPEN?

I SPOKE WITH THE DOCTOR'S OFFICE. A NURSE SAID THEY'LL PIERCE OUR EARS IF WE GET PARENTAL PERMISSION.

THAT'S NO PROBLEM...

Dear Doctor,
Okay! Let her have her dumb ears pierced. I am sick and tired of arguing with her.

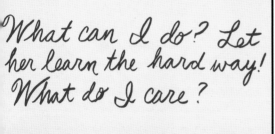

What can I do? Let her learn the hard way! What do I care?

THAT'S PERFECT, LUCILLE! IT SOUNDS EXACTLY LIKE A FED-UP MOTHER!

THIS IS NOT A GOOD IDEA...

DO NOT GO GENTLE INTO THAT GOOD NIGHT, SIR...

I DON'T GO GENTLE ANYWHERE!

AND STOP CALLING HER SIR!

GOOD GRIEF...

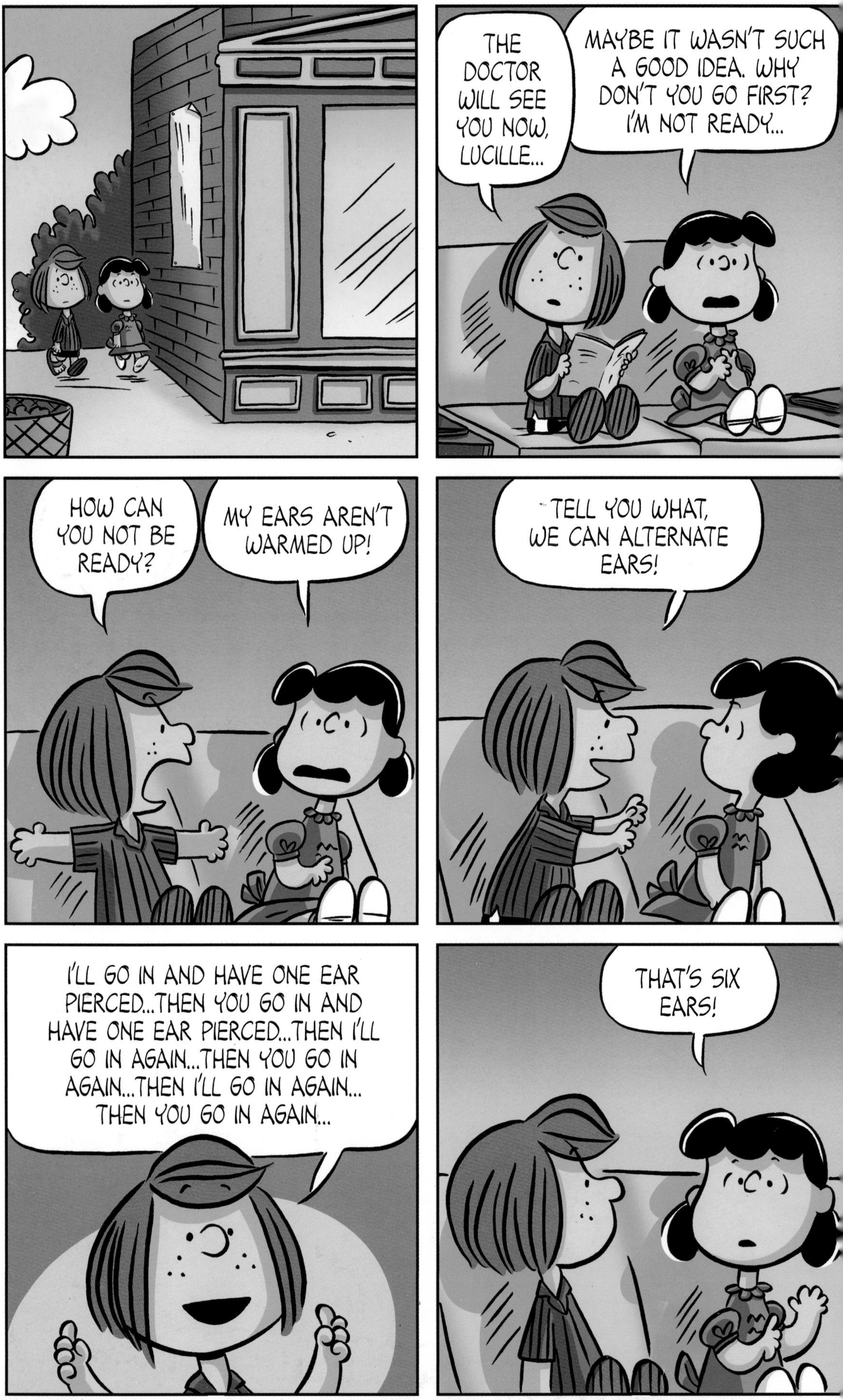
THE DOCTOR WILL SEE YOU NOW, LUCILLE...
MAYBE IT WASN'T SUCH A GOOD IDEA. WHY DON'T YOU GO FIRST? I'M NOT READY...
HOW CAN YOU NOT BE READY?
MY EARS AREN'T WARMED UP!
TELL YOU WHAT, WE CAN ALTERNATE EARS!
I'LL GO IN AND HAVE ONE EAR PIERCED...THEN YOU GO IN AND HAVE ONE EAR PIERCED...THEN I'LL GO IN AGAIN...THEN YOU GO IN AGAIN...THEN I'LL GO IN AGAIN... THEN YOU GO IN AGAIN...
THAT'S SIX EARS!

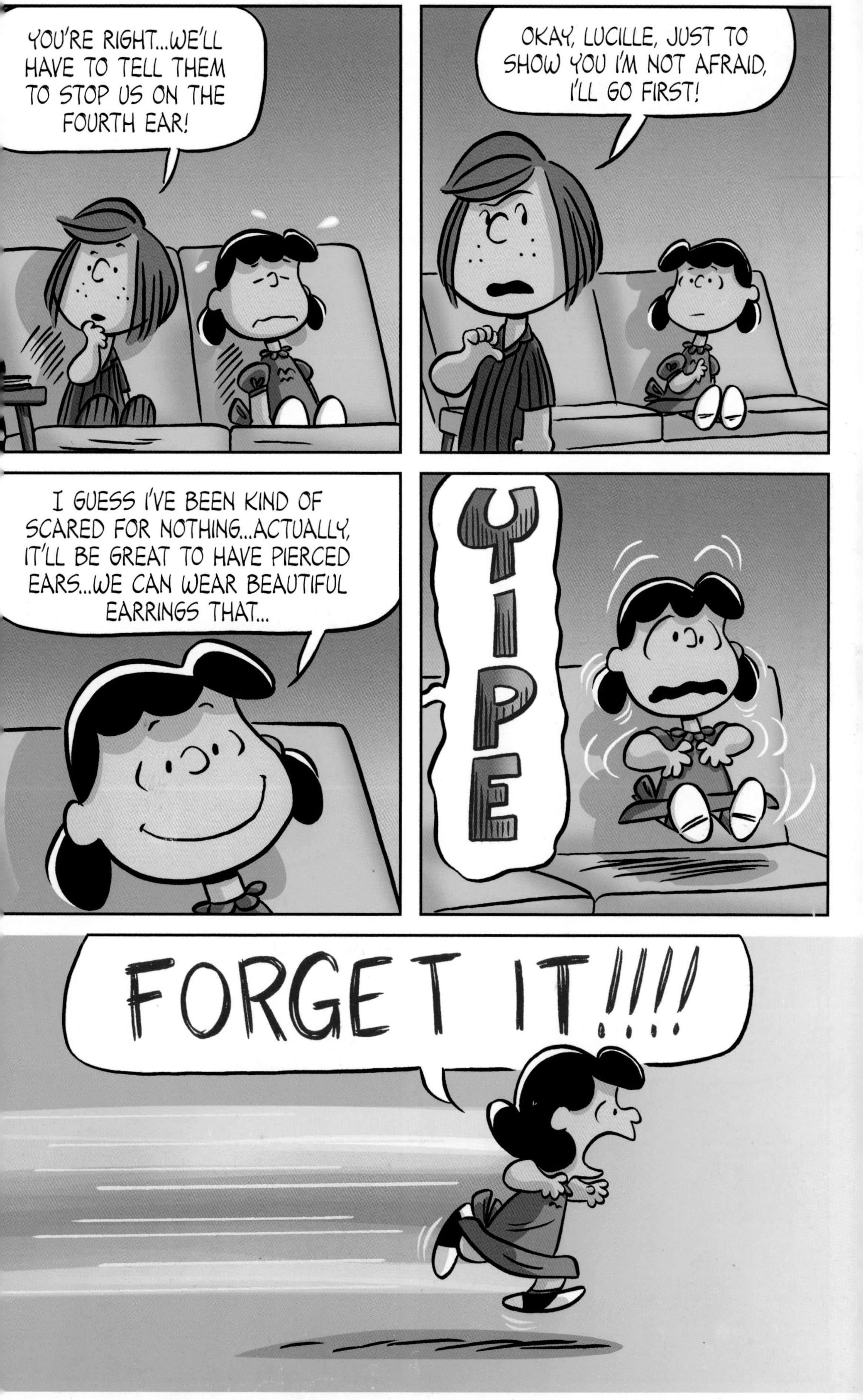
YOU'RE RIGHT...WE'LL HAVE TO TELL THEM TO STOP US ON THE FOURTH EAR!
OKAY, LUCILLE, JUST TO SHOW YOU I'M NOT AFRAID, I'LL GO FIRST!
I GUESS I'VE BEEN KIND OF SCARED FOR NOTHING...ACTUALLY, IT'LL BE GREAT TO HAVE PIERCED EARS...WE CAN WEAR BEAUTIFUL EARRINGS THAT...
YIPE
FORGET IT!!!!

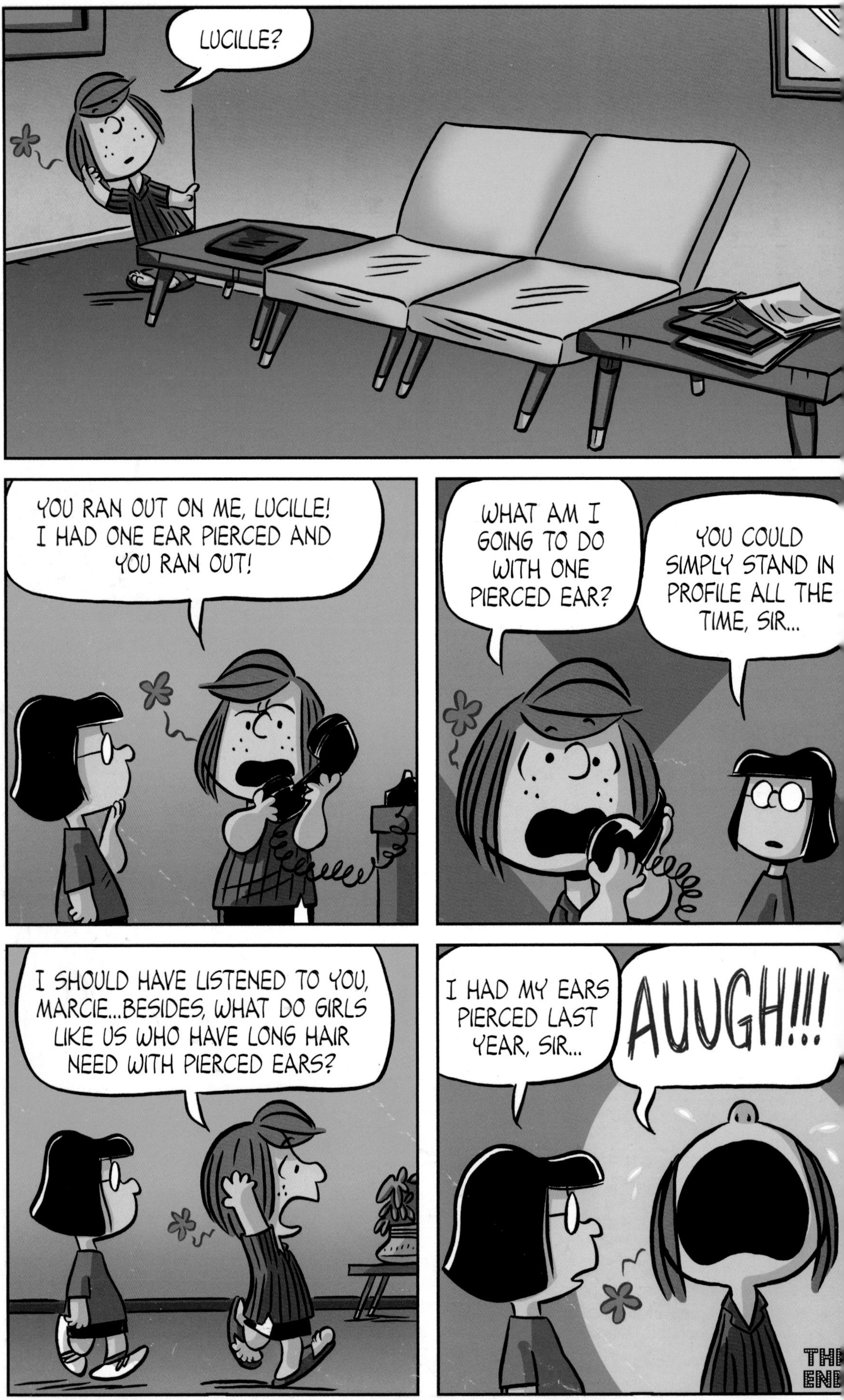

LUCILLE?
YOU RAN OUT ON ME, LUCILLE! I HAD ONE EAR PIERCED AND YOU RAN OUT!
WHAT AM I GOING TO DO WITH ONE PIERCED EAR?
YOU COULD SIMPLY STAND IN PROFILE ALL THE TIME, SIR...
I SHOULD HAVE LISTENED TO YOU, MARCIE...BESIDES, WHAT DO GIRLS LIKE US WHO HAVE LONG HAIR NEED WITH PIERCED EARS?
I HAD MY EARS PIERCED LAST YEAR, SIR...
AUUGH!!!

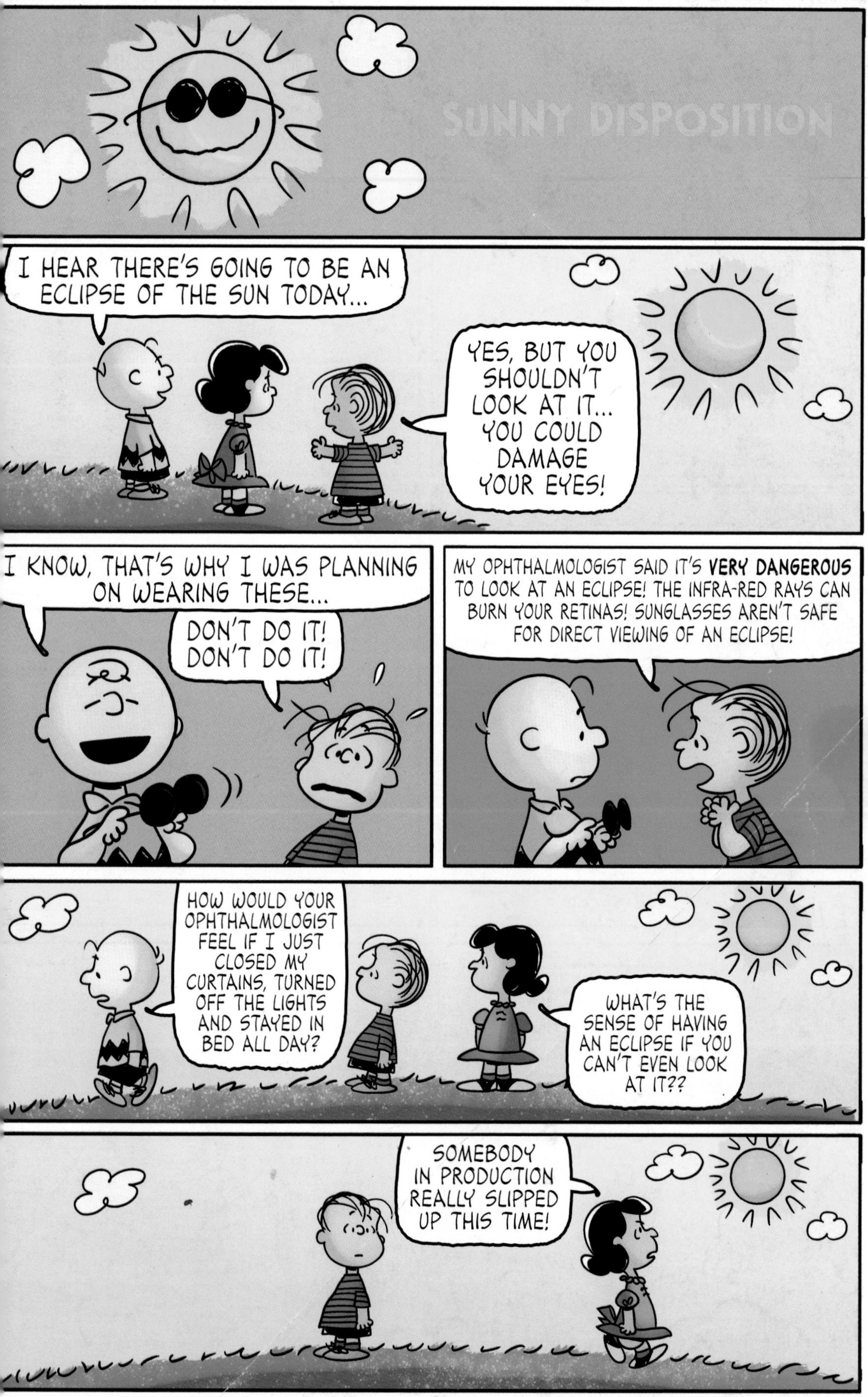
SUNNY DISPOSITION
I HEAR THERE'S GOING TO BE AN ECLIPSE OF THE SUN TODAY...
YES, BUT YOU SHOULDN'T LOOK AT IT... YOU COULD DAMAGE YOUR EYES!
I KNOW, THAT'S WHY I WAS PLANNING ON WEARING THESE...
DON'T DO IT! DON'T DO IT!
MY OPHTHALMOLOGIST SAID IT'S **VERY DANGEROUS** TO LOOK AT AN ECLIPSE! THE INFRA-RED RAYS CAN BURN YOUR RETINAS! SUNGLASSES AREN'T SAFE FOR DIRECT VIEWING OF AN ECLIPSE!
HOW WOULD YOUR OPHTHALMOLOGIST FEEL IF I JUST CLOSED MY CURTAINS, TURNED OFF THE LIGHTS AND STAYED IN BED ALL DAY?
WHAT'S THE SENSE OF HAVING AN ECLIPSE IF YOU CAN'T EVEN LOOK AT IT??
SOMEBODY IN PRODUCTION REALLY SLIPPED UP THIS TIME!

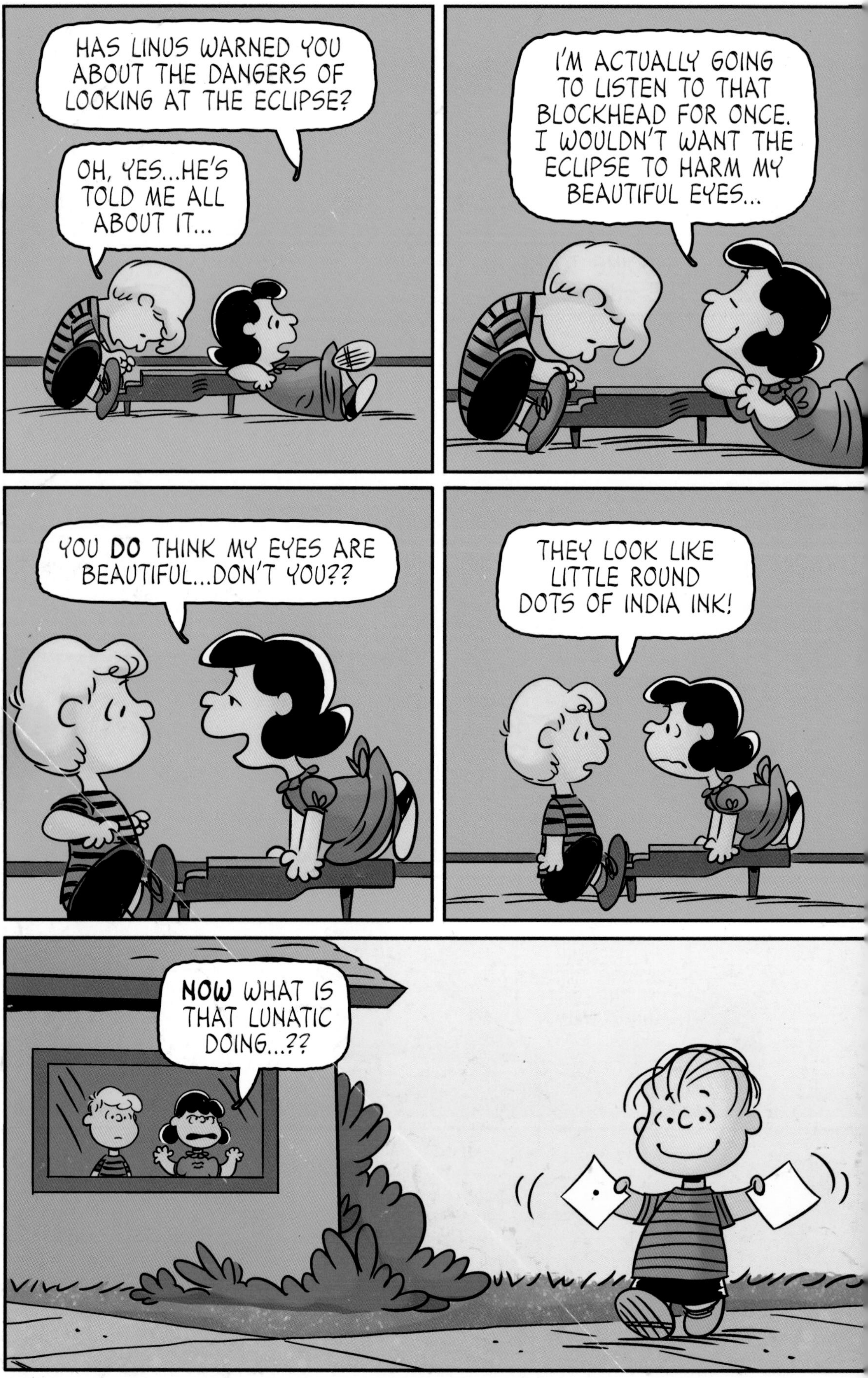
HAS LINUS WARNED YOU ABOUT THE DANGERS OF LOOKING AT THE ECLIPSE?
OH, YES...HE'S TOLD ME ALL ABOUT IT...
I'M ACTUALLY GOING TO LISTEN TO THAT BLOCKHEAD FOR ONCE. I WOULDN'T WANT THE ECLIPSE TO HARM MY BEAUTIFUL EYES...
YOU **DO** THINK MY EYES ARE BEAUTIFUL...DON'T YOU??
THEY LOOK LIKE LITTLE ROUND DOTS OF INDIA INK!
NOW WHAT IS THAT LUNATIC DOING...??

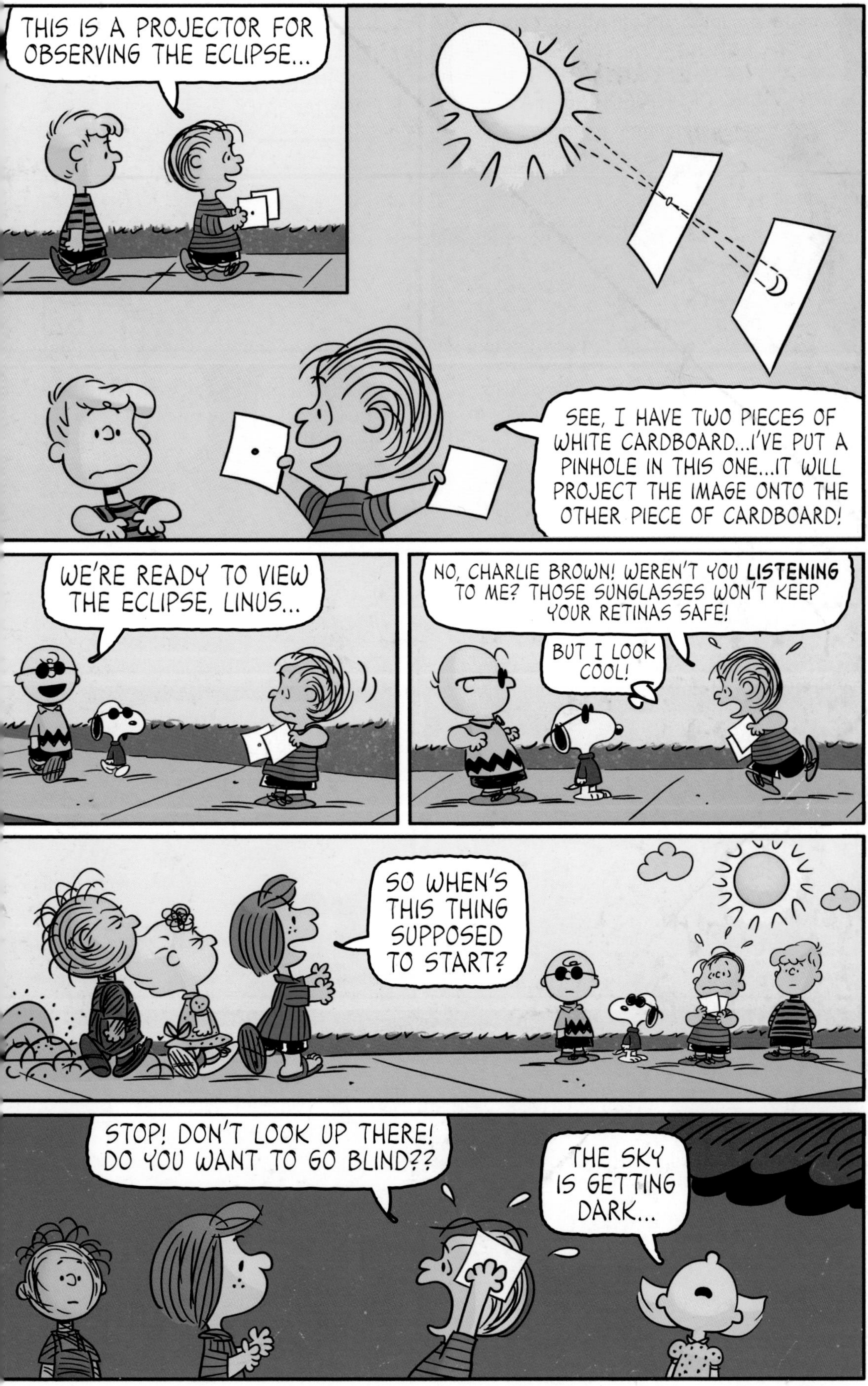
THIS IS A PROJECTOR FOR OBSERVING THE ECLIPSE...
SEE, I HAVE TWO PIECES OF WHITE CARDBOARD...I'VE PUT A PINHOLE IN THIS ONE...IT WILL PROJECT THE IMAGE ONTO THE OTHER PIECE OF CARDBOARD!
WE'RE READY TO VIEW THE ECLIPSE, LINUS...
NO, CHARLIE BROWN! WEREN'T YOU **LISTENING** TO ME? THOSE SUNGLASSES WON'T KEEP YOUR RETINAS SAFE!
BUT I LOOK COOL!
SO WHEN'S THIS THING SUPPOSED TO START?
STOP! DON'T LOOK UP THERE! DO YOU WANT TO GO BLIND??
THE SKY IS GETTING DARK...

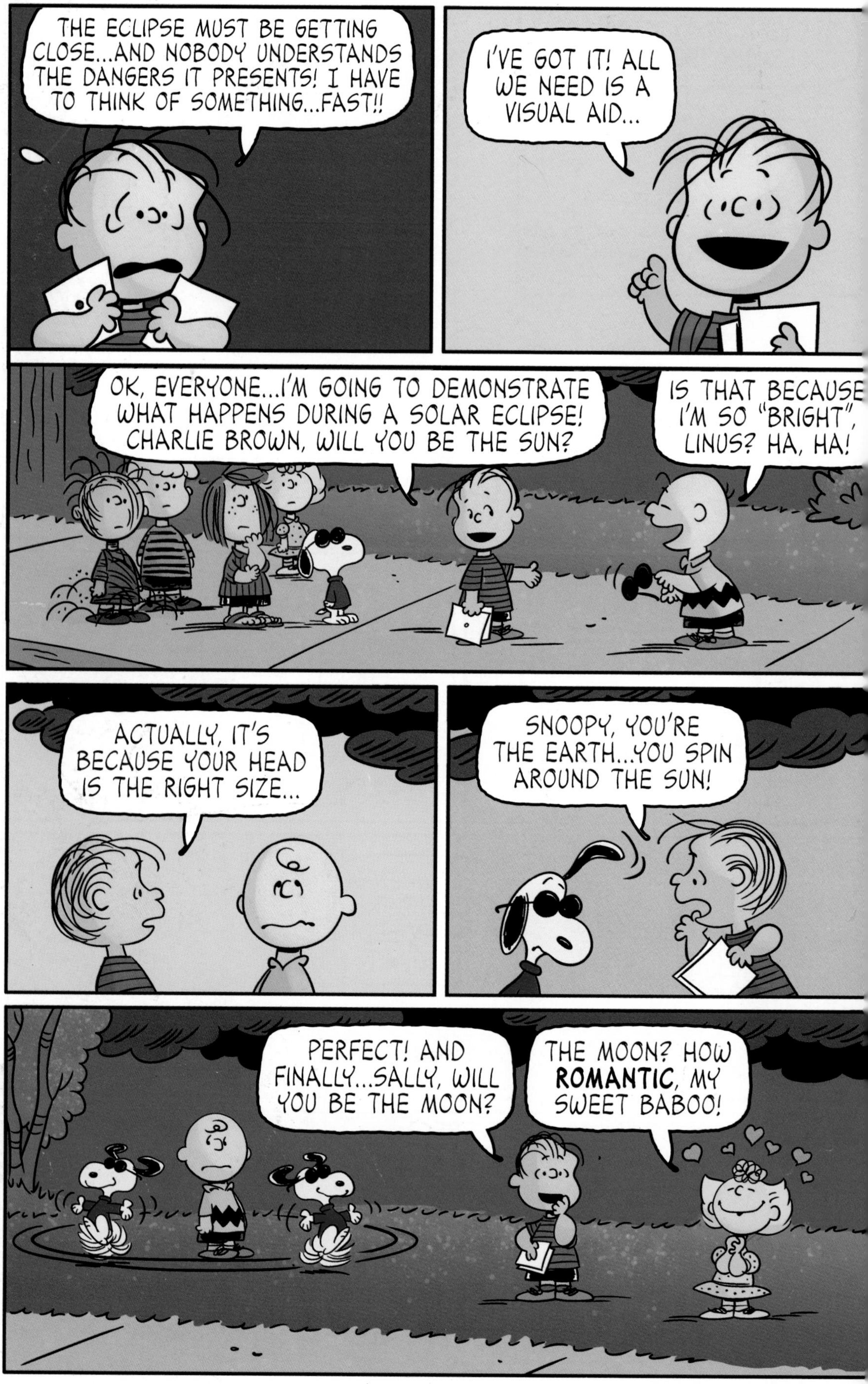
THE ECLIPSE MUST BE GETTING CLOSE...AND NOBODY UNDERSTANDS THE DANGERS IT PRESENTS! I HAVE TO THINK OF SOMETHING...FAST!!
I'VE GOT IT! ALL WE NEED IS A VISUAL AID...
OK, EVERYONE...I'M GOING TO DEMONSTRATE WHAT HAPPENS DURING A SOLAR ECLIPSE! CHARLIE BROWN, WILL YOU BE THE SUN?
IS THAT BECAUSE I'M SO "BRIGHT", LINUS? HA, HA!
ACTUALLY, IT'S BECAUSE YOUR HEAD IS THE RIGHT SIZE...
SNOOPY, YOU'RE THE EARTH...YOU SPIN AROUND THE SUN!
PERFECT! AND FINALLY...SALLY, WILL YOU BE THE MOON?
THE MOON? HOW **ROMANTIC**, MY SWEET BABOO!

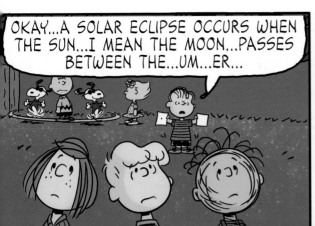

OKAY...A SOLAR ECLIPSE OCCURS WHEN THE SUN...I MEAN THE MOON...PASSES BETWEEN THE...UM...ER...

THIS ISN'T WORKING LIKE I HAD PLANNED!

SALLY, YOU'RE THE MOON! YOU HAVE TO PASS BETWEEN THE EARTH AND THE SUN!

I CAN'T! THE EARTH IS SPINNING TOO FAST!!

I'LL SAY IT IS...I'M GETTING DIZZY!

THIS MUST BE IT! IT'S ECLIPSE TIME!!

CRACK!

BOOM!

THAT IS ONE NOISY ECLIPSE!

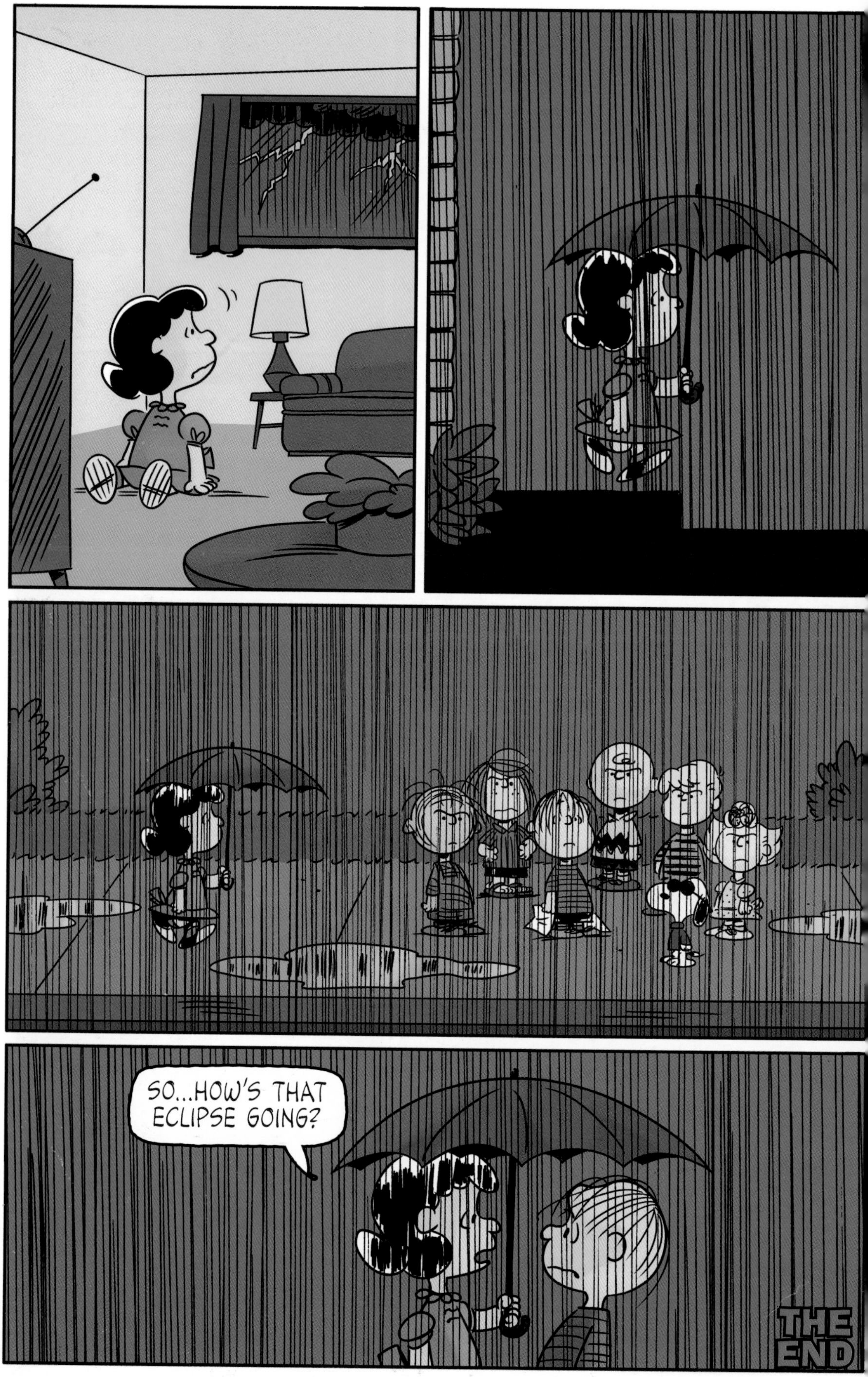
SO...HOW'S THAT ECLIPSE GOING?
THE END

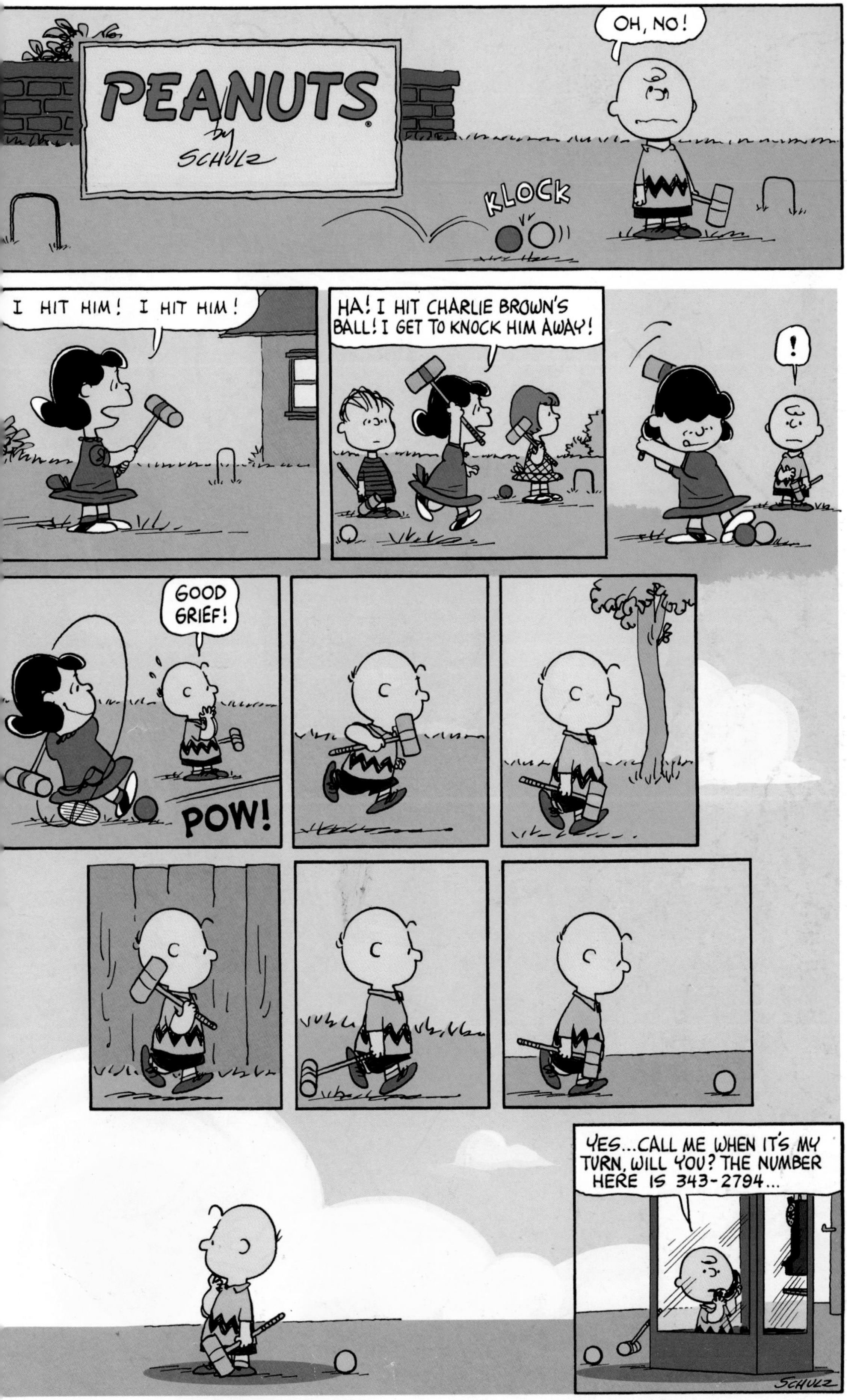
PEANUTS
by SCHULZ
OH, NO!
KLOCK
I HIT HIM! I HIT HIM!
HA! I HIT CHARLIE BROWN'S BALL! I GET TO KNOCK HIM AWAY!
!
GOOD GRIEF!
POW!
YES...CALL ME WHEN IT'S MY TURN, WILL YOU? THE NUMBER HERE IS 343-2794...
SCHULZ

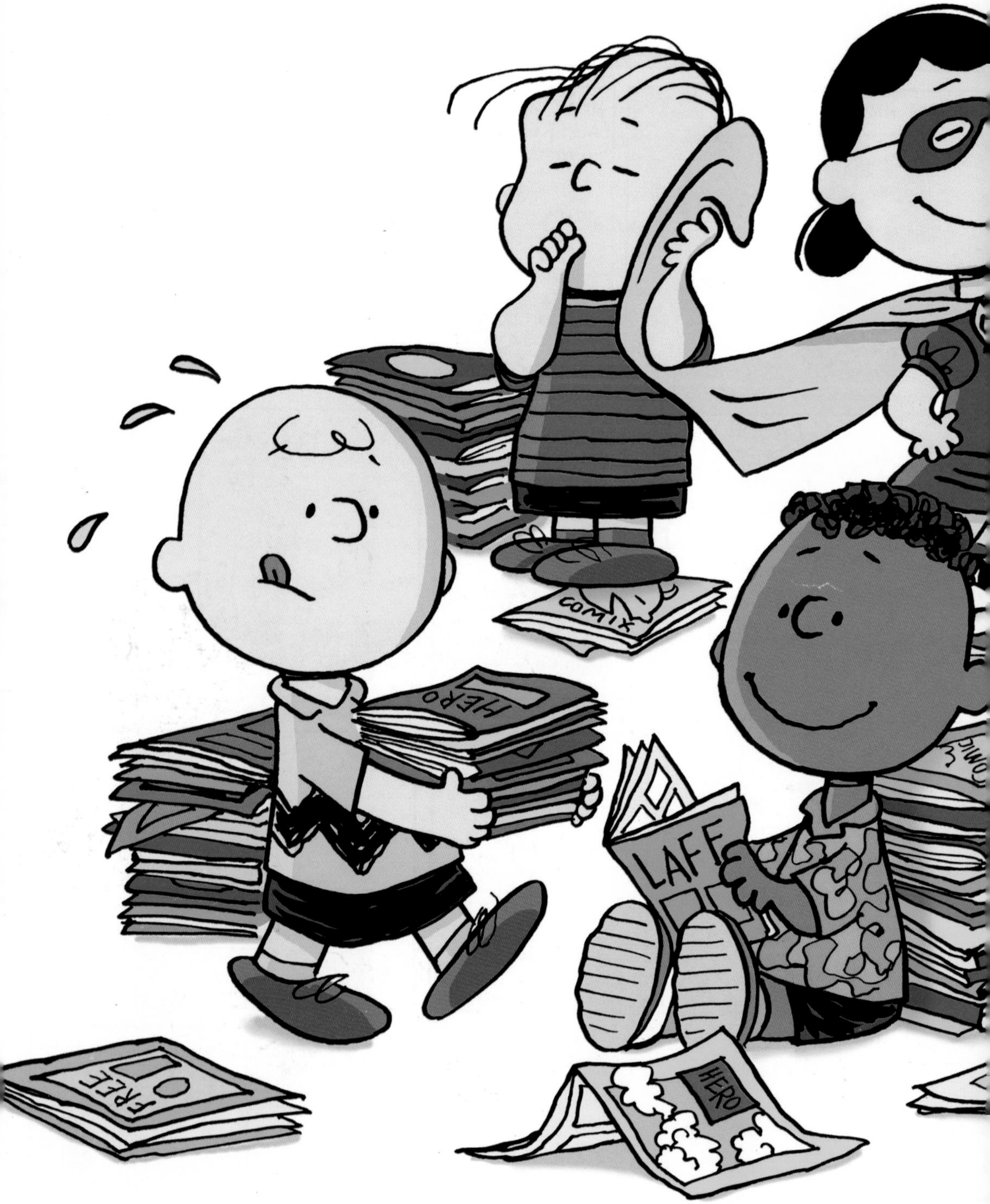
COMIX
HERO
LAFF
FREE
HERO

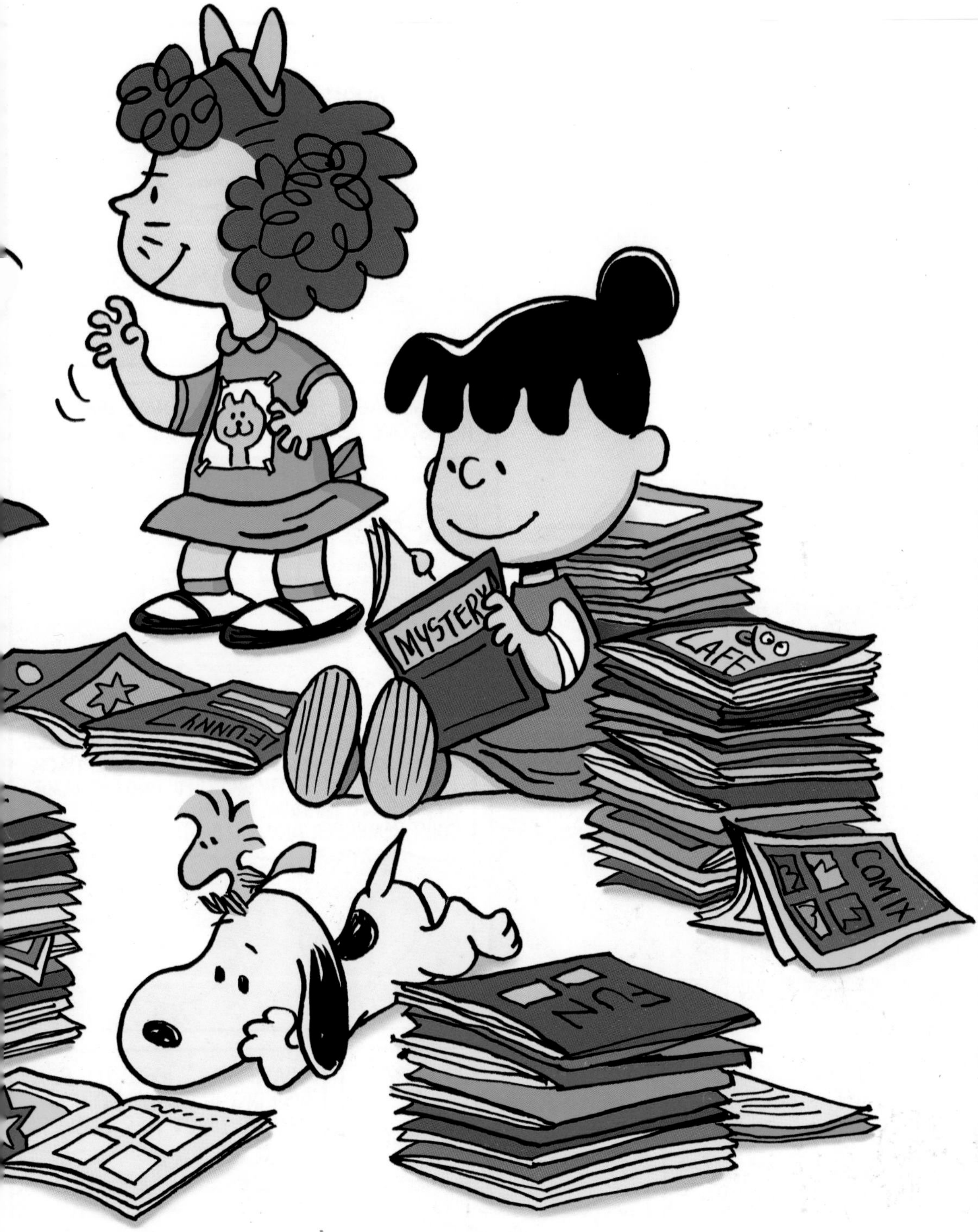

MYSTERY
FUNNY
LAFF
COMIX
FUN

PEANUTS
by SCHULZ

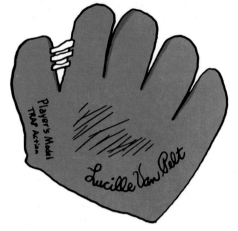

Player's Model
Trap Action
Lucille Van Pelt

OKAY, LET'S SHOW A LITTLE LIFE OUT THERE!

?

HEY, MANAGER...SOME KID MUST HAVE LEFT HIS GLOVE HERE.. IT HAS HIS NAME ON IT..

SEE? RIGHT HERE... "WILLIE MAYS".... HE WROTE HIS NAME ON HIS GLOVE, SEE?

POOR KID..HE'S PROBABLY BEEN LOOKING ALL OVER FOR IT..WE SHOULD HAVE A "LOST AND FOUND"

I DON'T KNOW ANY KID AROUND HERE NAMED "WILLIE MAYS," DO YOU? HOW ARE WE GONNA GET IT BACK TO HIM? HE WAS PRETTY SMART PUTTING HIS NAME ON HIS GLOVE THIS WAY, THOUGH...IT'S FUNNY, I JUST DON'T REMEMBER ANY KID BY THAT NAME...

LOOK AT THE NAME ON YOUR GLOVE

WHAT?

LOOK AT YOUR OWN GLOVE... THERE'S A NAME ON IT..

"BABE RUTH"...WELL, I'LL BE! HOW IN THE WORLD DO YOU SUPPOSE I GOT **HER** GLOVE?!

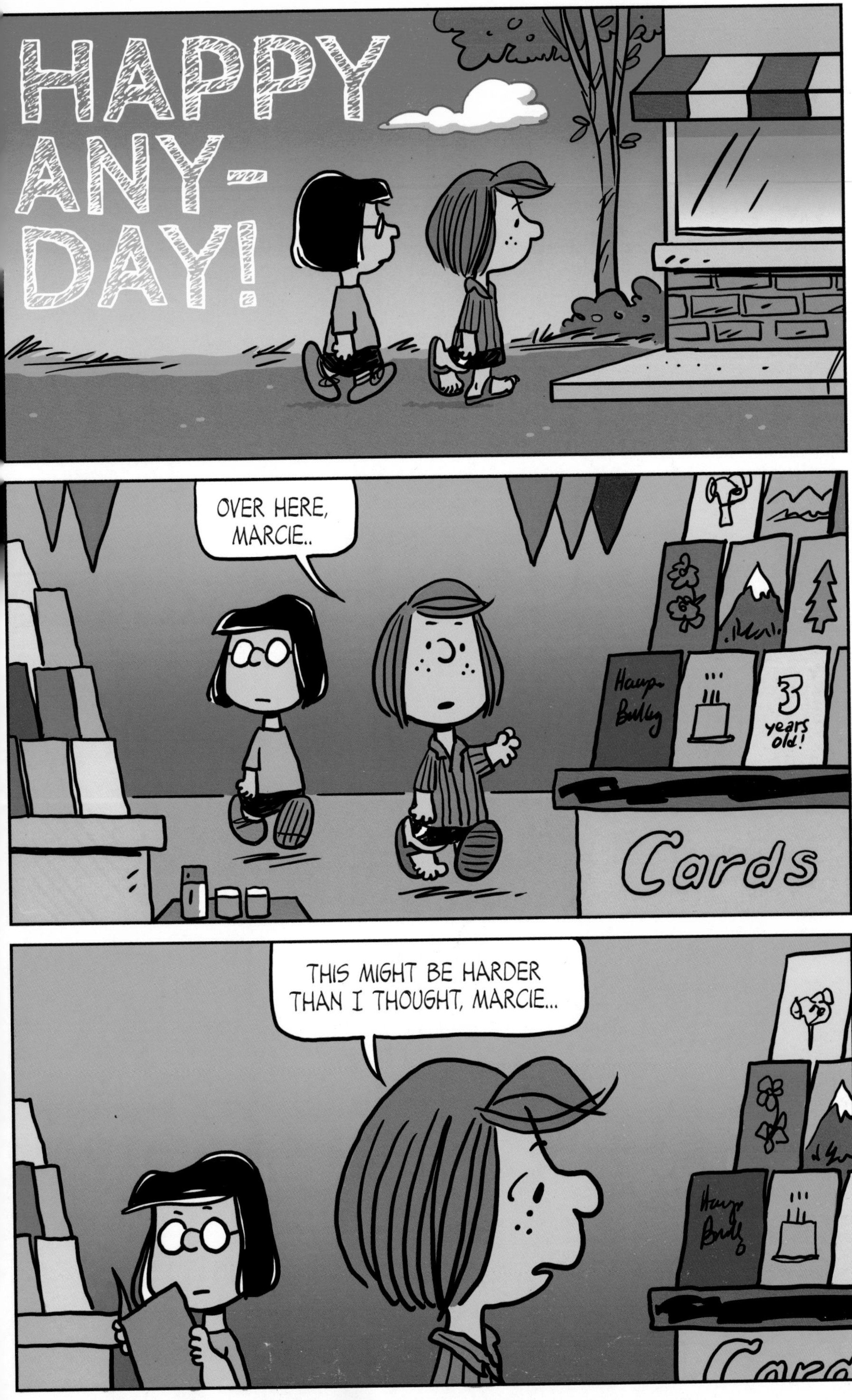
HAPPY ANY-DAY!
OVER HERE, MARCIE..
Cards
THIS MIGHT BE HARDER THAN I THOUGHT, MARCIE...

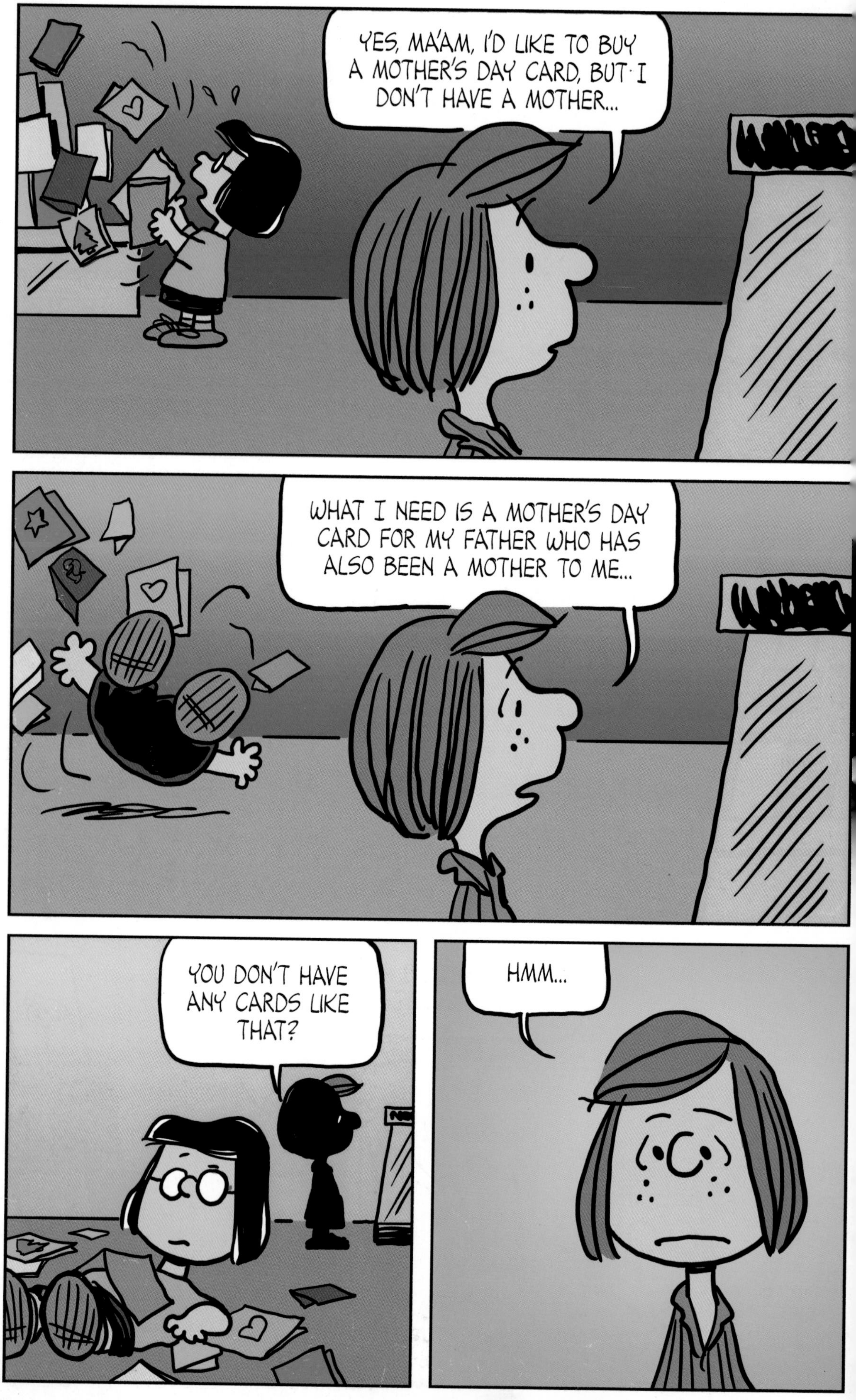
YES, MA'AM, I'D LIKE TO BUY A MOTHER'S DAY CARD, BUT I DON'T HAVE A MOTHER...
WHAT I NEED IS A MOTHER'S DAY CARD FOR MY FATHER WHO HAS ALSO BEEN A MOTHER TO ME...
YOU DON'T HAVE ANY CARDS LIKE THAT?
HMM...

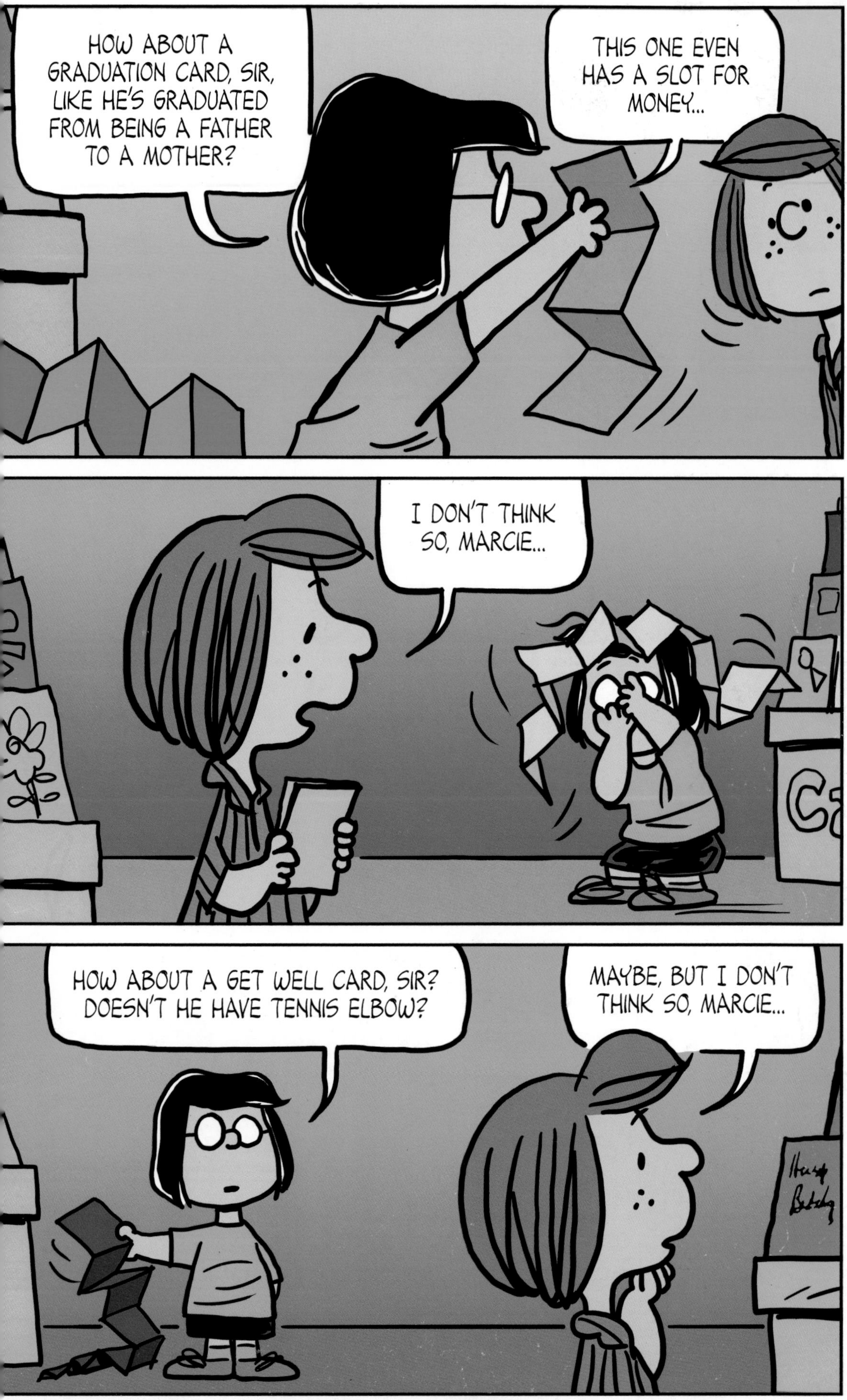
HOW ABOUT A GRADUATION CARD, SIR, LIKE HE'S GRADUATED FROM BEING A FATHER TO A MOTHER?
THIS ONE EVEN HAS A SLOT FOR MONEY...
I DON'T THINK SO, MARCIE...
HOW ABOUT A GET WELL CARD, SIR? DOESN'T HE HAVE TENNIS ELBOW?
MAYBE, BUT I DON'T THINK SO, MARCIE...

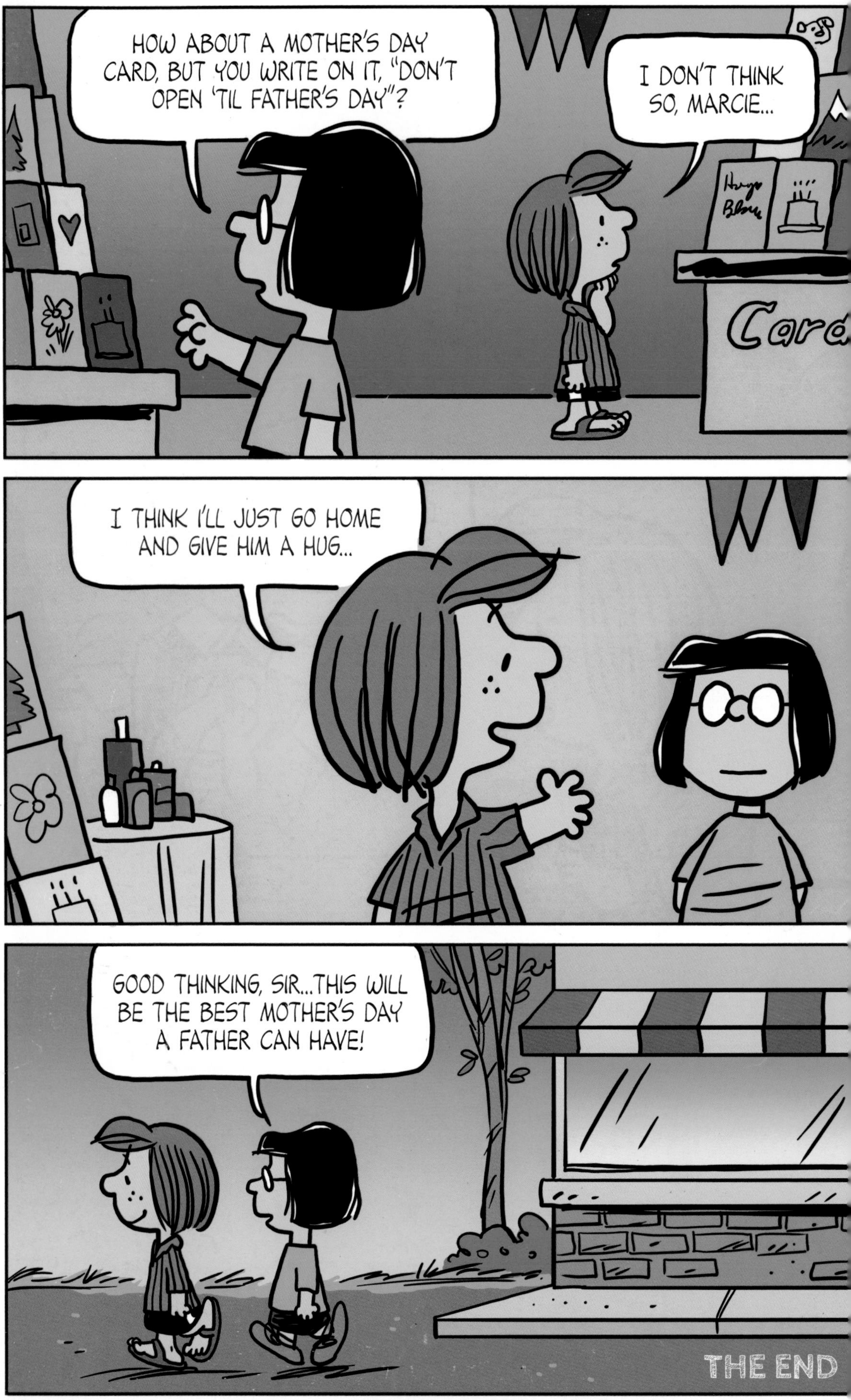
HOW ABOUT A MOTHER'S DAY CARD, BUT YOU WRITE ON IT, "DON'T OPEN 'TIL FATHER'S DAY"?
I DON'T THINK SO, MARCIE...
I THINK I'LL JUST GO HOME AND GIVE HIM A HUG...
GOOD THINKING, SIR...THIS WILL BE THE BEST MOTHER'S DAY A FATHER CAN HAVE!
THE END

PEANUTS.

by SCHULZ

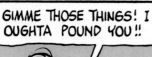
CLOMP CLOMP
CLOMP CLOMP

? ? ?

HEY, YOU DUMB DOG! COME BACK HERE WITH MY SHOES AND SOCKS!

GIMME THOSE THINGS! I OUGHTA POUND YOU!!
SLOOP!

THE LACES ARE GONE! WHAT DID HE DO WITH THE LACES?
LACES?

I DIDN'T KNOW WHAT THEY WERE SO I ATE THEM!

103

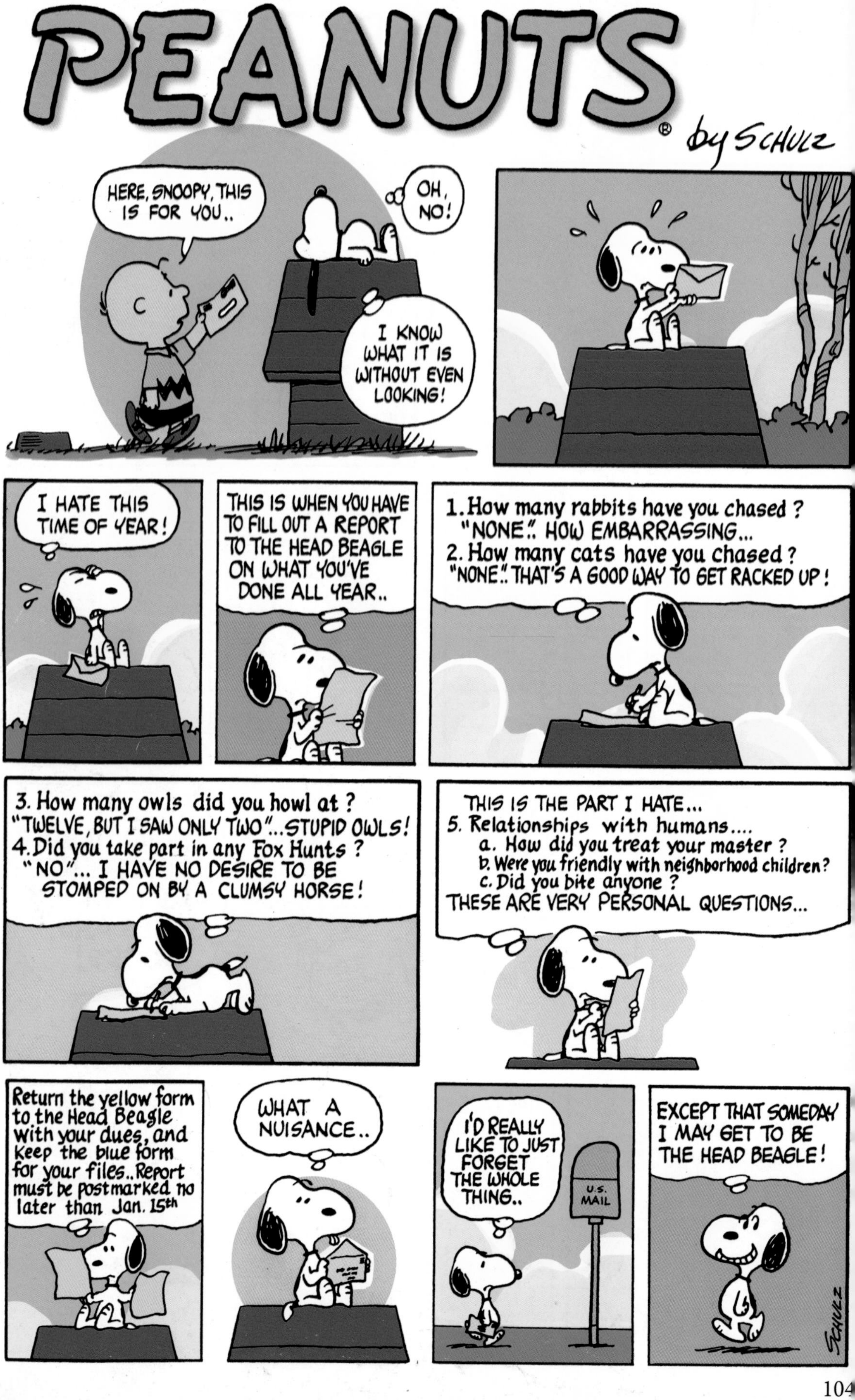
PEANUTS® by SCHULZ
HERE, SNOOPY, THIS IS FOR YOU..
OH, NO!
I KNOW WHAT IT IS WITHOUT EVEN LOOKING!
I HATE THIS TIME OF YEAR!
THIS IS WHEN YOU HAVE TO FILL OUT A REPORT TO THE HEAD BEAGLE ON WHAT YOU'VE DONE ALL YEAR..
1. How many rabbits have you chased? "NONE". HOW EMBARRASSING...
2. How many cats have you chased? "NONE". THAT'S A GOOD WAY TO GET RACKED UP!
3. How many owls did you howl at? "TWELVE, BUT I SAW ONLY TWO"...STUPID OWLS!
4. Did you take part in any Fox Hunts? "NO"... I HAVE NO DESIRE TO BE STOMPED ON BY A CLUMSY HORSE!
THIS IS THE PART I HATE...
5. Relationships with humans....
a. How did you treat your master?
b. Were you friendly with neighborhood children?
c. Did you bite anyone?
THESE ARE VERY PERSONAL QUESTIONS...
Return the yellow form to the Head Beagle with your dues, and keep the blue form for your files.. Report must be postmarked no later than Jan. 15th
WHAT A NUISANCE..
I'D REALLY LIKE TO JUST FORGET THE WHOLE THING..
U.S. MAIL
EXCEPT THAT SOMEDAY I MAY GET TO BE THE HEAD BEAGLE!
SCHULZ

Cover Gallery

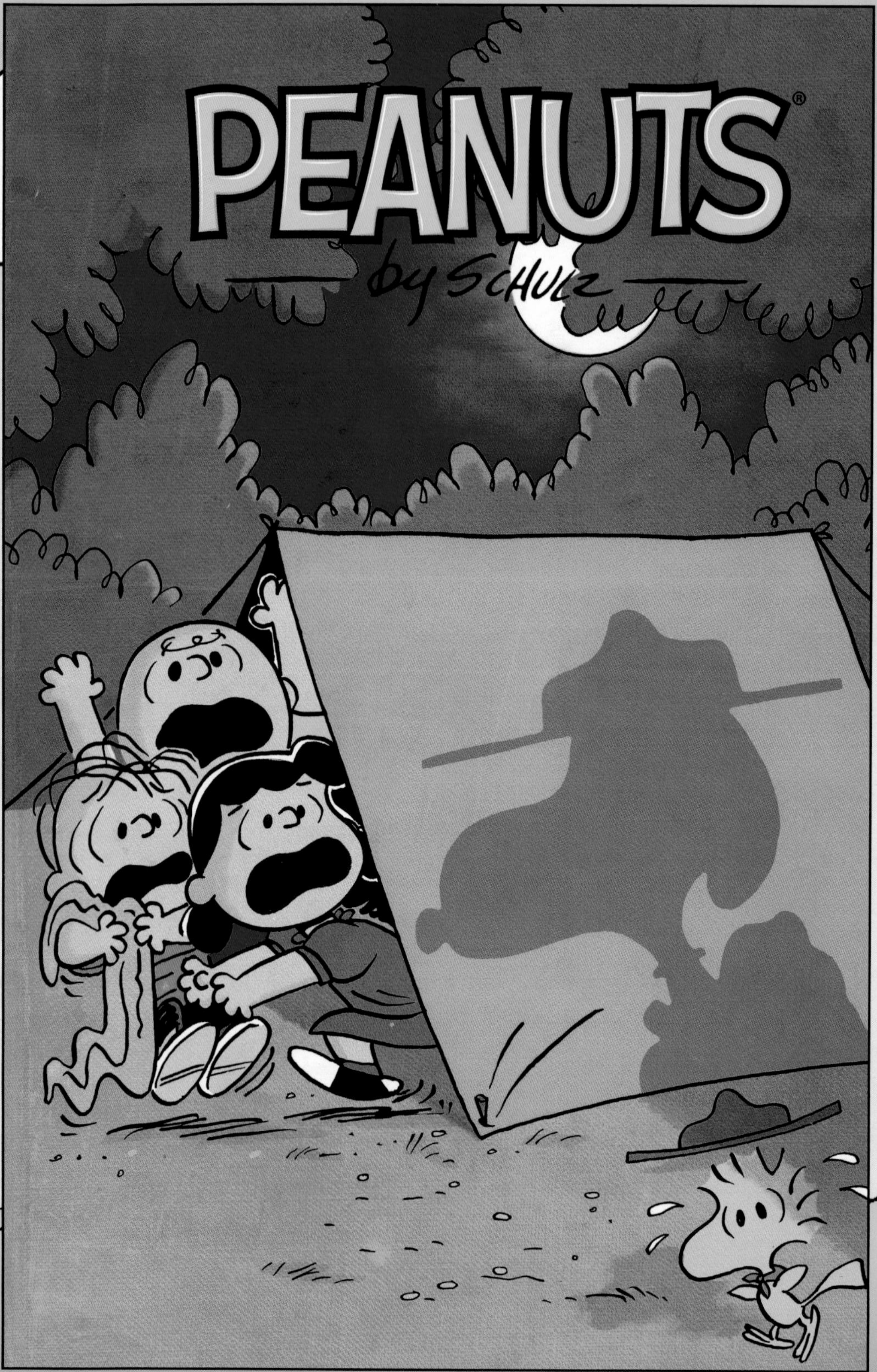
PEANUTS®
by SCHULZ

by Vicki Scott
Inks by Paige Braddock
Colors by Nomi Kane

Peanuts #25 Denver Comic Con Exclusive

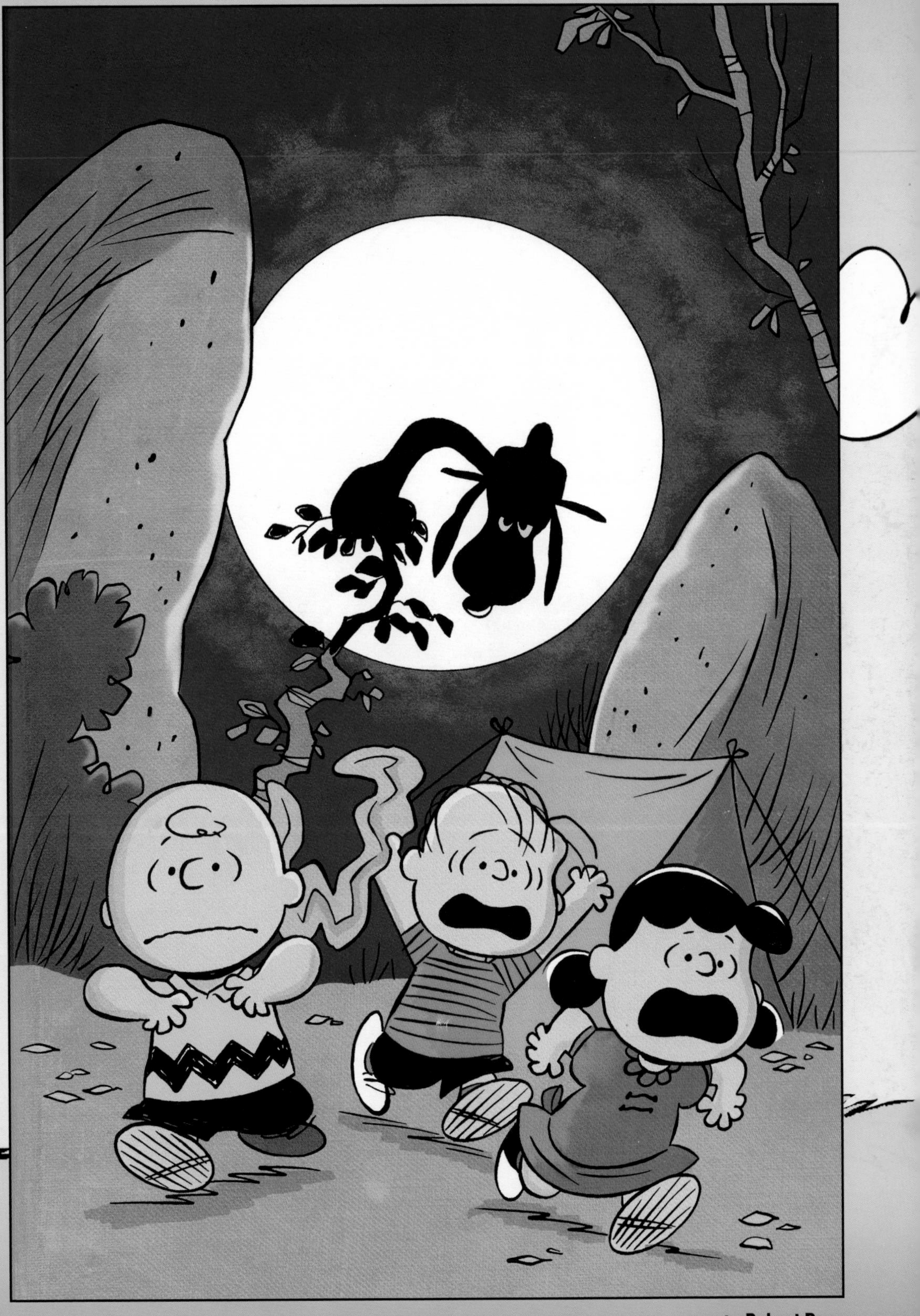

by Robert Pope
Colors by Nomi Kane

Peanuts #25 65th Anniversary

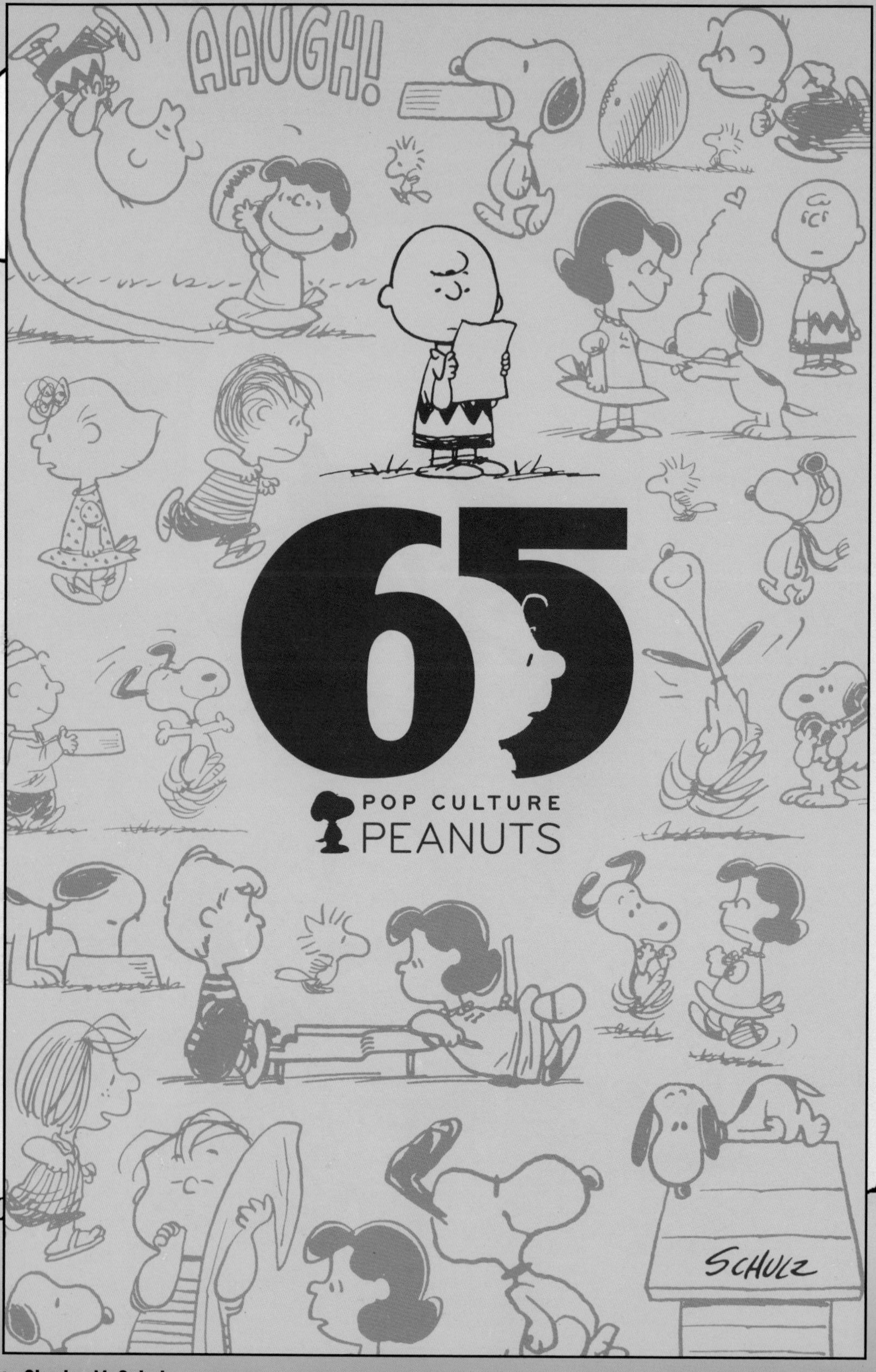
AAUGH!
65
POP CULTURE
PEANUTS
SCHULZ

by Charles M. Schulz
Design by Scott Newman

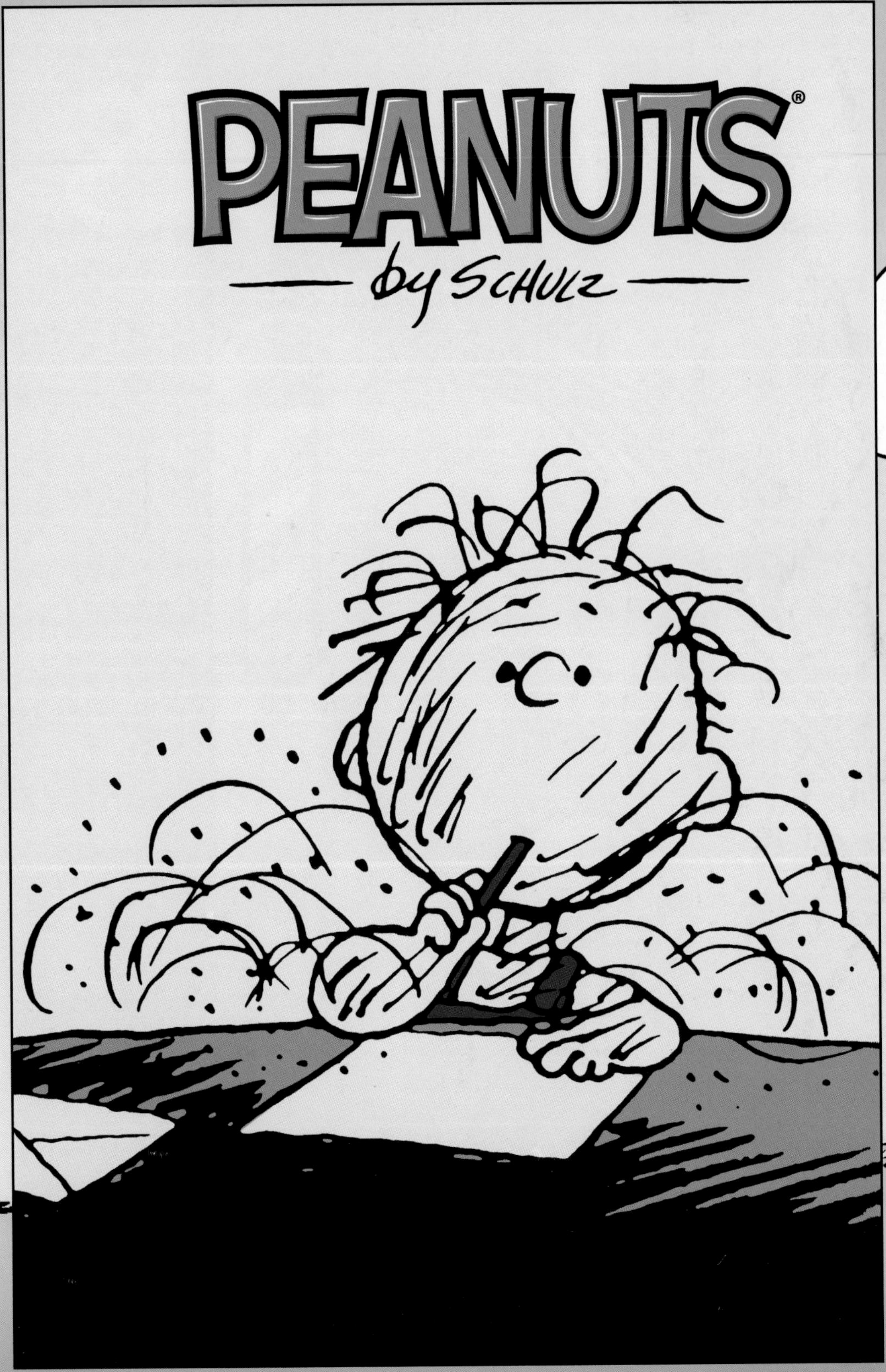
PEANUTS®
by SCHULZ

by Charles M. Schulz
Design & Colors by Paige Braddock

Peanuts #27

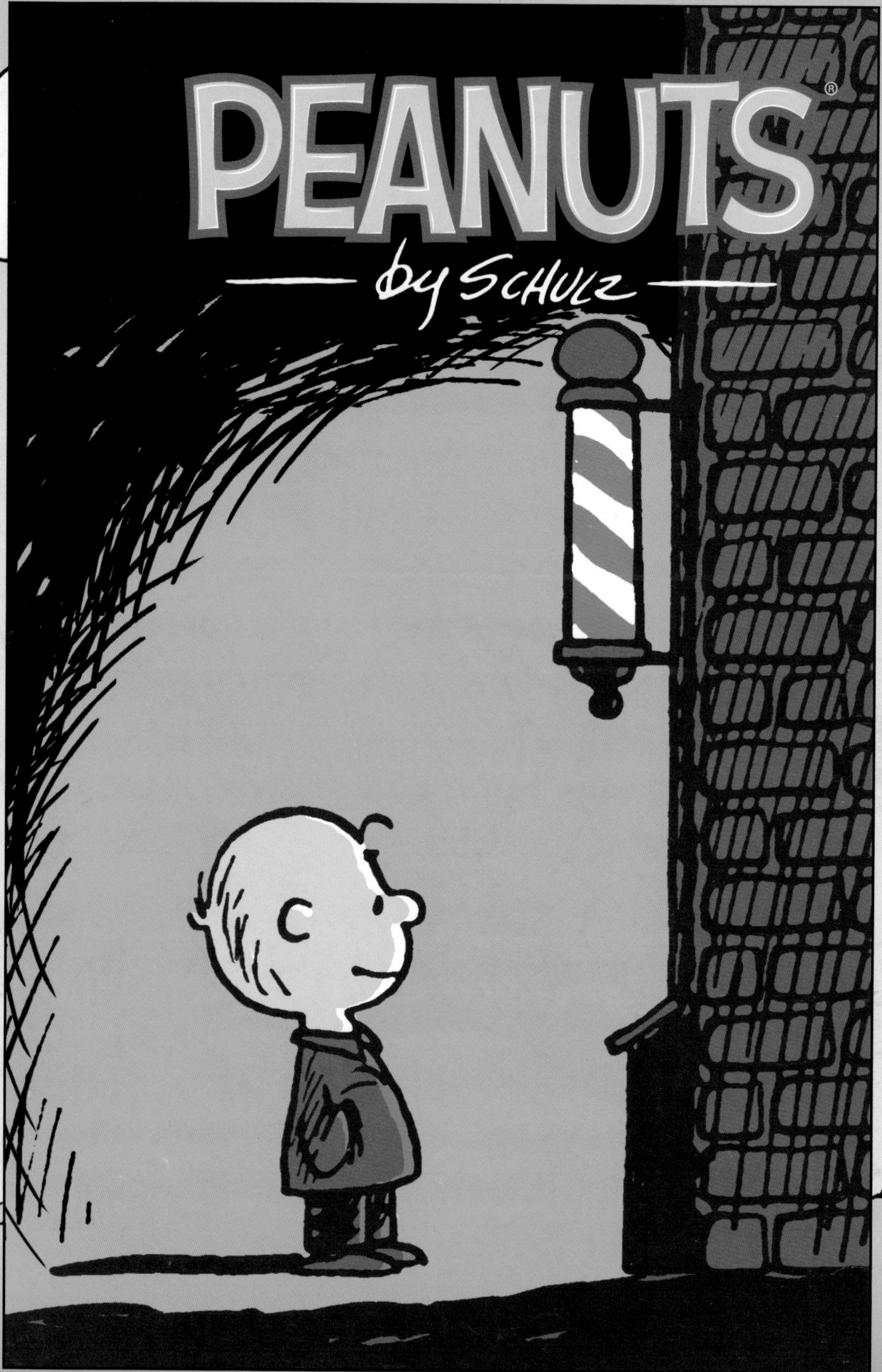
PEANUTS®
by SCHULZ

by Charles M. Schulz
Design by Donna Almendrala and Scott Newman

Peanuts #28

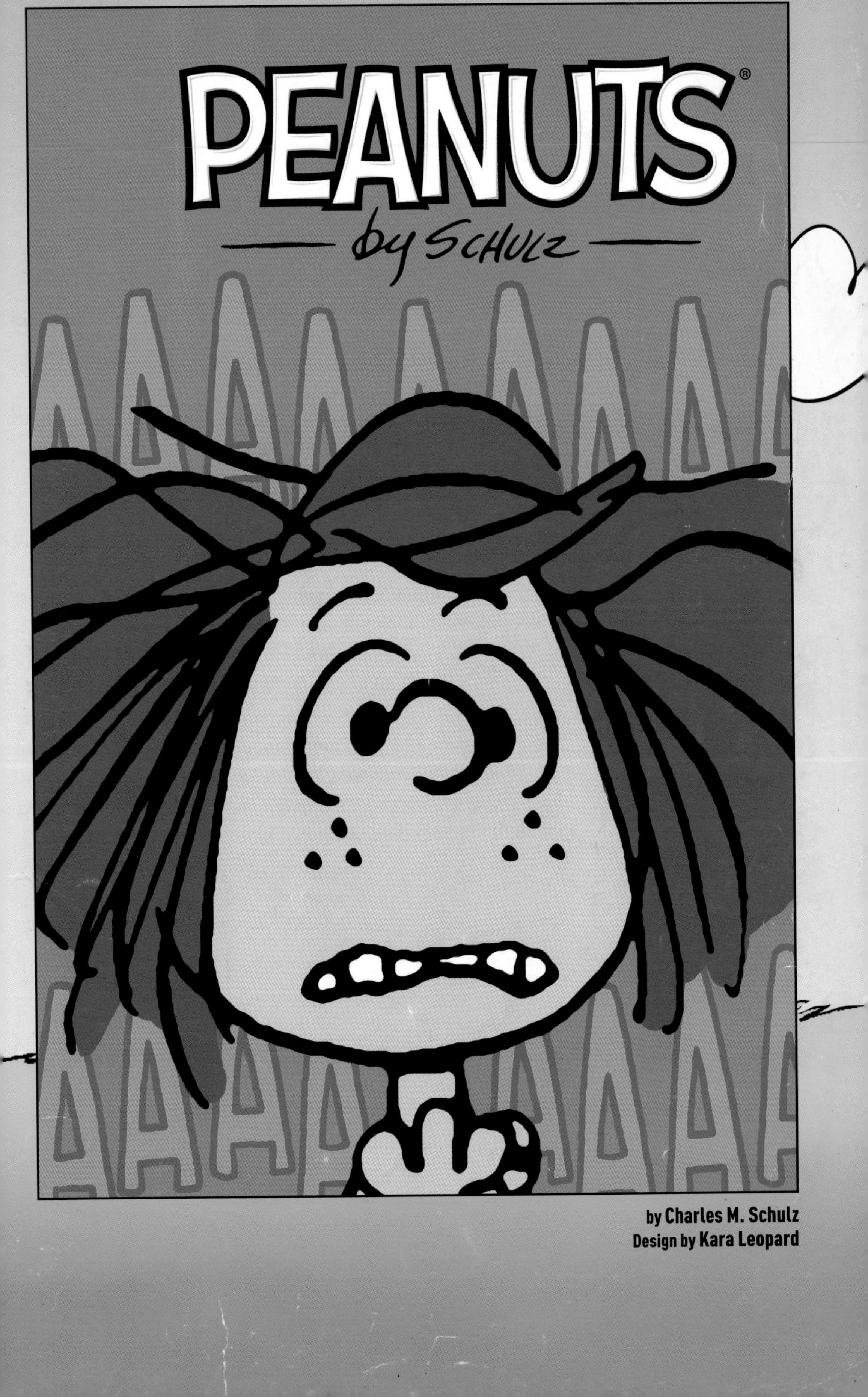
PEANUTS®
by SCHULZ

by Charles M. Schulz
Design by Kara Leopard

Charles M. Schulz once described himself as "born to draw comic strips." Born in Minneapolis, at just two days old, an uncle nicknamed him "Sparky" after the horse Spark Plug from the "Barney Google" comic strip, and throughout his youth, he and his father shared a Sunday morning ritual reading the funnies. After serving in the Army during World War II, Schulz's first big break came in 1947 when he sold a cartoon feature called "Li'l Folks" to the St. Paul Pioneer Press. In 1950, Schulz met with United Feature Syndicate, and on October 2 of that year, PEANUTS, named by the syndicate, debuted in seven newspapers. Charles Schulz died in Santa Rosa, California, in February 2000—just hours before his last original strip was to appear in Sunday papers.